NIGHT COMES DOWN

READ ORDER

203   41   53

33(8)   67   81

137   247(14)

261(12)

95   13

213   113

229   151

177

Joseph D'Lacey

Bev Vincent

Robert E. Weinberg

Nate Kenyon

DARKARTS

B O O K S

Table of Contents

Powered By Brains

First, for all of you hopeful zombie fans out there, let me state clearly that these next few paragraphs will have absolutely nothing to do with the actual eating of human brains. Absolutely nothing. Really.

Instead, the subject of tonight's lecture will be the incredible elasticity of our old friend, the humble horror story. Or, to sharpen the point a bit and frame the question: what is it that makes scary stories so endlessly enduring?

The answer can be found in the unbelievable range of the horror story. Since we're going to be dealing in blanket generalizations, let's mix the metaphors and paint with the biggest brush we can find. Horror stories are unique as a genre in that they don't really operate under an iron-clad set of "rules." A romance, in all likelihood, is going to have a headstrong heroine, a mysterious and maddening foil for that heroine, and, at least, have a kiss somewhere in it. A Western will most likely have a taciturn lawman or a taciturn stranger or a taciturn gunslinger, any of whose sixguns speak much more eloquently than they do themselves. A detective story will have a case to be solved, usually by a down-at-the-heels gumshoe and a double-crossing dame to boot. The case might be solved, but curiously enough at the end, the detective will be less well-off financially as well as slightly battered. A mystery will also need to be solved, with plenty of clues and suspects and red herrings and a solution that was right there in front of the reader the whole time.

This is not in any way to denigrate or minimize the pleasures to be found in reading any of those genres. My point is simply that a romance without a feisty heroine, a Western without a reluctant savior, a detective story without a detective—well, they just sort of can't be. And, to be honest, some of the pleasure found in reading those genres is the comfortable familiarity that allows us as readers to slip into the stories like a comfortable and cozy old flannel robe.

Horror tales on the other hand, have no universal set-in-stone array of characteristics. While there are plenty of recurring characters – the suave vampire, the homicidal, cannibalistic inbred mutant, the evil or possessed child – there are no rules or conventions that define a piece of fiction as a "horror story." I suppose the argument could be made that the one and only requirement is that a horror story be "scary."

And therein lies the rub, (as someone famous once said.)

Because there is no one universal definition of "scary," there is no one universal boilerplate for the horror story. What powers the horror story, then, is the endless energy and inventiveness – and astonishing variety of fears – manufactured by the human brain.

What I find absolutely terrifying, you might be totally blasé about. Similarly, what makes you quake with fear in the darkest hour of night might make me giggle at its (to me) sheer ridiculousness. Thus, the secret of the enduring nature of the horror story – the cockroach of the literary world (not because it's gross, but because it primarily comes out at night and is very, very hard to kill) – is that it is ever-changing. Indefinable, yet dark. Powerful. Transporting.

Horror stories are driven by the excesses of the paranoid imagination – of both the writer and reader. In some cases, that means the writer uses his or her imagination to generate some of the most twisted and graphic visions possible. Think you have a strong stomach and nerves of steel? Read Jack Ketchum's brilliantly tense *Off Season* or Edward Lee's equally-twisted but so over-the-top it's both humorous and gag-inducing, *Header*. One has a murderous family of modern cannibals and the other is predicated upon the title act which cannot even be discussed in "civilized society." Buckets of blood, heaps of entrails and pages upon pages of unrelenting and unflinching human suffering make for harrowing reading experiences that seemingly push the limits of "horror" beyond the extreme.

Conversely, at the other end of the spectrum, there are horror stories where the impact is just as powerful, but the "horror" is kept off to the side, only partially unveiled. In Shirley Jackson's absolutely terrifying story "The Summer People," the most overt thing that happens is a car won't start; a phone line won't work. That's it. But, that story has a hidden depth; it resonates and stays with the reader long after the last paragraph has been read. Similarly, in Roald Dahl's "Man from the South," the action involves the repetitive striking of a lighter flint and wheel, to see if the lighter will successfully light 10 times in succession. That is about the extent of the action. But with that, Dahl creates unbearable suspense and an almost-perfect short story. In T.E.D. Klein's long tale "Petey," 95 percent of the action takes place at a sort of housewarming party for a couple who have purchased a "country estate" deep in the woods, and most of the dialogue is seemingly inane cocktail party chatter. Much like that other great example of quiet, understated horror, "The Monkey's Paw," the story ends with a door being opened. But, oh, what is on the other side of that door?

In between those two poles lie every conceivable kind of horror story – vampires, werewolves, mummies, zombies, serial killers, devils, giant monsters, some who lurk in the shadows and some who take center stage. Yet, each is potentially equally as formidable, since if done right, they all are powered by the unquenchable fuel of the human imagination to give them their power.

One of the things that we have deliberately set out to do with our titles at Dark Arts Books is to celebrate both the power of the imagination and the endless variations of what truly constitutes a "horror story." We try to encourage our authors to take risks, to explore any aspect of their creativity they wish; the results are always rewarding.

For our sixth collection, once again we've assembled four authors with very distinct voices and very distinct ways of approaching their craft.

Joseph D'Lacey works in the realm of pure ideas. His mind is like a Hadron Collider of the imagination, where various ideas and thoughts are accelerated and smashed together until a new super-hybrid emerges unlike anything seen before. Stories like "The Unwrapping of Alastair Perry" and "The Quiet Ones" are not only wildly effective tales, but they stay with the reader long after the book is closed – no matter how much the reader may wish to escape the thoughts D'Lacey has planted. "Etoile's 's Tree" reads like a hallucinatory fairy tale, while "Introscopy" wears its social commentary proudly as a badge of honor. The breadth of scope that D'Lacey explores – and excels at delivering to the reader – is truly amazing. Powered by brains, indeed.

Bev Vincent is, among other things, an award-winning nonfiction writer and an accomplished scientist. He brings this clear-eyed no-nonsense approach to his fiction. Bev's stories, no matter how bizarre or improbable the situation he supposes, simply reek of rationality and plausibility. And, because of that, we as readers willingly go along on the journey, believing all the way. A story of the fantastic, told with simplicity and straightforwardness is that much more effective. Like Shirley Jackson, Bev doesn't need complicated sentences or linguistic pyrotechnics to perfectly create the mood he desires. In "Knock 'Em Dead," Bev takes what seems to be an old chestnut – the artist desperate for success no matter the cost – and infuses it with a whole new spin. "Purgatory Noir" takes another well-known archetype – the hard-boiled detective tale – and gives it a subtle twist that transmutes it completely. And, in "Silvery Moon," Bev pulls off what may be the neatest trick yet – but for that one, you'll have to read the story. Powered by brains, indeed.

Robert E. Weinberg, quite literally, needs no introduction. Seventeen novels, sixteen non-fiction books and more than 150 anthologies edited, plus countless tales published in all of the greatest magazines – his bibliography reads like a veritable "Who's Who" of the great fiction publications of the 20th (and 21st) century. Since Bob prefers to write whatever interests him (and his interests are legion), his output is amazingly varied and diverse. Having cut his writing teeth when he did, one of Bob's major loves will always be the pulps, back when that word had a real meaning. Two-fisted stories of action and terror, brave wisecracking heroes and impossibly voluptuous dames, squared off against cackling professors, craven magicians and large monsters. Those were the days! With the long tale "The One Answer That Really Matters" Bob effortlessly transports us back to those times of inspired yarning. And, then, just as quickly shifting gears, Bob gives us one of the great stories about horror writers and horror conventions – Elevator Girls," which is kind of like "The Player" for the horror community. With monsters. Powered by brains, indeed.

There's a reason Nate Kenyon keeps being described in gushing terms as "up and coming" and nominated for awards and compared to Stephen King. Whatever that mysterious "it" is, Nate has it – in spades. These are 21st century horror stories at their most basic and brilliant; modern, taut and sharing a classic commonality with William F. Nolan's great, no-nonsense short stories like "The Partnership," "He Kilt It With a Stick" and "The Train." In "Gravedigger," Nate takes the increasingly tired zombie story into an entirely interesting new place. The one thing about Nate's fiction that makes it so compelling is its immediacy – the reader is thrust, like it or not, into the circumstances of the story and can almost taste the blood and smell the rot. In "Breeding the Demons," Nate looks at notions of art (or, perhaps more correctly, "Art") and combines that with a fearsome world of patrons who make the Medici family look like Ozzie and Harriet. And, fittingly in the closer to this collection, "The Buzz of a Thousand Wings," he explores Cronenbergian themes of physicality and mentality in revolt, and ends with a conclusion that resonates long after the book has been put back on the shelf. Powered by brains, indeed.

But more than being a bunch of "smarties" – the prize pupils of the horror story class – these four writers are first and foremost unbelievably talented tellers of tales. The single most important criteria for a story to be successful remains "is it entertaining and interesting for the reader?" With these sixteen stories, we have sixteen cases where the answer is a resounding "yes." Some are graphic, some are quiet, some are complex constructions, some are simplicity itself. But all are "good reads."

Enjoy.

– Bill Breedlove
Chicago, Illinois
February 2010

JOSEPH D'LACEY was born in London and has spent most of his life in the midlands. He is the author of *MEAT*, *Garbage Man* and *The Kill Crew*.

"My mother warned me never to tell stories that aren't true. It's been great fun ignoring her advice."

By day he runs an acupuncture practice – sticking needles into people and making little dolls scream. Between victims he writes all manner of disturbing fiction.

He lives in Northamptonshire with his wife and daughter.

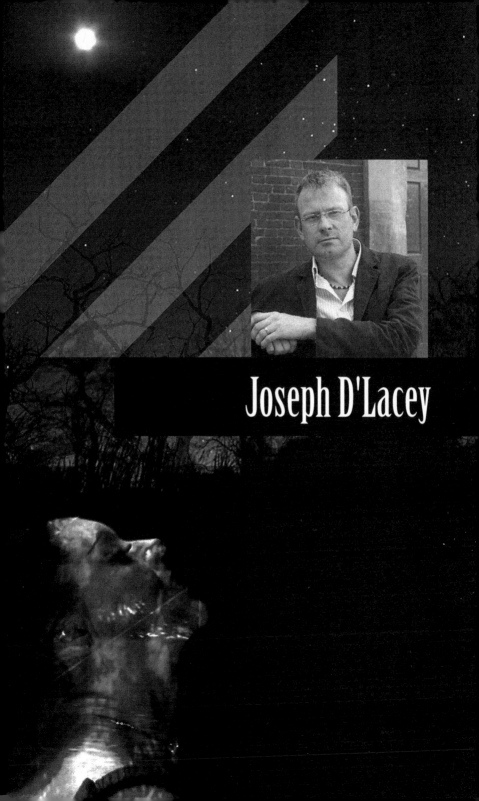

Joseph D'Lacey

The Unwrapping of Alastair Perry

*L*ooking back now, I see there was never any reason for me to be afraid.

As I sit here, momentarily sated and surrounded by the rubble that was once a North Yorkshire village, I rest and contemplate the feasting to come. Decades of it, perhaps. Until all form is gone. We are hungry.

~φ~

My eyes were different that morning, hinting at the changes that were to come.

With droplets of water dripping from my chin, I sprayed a mound of white foam into my left hand and squeezed my palms together, making a marshmallow sandwich of the minty soap. I noticed my eyes in the mirror as I began to apply it.

I stopped and studied myself. All that moved in the reflection were my eyes. They were the same colour green, the same size, the same shape. At least, I thought they were. When I looked in the mirror that day, it felt like the first time I'd ever noticed them. They weren't exactly different, I simply didn't recognise them.

I was a little hung over after yet another failed speed-dating event. I got on fine with almost all the girls – flirted a little, made them laugh – but only chose two of them as possible future dates. Mine wasn't the carpet-bombing approach. I picked ladies I really liked; ones I thought liked me too. But it was my fourth speed-dating session in as many months and I hadn't been picked by anyone. Not as a date. Not even as a friend. I'd moved on from the glitzy, hormone-spiced charade and ended up in Tito's Place two blocks from my flat. I stayed there until I was good and forgetful.

I spread the foam across my sandpaper skin and worked it in. My mouth was a raw pink gash in the whiteness.

A little hung over? Bullshit. I was sweating sour liquor from every pore. When I breathed out, I could smell it. Looking at my reflection started a thump in the back of my skull. More sweat prickled followed by a flood of body paranoia. I feared a brain hemorrhage.

Needing to get myself together, I reached for my granddad's straight razor. My hand tremored. Concentrating on the shave would restore the equilibrium. The requirement for poise and precision, the delicacy it demanded, the danger it presented; a straight razor shave was a must on that kind of morning.

I stropped the razor to an evil gleam on an old brown leather army belt, tilted my head to the left and laid the blade to the skin below my right ear. I caught sight of my eyes again and blinked. Seeing those unfamiliar eyes must have made me falter. When I made the first stroke, instead of sliding with a satisfying rasp across my whiskers, the blade bit into my neck. I winced waiting for the pain and the blood. Poppy droplets in snow. Neither came. I couldn't have felt less if I'd had a local anaesthetic. Blood that should have welled and then poured did not. Moments passed. I dared not move in case the blade itself was holding the wound closed.

I couldn't stay that way all day.

I withdrew the razor the way a man with his front wheels over a cliff reverses his car. The cut was dry. I set the razor between the taps and swabbed some foam away with my fingertips expecting a delayed rush of blood. Nothing happened. No pain. I could feel my face but it was the wrong kind of sensation. The surface was dead but beneath it, something lived. Careful not to stretch or jolt the cut, I rinsed away the foam with gentle splashes from the sink.

The cut was three inches across, stretching from the angle of my jaw diagonally downward towards my adam's apple. Nothing more than a very neat groove in my skin. Feeling along its edges, I discovered sensitivity. There was facial tissue inside the cut: that skin was belly-smooth. Young, strong and elastic. Still feeling no pain, I explored deeper and my fingertips found firm, healthy resistance. Not a wrinkle. It felt like the skin of a younger man.

Tentatively, I nipped a hold of the lower edge of the cut between my right thumb and index finger and tried to pull it open a little wider. There was no pain but there was no give either. I tugged harder at the lip of the cut trapping more wounded skin in my grip. Leaning closer to the mirror and tilting my neck away, I peered from the corner of my eye at the reflection of the wound. I could see the skin inside it. No blood. No damage. No naked meat.

But I couldn't go to work like that.

How long would it take to heal? What about speed dating?

No. I'd started something. I had to finish it.

I shook the blue and white aerosol of shaving cream and squirted a second, smaller mound into my palm. I worked the lather into my neck and picked up the razor. I felt a strong but bizarre sense of purpose. I did hesitate before I placed the blade back into the cut. But only for a moment.

Perhaps I'm not unique in history but I must be a rarity. Plenty of unfortunates must have had their faces removed forcibly but there can't be many who have done it willingly and by their own hand.

The process transported me to childhood. 'Helping' my father with his carpentry. Rather than pay attention, I would squirt wood glue onto my hands, blow on it until my palms no longer felt cool, then peel it away, trying to keep it in one piece. Then I'd have a snakeskin handprint and the palm below felt clean and pure. Watching my mother peeling strips of brown skin from mushrooms by trapping a layer between her thumb and a short-bladed knife. Below was a pale, healthy mushroom every time. In my teens, I'd been drawn to circumcision but my parents had been dismayed. They refused to discuss it after the first argument. When I was twenty-one, I paid to have it done. It hurt a hell of a lot more than cutting off my face.

There was no scraping sensation when I drew the razor down towards my clavicle. Something wrinkled and heavy, began to fall away. Below it was a new skin.

Someone else's.

No, mine.

When the stroke reached the bottom of my neck, the dead flap came away and plopped into the half-full sink.

Each careful downward sweep of the blade outed the new face beneath. Was this my true face, I wondered, hidden for all these years below a dishonest disguise? My fingers still trembled but now it was with excitement rather than toxicity. The face that I was revealing, one slough of unhealthy skin at a time, was paler. I stroked my neck and it was smooth; no more than a peachy down covering it. My adam's apple, an obstacle I usually nicked with the razor, was barely palpable beneath my fingertips.

I flayed the right half of my face in three confident passes, the left in only two. My chin was more challenging. When the old skin dropped away it removed a layer from my lower lip. When I shaved the area below my nose, the skin of my top lip peeled off. My new lips were soft and proud, pinker than the old ones. My teeth were whiter and straighter.

I stepped back. I had the hair, forehead, ears and nose of a man. I had the eyes, lips, cheeks and neck of a young woman. The mixed genders in my reflection made me queasy. The hangover kicked back in. I couldn't leave it like this.

I cut a flap beside my ear lobe and pulled with my fingers. It wouldn't come away. I traced a cut below, behind, over the top and back down to the lobe again. This time when I pulled the flap, the surface of my ear came loose and a new one popped free as if drawn from a latex wrapper. I dropped the old ear into the sink where it lay on a sloppy pile of greying skin and foam.

Nauseated, I sliced into my forehead on the left hand side and scraped the blade all the way to the right in one movement. The skin came away in a single greasy ruffle. Below it was a smooth brow. My male hair looked like shit against this femininity. That upset me. I made a horizontal incision at my hairline from ear to ear. Then, angling the blade under my scalp, I drew it back like a comb. Beneath my old scalp I was blonde. I liked it.

I shaved downward from my eyebrows, peeling the last of the skin away and feeling the razor's edge make contact with my eyeball both times. My eyes had already changed. I was relieved not to have to dig them out.

The muck in the sink had begun to smell rotten. I kicked open the lid of the toilet, scooped the dregs of my old face up in a double handful and dumped them into the pan with a splat. One flush took all the evidence away. I rinsed my face, already feeling the need for a cleansing moisturiser, and took a good long look at the new me.

I was gorgeous, the kind of girl I'd never have had a chance with. The kind of girl I met speed-dating and never saw again. It made me hard just imagining myself naked. I looked down at my man's body with this stunning woman's head, perched petitely on top of it. If the magic stretched to the rest of my body, there was a lot more plastic surgery to be done. If it didn't, I was going to start wishing I hadn't flushed my old face away.

I started with a place no one would see if the cut went wrong. Believing my luck couldn't possibly hold, I made an upwards stroke from my knee to my groin along my inner thigh. This yielded a painless flap of hairy man-skin and revealed more woman below. I think that was when my hangover was cured for the day.

Before continuing, I checked my voice – it was still manly – and dialled work.

"Gloria? Hi, it's Alastair..."

"Heavens, not another liver crisis."

"No... Nothing like that."

"Don't tell me you finally beguiled some poor lass into sleeping with you."

"Uh, not exactly."

"Alastair. I'm impressed."

"Honestly, that's not what happened."

"Don't panic, darling. Auntie Gloria understands. Actually, Auntie Gloria is suddenly a mite jealous. Now, what do you want me to tell Mr. Crowther?"

"Tell him it's a... skin condition."

"That doesn't sound very serious."

"Believe me, it is."

"I'll make it sound life-threatening."

"Thanks, Gloria."

"Don't mention it, stud."

~φ~

I was in the bathroom two hours.

Over the years I'd had terrible nightmares about castration. I never once imagined a time would come when I'd be slicing off my own carrot and onions with a straight razor.

The time came that very morning.

It didn't hurt a bit.

And then I was a woman. Or so I thought.

~φ~

I spent much of that day in front of the mirror in the bedroom checking out my bottom, my tits and especially my pussy. It was like being handed a woman I could do anything I wanted with, my own living doll. I discovered why women have more fulfilling orgasms than men. I did all the things I'd read in sex manuals that would drive a woman crazy with pleasure.

The manuals were right.

As the day passed, I lost the ability to see myself from a man's point of view. I decided my face looked plain and my arse was too prominent. I'd have looked more desirable with a tan. My stomach wasn't as flat as I'd have liked it to be. I craved chocolate and felt guilty about it. What I required was a diet. But before that I wanted magazines and make up.

And I needed an emergency appointment with a hairdresser.

~φ~

I didn't go into work the next day. Who was going to understand when a woman took her place at my desk? I pulled on Alastair's old jeans, turned them up and wore them as hipsters. I tied one of his flowery shirts around my middle instead of buttoning it. My feet weren't too much smaller so I slipped on a pair of his leather flip-flops.

Instead of going to the office, I did things that made me very happy. I bought new underwear, clothes and shoes – shoe shopping was the best. I bought make up and perfume, facial cleansers and toning lotions. I had my hair styled and low-lighted.

The following morning the phone rang.

"Perry residence," I said.

"Put Alastair on the phone, please."

I recognised the voice.

"Who's calling, please?"

"This is Bob Crowther, his employer."

I said nothing for several seconds.

"Mr. Crowther, I'm Alastair's sister. He's…gravely ill." I began to cry. "The doctors say there's nothing more they can do."

I heard him chewing back the bollocking he'd prepared.

"I had no idea it was so serious."

"Could I call you back when he's… when… I just can't deal with this right now."

I screeched, demented and bereaved, and hung up.

~φ~

Calling myself Alison Perry or sometimes A. Perry, I built a new identity using the same address. It was incredibly simple. Library cards, gym memberships, dating services. With electricity and telephone bills, more doors opened. I got on the electoral roll and opened a new bank account. The confidence to be a real woman came easily and quickly. The need for something more was building inside. I thought I knew what it was.

I went speed-dating.

~φ~

Getting a man was the easiest thing I've ever done. I picked the best looking guy in the place – Jeremy. When the dates were over and informal drinks were being served, I made eye contact with him. A couple of hours later I went home with him. We drank more wine and my inhibitions evaporated. I was dying to know how it felt to be fucked. I did everything I would have wanted a woman to do to me. I wore him out. While Jeremy was still asleep I left. I left no contact information. It wasn't a relationship I wanted, after all.

I wanted money. A way to get out of the dead-end life

Alastair had been living. He'd bled away his twenties on beer and porn and late nights. He had nothing to show for the time he'd spent in the sales department of Crowther's Fitted Furniture.

Believing I'd discovered the source of my yearning, I planned to change that.

~φ~

The high end of the escort business can bring in two to three thousand pounds a night. If you're prepared to work on your own, without protection, you can make even more. I knew exactly what men would pay for.

Over the next six months, I sucked, fucked and milked my way to two hundred grand. I developed a regular client list of very wealthy men and earned fabulous tips when I performed the way they wanted me to. It was the quickest, easiest money in the world.

And I enjoyed earning it. We ate in the best restaurants, flew and yachted all around Europe. A couple of my clients set up expense accounts for me, enabling me to save almost everything else. The cash built up under the floorboards in my flat. Some went into the bank to mimic a normal salary.

~φ~

There was often an emptiness within me, something I couldn't satisfy with pleasure and money. When it was bad I destroyed things, smashed plates and windows, ripped curtains and bedding. I'd put feathers and torn cloth in my mouth, lacerate my tongue crunching shards of crockery and glass. The emptiness never filled.

~φ~

Being a hooker, even a classy one like I was, is a solitary business.

The pleasure and companionship only go so far. There's a

point beyond which you never step with any client if you want
to keep making money. When I'd made three million, I wanted
a change. I wanted to do something with my life before it was
too late, something more meaningful.

I became Mavis Taylor – a 'childless divorcee' from east
London and bought a large cottage in north Yorkshire. I con-
verted the outbuildings into a studio. Each morning, with a cup
of black coffee scalding my palms, I would stare at an eight-
foot high block of marble for a few minutes and then sculpt. I
worked until lunchtime every day and did what I pleased with
the rest of the day. Long walks across the moors, shopping trips
to nearby Harrogate, reading novels curled up in my favourite
armchair.

Still, I was not content. I had only an emerging figure in
stone for company. The yearning to share my life grew strong,
especially in the long nights. There was something else; time was
a factor. Mavis harboured a desire Alison had been concealing.

~φ~

How I hungered.

I began to take folic acid and other supplements to make
sure I was healthy and prepared. I didn't plan to prolong things
if the right man came along. My only chance of meeting a partner was to get out more. I joined a nearby private golf club and
took lessons. I made my presence plain in the nineteenth hole
at least twice a week and checked out my options.

A lot of them were older than I'd anticipated but some
were young enough to fill my belly with a new generation. The
problem was that most of them were already married.

Hell, that hadn't stopped them when I was a whore, why
would it now?

~φ~

I played cat and mouse with Thomas Towers the architect
for a few weeks before 'bumping' into him in the Hadliegh Golf
Club car park. I gave him my number and walked away before
he could protest. Leave a man with temptation long enough

and sooner or later he'll give in. Thomas Towers made me wait three weeks before phoning. I let him leave a message.

"Listen, Mavis, I'm only phoning to say that this is not going to be what you think. I'm married. I've got two great kids and I don't want any complications in my life. However, the least I can do is buy you dinner. How are you fixed for Tuesday? Say, seven-thirty? I know this great Italian place near the river."

Tom was a gentleman. Well brought up, well educated, well spoken. He even tried to restrain his manly urges. I played innocent, making out that all I wanted was friendship. At the same time my eyes met his lingeringly. Secretly, all manner of tempestuous sexual images went through my mind. Perhaps he could see them flickering in the darkness of my pupils.

If he could he didn't mention it. Instead he explained his passion for definition and form. He told me how he loved this world of clay and how men shaped it to their will. As though they were the very hands of God manifest. Something about that offended me in a way I wasn't able to express until later.

He didn't come home with me. Had to go back to Mrs. Towers, no doubt, to tell her how his after-hours business meeting went.

I had my own after-hours business planned for him.

On a quiet Monday morning at the golf club, I played an early nine holes with him. We were first there and no one teed off behind us. I offered my arse like bait on every stroke, knowing he was standing behind me and seeing it all. On the sixth, I hooked my ball into the woods. A foursome were a couple of holes behind us playing leisurely shots. There was ample time to search for my ball amid the pines. After a minute or two, Tom came to help me. I goosed him as he bent to look in a thicket and he leapt upright.

"Jumpy, are we?" I said, mocking him. "Afraid to be alone in the forest with me?"

He looked both angry and frustrated but said nothing. I stepped up and laid my leather-gloved palm against his crotch. He didn't stop me. I knelt on the dead pine needles and gave him something to think about when he was lying awake next to his wrinkled, disinterested wife. After that, his game went to hell.

I invited Tom out to my cottage and we went walking on the moors. It became a routine, him making an excuse once every week or two and spending an afternoon or morning with me. We went walking regardless of the weather. There was nothing so scrumptious as coming in soaked or chilled, showering in steaming water, then lying on a rug by the fire drinking red wine and making love. It must have got to him.

After a couple of months he began to wear a pained expression for much of the time we spent together. He smiled through it but I knew he was beginning to realise there was a choice to be made. A choice he'd never anticipated when he took his marriage vows. I said nothing about it. Let him suffer, I thought, let him come to me willingly. Considering all I knew about being a man, giving him every reason to choose me was easy. I liked watching him squirm. Could I have a child with this man? I often asked myself. The answer was always yes. Could I spend the rest of my life with him?

Well. Maybe.

But what did that matter? Wasn't a family what I wanted? I thought it was.

Tom dithered and wrestled with himself for another couple of months and I began to get bored with waiting. One day I brought him close to orgasm with my mouth, stopping at a crucial moment.

"You don't need to wear anything today," I said. "I'm due on tomorrow. It's safe."

"I shouldn't," he said but it was clear he wanted that membrane-to-membrane touch we'd never shared.

I turned over on all fours, laid my head on the rug and opened myself.

"Just do me, Tom. Do it hard."

A little lie was all it took. About six weeks later I bought a pregnancy test. It confirmed I was on my way to motherhood.

~φ~

Sometimes I patrolled the cottage studying its structure and contents. The beams and bricks. The TV, the phone, the washing machine. The windows and doors, the way everything fitted together. The way it all worked. I hated the cleverness of these man-made things. I wanted to smash them. Everything constructed, everything technical, everything unnatural. I wanted to destroy it all.

Behind all this, a rapacity; a need to be satisfied. Even the thought of my child was not enough to assuage my wanting.

~φ~

I understood what men wanted sexually but I'd misjudged their emotional requirements. I discovered this when Tom told me he wasn't leaving his wife for a woman who had tried so blatantly to trap him. *Fuck you, Tom*, I thought. *Keep your crusty, cellulite-ridden, shapeless bitch of a wife if that's what gives you comfort.* It wasn't a man I wanted. Not a man like him.

At least I had my baby.

~φ~

I stayed at home and worked on the sculpture.

The marble was hard. I didn't have Alastair's strength to chip off huge chunks but something was definitely emerging; a figure I could sense but not visualise. There was a soul in the stone. I freed it a shard at a time.

The workshop was dusty with a fine layer of marble powder. It clung to everything even after I'd swept. There was an odd smell in there – dampness from before the conversion. It affected my tools, covering them with reddish brown spots within hours of me cleaning and oiling them. Must and dust and rust. The odours of sculpture.

Soon, a dislike of the sculpture grew. Not a dissatisfaction with my ability. On the contrary, I felt I'd been reborn with artistic genius. I began to hate the statue itself; the very search for the life within in the stone. One day I would find it and what then? Part of me doubted there was any more meaning in a sculpture than there was in a bridge or a desk or a computer. There was no life in it. No nature. It was no more than another meaningless structure. Something men might congratulate themselves about. Something without purpose.

I'd already achieved so much as a woman: the money, the lifestyle, the imminent child, the art. What would my purpose be after the child was born? What else was I meant to do?

The questions were a little premature.

~φ~

Just because I'd stopped seeing Tom and just because my stomach had turned into a space-hopper didn't mean I let myself go. I still went to the hairdressers and beauty salon. I lay on my tanning bed at home. I avoided overeating. I kept my legs and underarms smooth. My granddad's razor represented the end of Alastair's life and the origin of mine. I still used it.

One evening in the aromatic steam of the bath, I soaped my legs, made the first upward stroke from ankle to knee and tore off a long strip of skin. There was no pain. If there had been I would have stopped before the stroke was complete. Instead I sat there, one leg up in the air, the blade against the outside of my knee and a scrunched flap of tanned shin skin, slightly stubbly, hanging down into the water.

Beneath was something unrecognisable. The revealed layer of skin – if that was what it was – was the colour of pale, cloudy pondweed; something that might grow in a stagnant rut. It was marbled with deep green tributaries.

I could live with hairy legs and a bushy crotch but there was no need to expose the rest of whatever now lurked beneath my hide. In case it was infected, I drenched the newly exposed area with hydrogen peroxide. I waited for the acidic sting and fizzing but neither came.

No brain, no pain.

I wrapped my leg in a gauze dressing, secured it with zinc oxide tape and retired to bed with a brandy. I slept but not deeply. While my body was unconscious, another part of me paced the room, watching me impatiently. I awoke exhausted but unable to fall back to sleep.

The baby kicked hard, hurting me.

I made coffee, extra strong, microwaved a Danish pastry, slathered it with marmite and went out to the studio still in my dressing gown. The pastry tasted great with the saltiness of yeast extract and the coffee sharpened me up. I hefted the hammer and chisel, already carrying a patina of rust from the previous day, and smashed compulsively into the marble.

For all the effort I put into it, the chips and fragments coming away were no bigger than usual. The work progressed far too slowly. My arms ached. My hands cramped closed. I forced myself to continue, hating the emerging figure but desperate to complete it.

At lunch I ate ice cream and kosher dill pickles, one from the box the other from the jar. I alternated mouthfuls, craving the clash of flavours. My right leg was numb below the knee. It didn't belong to me. I ignored it and hammered away the dross marble, inching one frustrating stratum closer to releasing the soul in the rock with each blow. I was so hungry I could have eaten stone.

That night I slept in utter fatigue but the sense of watching myself was stronger. There were two of us in that room. Lost in the night I imagined it was the baby, impatient to be born, desperate to begin its life's mission. Morning found me as exhausted as the day before but worse off because my arms and hands were stiff and sore from the previous day's efforts.

Breakfast was crazy – an omelette with dark chocolate stirred into it. I ate it with sweet chilli sauce and mustard. Unwashed, ragged with unrest, I took my triple strength coffee to the studio and began to work immediately. I hadn't bothered to clean my tools the night before and the rust lay over their surfaces like old menstrual blood. The first few strikes elicited both white and brown dust. I coughed and continued.

Before lunch I stepped back to assess what I'd achieved and fell over, sitting down hard on my tailbone. My partially peeled right leg had given out. A deep ache began in my abdomen. The ache became a cramp and the cramp became a contraction. I bled for the next four hours, checking the flow again and again. Nothing solid came away.

I dared not go to the hospital as I was. I could only pray that the baby was still all right. It felt like sabotage. Did part of me not want the child?

~φ~

On the third day, the bandage began to look juicy. It smelled of sweet mould and blue cheese and was the colour of a grass stain. I unwrapped it in the bathroom. The bandage was damp and hung heavy from my fingers as it peeled away. It came grudgingly, bringing my skin with it.

If there was an infection, it was in my skin. Where the now untidy edges of my scrape-wound met the new flesh below, there was decay and purulence. The yellow-green softness of a wet scab. The rest of my lower leg was just as numb and the skin just as dead. The bandage had been holding it on. Now it fell away like the slippery skin of a poached hen. When I'd removed my face, it had required commitment and the use of the blade. Now, my skin was falling away and I couldn't stop it. Already it was discoloured and loose above my knee.

I just wanted a little more time. I re-wrapped the leg in bandage all the way up to my thigh and went back to work.

~φ~

The figure I was discovering in the marble appeared to be human or at least humanoid. Masculine too. I hammered with all my strength, listening carefully to my intuition for where to deliver each strike. There was a man in there somewhere, struggling to be free of the stone. I wanted to see him and then… I didn't know what then.

I used a breakfast barstool to stop me losing my balance because the numbness had reached my groin.

I was afraid.

~φ~

I couldn't ignore the discoloration seeping through the bandages any longer but I whimpered when I peeled the rest of the skin from below my knee. Beneath the rotten dermis there were two sap-green lower limbs; strong and skeletal.

Reptilian.

~φ~

When I'd discovered a woman inside me, I was overjoyed at the possibilities. Now I'd found something unknown and I didn't want to go through with it. It was not, however, a matter of free will. Inside the woman something new needed to be recognised, demanded its freedom and dominion over the femininity I had revelled in.

Reduced to practicalities, it made far more sense for me to remove my dying skin as I had before, rather than waiting for it to rot off me.

Once again I found myself in the bathroom with my granddad's razor in my hand. This new bathroom of mine had a full-length mirror I could shave in front of. There was no need for foam or soap or cream. My new self, the one I did not know, cried out for the blade. My hand trembled as I brought the razor to bear on what was left of my skin. Before I did what had to be done, I wondered what granddad would have said if he could see what I was using his old razor for. I heard his voice clearly:

You keep peeling that onion, lad, and you know what you'll end up with.

It didn't change anything; one way or another my skin had to come off.

I flayed myself one frantic strip at a time, weeping a woman's tears over her lost beauty.

~φ~

The tears disappeared with the last of my old face.

I stood naked and new in front of the bathroom mirror, the remains of a woman shed around me in foetid, wrinkled piles.

This was what I saw:

I had four pale green legs but was able to stand upright. My feet had four toe-pads, three splayed at the front and one at the back. At the end of each of the three front pads were emerald talons the shape of rose thorns but much, much larger. The rest of each foot was like a long shin articulating forward from the ankle joint. My legs were like the hind limbs of some tall, balancing canine. But they were smooth-skinned, hairless.

My crotch was flat, no outward sign of genitalia. The pregnant bulge that had become so cumbersome was much reduced. I believed the thing I'd become was not only not pregnant, but also incapable of ever being so; an androgen. There was a swelling in what I took to be my abdomen but it was covered with slablike musculature. I had no breasts. No nipples.

My chest was huge, much larger than Alison's, even larger than Alastair's. The muscles bunched and twitched whenever I moved. I had four huge, bough-like arms each with two elbow joints and hands with six fingers. Each hand was a hybrid of a shovel and a garden fork; flat, wide and sharp at the fingertips. But they were dextrous hands. I moved the fingers and felt capable of minute delicacies and gross acts of violence.

My neck was short and wide to support my huge head. I stared with two bulbous eyes from the control centre of my new self, a cranium of bone so heavy and thick that it would have taken several men with jackhammers to breach it. It was broad and squat, the head of a giant, armoured praying mantis perhaps. The mouth was almost as broad and opened so wide I could have put a football in it. I had two large black teeth in the top of my mouth and two tiny ones opposing them in the lower jaw. Each was a needle-sharp fang that broadened to the width of a wine cork before disappearing into charcoal grey gums. Behind them were dozens of black molars that looked like they could crush a safe. A loose mass of mucus-covered tongue tissue quivered between them. I had no nose, only two nostrils on my flat new face. My eyes moved behind a hard clear surface. When I blinked, I blinked beneath a protective sheath.

Something moved inside my abdomen. I was ravenous. No amount of ice cream and pickles was going to make the feeling go away.

~φ~

I looked in the fridge but nothing inside interested me. I lifted several items to my nose in succession with each of my four hands. Nothing smelled good. Looking around, I was drawn instead to the radio, the crockery, the kitchen knives, the furniture and ornaments, the microwave. My hunger made no sense.

Something beckoned me to the studio.

There, I pulled the sheet from the sculpture. I sniffed the air. My abdomen twitched and juddered beneath the plates of muscle. From the hanging rack of craftsman's implements I selected two hammers and two chisels. They felt as light as plastic toys. I placed the chisel heads against the marble in two places and made two simultaneous strokes with the hammers. Particles and rock flew. I sniffed at the dust-heavy air.

In the corner of the room a chip of marble had come to rest. I walked to it on four strange legs, already becoming nimble. I passed a chisel to a hammer hand and with the free one picked up the marble shard. I turned it over in my fingers. I held the broken rock to my nostrils and sniffed again. My insides spasmed. Before I knew what I was doing, I'd thrown the rock into my mouth and was biting down on it. I wanted to stop myself, afraid I'd break my teeth and slice up my tongue. The rock crumbled like dry fudge and melted over my tongue. It tasted of intention and the inspiration before creativity, of something to be wrought: the theft of form from nature's purity. I swallowed and the rock was gone.

There were two giant plastic bins where I put all the shards and swept-up marble dust, both at least half-full. I reached in, took four huge handfuls of broken rock and piled them into my mouth. I crunched and mauled my jaws. The rock disintegrated like candy.

I chewed through one bin and fell asleep on my back.

~φ~

I awoke and my abdomen was serene. It seemed larger, but there were no tremors below the surface. My head was clear and I felt strong. There was work to do.

~φ~

By dusk the statue was finished. My strength and dexterity enabled me to finish in a single day what would have taken two more months to complete as a woman. The figure was very familiar but it belonged to another time. It was distant the way childhood can feel distant; when the memories of youth might be those of some other person.

In the marble was a perfect representation of the man whose name was Alastair Perry. I'd picked out every detail.

He stood with a face of stone, looking into a mirror of stone. In his hand was a straight razor. He was about to make a cut below his right ear. He looked bleary-eyed and tired, like a man whose life is going nowhere. His muscles were slack and weak with disuse, his face prematurely aging. Despite the lack of colour, he looked more real to me than my own face had in that mirror those few years previously.

Alastair Perry was someone I would never be again. Had I still been Alison, I might have felt something to see him standing there, poised on the cusp of his re-creation. In my new form, his image barely touched me.

And yet, it was significant.

A sudden pain ripped through me. Deep within my abdomen, something was moving. I howled and every window in the studio turned cloudy with cracks before falling from their frames like a billion diamonds. I fell to my four knees. In spite of the pain I saw one of my hands reach out and pick up a handful of glass crystals. I threw them into my mouth, ground them to a savoury powder and swallowed.

The pain spread from my crotch to my neck and through to my back. My entire torso felt like it was being forced open. I howled again and heard glass shatter in the cottage. I looked down at my body and saw a central partition of muscle separating from the rest. A crack opened up around it and a gruel of watery mucus dripped to the floor. Near my crotch, the muscle remained attached but the rest of it opened like a living trap door and out tumbled a hundred pale green miniatures of myself. Their heads were disproportionately large for their tiny bodies but they had no trouble supporting themselves.

They moved with hyperactive intensity. After only moments of orienting themselves they made straight for the statue. Soon the effigy of Alastair Perry was covered in my tiny babies. They scaled his ankles, his knees, his crotch, his stomach and back and all the way up to his head. Like caterpillars on cabbage leaves, they demolished him. It took minutes.

I lay back against the leg of a workbench and watched. Slowly, my abdominal hatch closed up and sealed. Soon there was no sign it had ever been breached. I was leaner and felt lighter. I knew when I'd rested and eaten I'd be stronger than ever.

When there was nothing left of the statue. The babies began to howl in tiny plaintive voices. I stood up and led them to the broken glass. They devoured it in seconds and looked at me for guidance. I stepped outside and with one hand I gouged a hole in the stone wall of the studio. I put the excavated handful in my mouth. It was exquisite. My babies clambered over each other to reach the wall but some of them started on the tools and the old kettle. The sound of destruction soothed me.

~φ~

When my property was swallowed, we converged on the village.

Alastair Perry is gone and I have reached my final morphology. My children grow larger and stronger each day. I know what I am now. I know what we are. We will multiply.

We will devour this polluted world, misshapen as it is by structure and the interference of human inspiration. We will return it to a world of clay.

Etoile's Tree

There were many mango trees on the island but the one that grew in front of Etoile's hut was the largest. It had been there since before his great grandfather was born and Etoile knew it would be there long after he was gone. In the morning, and in the evening after he had sold his catch, he would sit near the doorway with his back to a wall of woven palm leaves and watch the tree and the creatures who made use of it.

When the wind blew and sometimes in the calmest, blackest hours of the night the tree would speak and Etoile, lacking any human company for most of every day, would answer. The words of the mango tree became a refrain, chanted over and over in his mind as he repaired his fish traps or waded into the luminous shallows to place them. The words were on his lips while he slept, as he waited and when he waded out once more to bring the fish traps in.

Every islander knew where to come for the best fish. He would sell them by the track that ran between his tin roofed house and the palm-lined shore. Etoile always kept a couple for himself which he would grill over an open fire and eat with boiled cassava root or rice. Sometimes he would walk the sandy mile along the track to the shop and buy himself an ice-cold bottle of Coke. The girl would open the bottle for him and he would sit by the road watching the people come and go.

The people of the island did not know Etoile well. They knew where he lived and the history of his family. They knew his fish were fresh and delicious. But these were things that people might know about anyone on the island. The rest of Etoile, if there was any more to be known, was a mystery and the islanders made stories up to fill in the holes in their knowledge. The stories were wicked but they made the islanders feel safer. The stories allowed them to speak of Etoile and in doing so keep themselves apart from his mystique. They used Etoile as a threat when their children would not behave.

He has the power of the woods

He speaks the language of the dead

Etoile will take you in the night and feed you to the fish, that is how they taste so good

He will put his curse on you and the forest will take your mortal soul

The children avoided Etoile when they saw him drinking his Coke and if they had to pass his house they would do it at a run. Some of the boys threw stones into the forest where his house was, crying out in delight if they heard the sound of stone on tin but they never heard the sound of stone on Etoile.

~φ~

"Why won't you let me swim with you?"

Jules had been hanging around the other boys for half of the morning and they were keen to be rid of him.

"You are not a man, Jules. Only men can swim with us. Look at your foot, how can you swim with that?"

Jules ignored the reference to his dropped foot. Even he knew that being crippled could not stop you from being a man.

"I am as much a man as any of you," he said and regretted his boldness in the next instant. The boys were cruel and full of mischief.

"You can prove you are a man. Bring us a mango from Etoile's tree. Then you can swim with us."

"But Etoile will be there now," he said.

A beating would have been better. If they'd told him to swim to Long Rock and back, braving the sharks and the currents he would have been more willing. Etoile was a sorcerer. How could he become a man if Etoile took his soul?

The choice was already made for him. He could face this challenge or face the rest of his life as an outsider. Jules knew in his heart that even completing their task might not mean true acceptance. His foot would ensure his separation forever.

Without any more complaints, he turned away from the lean, brown bodies of the group, every one glistening in the water, and walked towards Etoile's house. The boys giggled at first but they could see where his steps were leading him and soon they followed, their swim forgotten. They saw him disappear into the bushes on the other side of the sand-covered track and that was as near as any of them would go.

~φ~

Jules crept through the clinging mesh of undergrowth, past the cinnamon trees and vanilla vines and under the paw paws and red banana trees. He tried to make no sound but his deformed foot often caught on exposed roots and dragged across fallen palm leaves causing them to rustle. Each time he made a noise louder than his own breathing and his own heart beat, he would freeze, lizard-still and sweating before moving again.

On the other side of the track by the beach, the waiting boys heard nothing. They could only imagine Jules' fear and each was secretly ashamed that they did not have his courage. For once they were silent and still. No jeering or pushing. No pitiless laughter.

The sweat stung Jules' eyes and he used the back of his thumbs to wipe them clear before moving on. The foliage broke open before him and he found he was in the clearing where Etoile lived. There, he saw the hut with no door and no glass in the windows. There, he discovered the ancient mango tree and in it the largest mangos he'd ever seen. Of Etoile there was no sign.

There was no more cover for him now. He had to cross the open space and climb the tree to take his prize and then the others would see he was a man. Knowing it would look foolish but not being able to keep from doing it, he bent almost double as he slunk across the exposed distance to the base of the tree.

When he reached it, he was so unsettled that every sound of the forest made him start like a hunted animal. His next challenge was the tree. Now that he was beside it he could see the tree was even bigger around than Etoile's hut. The bark was rutted and rough but he could find no purchase on the broad trunk. His dropped foot had the strength to support neither his desire to climb nor the weight of his body.

He began to realise that his attainment of manhood might be far out of reach but, unwilling to give up, he concentrated his efforts and tried every approach to reach the first separation in the tree's trunk. He could not hold back his tears of frustration and the curses against his foot that his mother would have slapped him for had she heard them.

"There are easier ways to pick fruit," said a voice behind him.

In his efforts to climb Jules had forgotten where he was, forgotten that he was trespassing and attempting to steal. Now he stopped struggling and turned with his head dropped and his eyes downcast. He could have tried to escape but he did not.

"Look at me. Let me see the face of the man that tries to climb this mango tree."

Jules lifted his heavy head until he could see Etoile properly. The man was old, his face wrinkled from day upon day of equatorial sun. He wore only a pair of ragged shorts, mended many times and crusted white with sweat and the salt of the sea. His beard was thinning; yellow and grey had crept into it. His limbs were tight and sinewy but the skin over them was slack with age. Like most people on the island, he wore no shoes. He smiled a little through broken and missing teeth.

Their eyes had met now and Jules was not so afraid as he thought he would be. Perhaps losing his soul would not be so terrible a thing. He sensed a gentleness from the old man, a calmness that reminded him of the flatness of the lagoon on a moonlit night in the hot season, no breeze to wrinkle its mirrored surface.

"The mangoes from this tree are very special," said Etoile, looking upward with meaning. Jules followed his gaze. There he saw a clump of green and pink-skinned fruit twice the size of any on the island. He saw Etoile hold out both hands as if offering him something and a huge mango fell into each of them. "All you need to do is ask." He handed the fruits to Jules whose small hands were weighed down by the fragrant burden.

"Taste one. Then take the other to your friends."

Jules lifted his right hand to his lips and bit through the

skin. His teeth sank through the soft, sweet flesh and a flood of saliva filled his mouth. The scent of ripeness burst below his nose as the pulp melted on his tongue. He spat out the skin and took another bite and another until nothing but the fibrous heart remained.

When he looked up, Etoile was no longer there. He ran back through the undergrowth to where the other boys were waiting. He ran as the man that the other boys would never be. He tossed them the mango and went to swim by himself. He no longer cared what they thought of him. They noticed the condition of his foot long before Jules did. He was running and swimming more strongly than any of them. He limped no longer.

A day later, the old man found a freshly butchered and gutted suckling pig laid across his doorway, a gift from Jules' mother. He had no use for so much extra food so he buried it near the trunk of the mango tree where he buried his old fish bones. He knew the carcass would be rich food for the tree.

~φ~

Etoile sat on the weathered log outside his hut. His backside had polished the wood smooth over many years. He waited for the rains the way he waited for everything, knowing that in time every season would come to him, knowing that he could neither spin the world faster nor prevent it from showing him the way to his grave.

In the clearing below the tree, all was shade. Etoile watched the bandit-faced mynah birds bounce and chatter as they searched for food. They were thieves who would tip eggs from the nests of other birds and then fly down to eat the smashed results. Their opportunism was boundless.

As some of the heat went out of the day in the late afternoon, the fruit bats arrived in the forest. About a dozen landed in the mango tree where they hung upside down in the branches and clambered after the many prizes to be had. In spite of the great numbers of fruit they always tried to eat the same clusters and ended up squabbling and biting, high in the limbs of the tree. Now and again a partially eaten mango would fall from their claws to the ground below, other times a squirt of urine or guano. Etoile's seat was well out of the way.

On the trunk and limbs columns of ants attended to endless business. Large green geckos chased insects and wasps made their daubed homes. Colonies of palm spiders wove their huge webs high in the tree and in the sunlight, their creations shone in complex gold geometry.

When he had waited and no rain had come, Etoile went to collect and sell the day's catch.

~φ~

A week later he sat once again on his seat, shaded from the midday sun by the outer limbs of the mango tree. The air gathered density around him pressing close and forcing the sweat from his skin. There had been no wind for days. He told himself he would walk to the shop for a Coke but his legs did not respond. Instead he waited. The air clung to him, wringing him like a clenched fist. It forced its way into him, heating his airways and his head.

Above him, behind his back, the exposed, rusted roof of his house rippled in the heat. The sun was crushing everything with its glare.

The first drops fell before the clouds could cover the sun. When they hit the corrugated tin of his roof they sizzled and evaporated, but they were followed by more and then by a slight breeze and Etoile knew that his waiting was over. The spatters of rain increased their finger drumming. The breeze became a wind and enough fat drops of rain fell that the roof steamed instead of sizzling.

The leaves of the mango tree shifted and the branches nodded gently. A whisper sprang up through the jungle all around, a rumour of rain. The air filled with the smell of ozone. Etoile looked around. The world was in shadow now; the wind sent a shiver across his skin.

For a moment everything stopped; the wind, the sighs of the leaves, the swaying of the branches, the drops on the roof, the strangling of the air. The world was withering. Then the rain unleashed itself, thundering onto the roof and the leaves of the trees and rumbling onto the ground turning the dryness to mud.

Etoile turned his face to the sky and drank deep of the rain, let it wash the cracks in his skin. He threw off his shorts and ran, dancing around the trunk of the mango tree. He let the rain give everything, let the rain take everything away.

~φ~

The storms of the monsoon were fierce that year, blowing down palms all over the island, taking away houses and sinking boats. The gift of rain was costly.

Etoile's house and clearing were well sheltered and he suffered no damage but the mango tree did not escape uninjured. It lost many dead braches and one small, green branch that was struck by a heavier one as it fell.

Etoile picked up the young branch and shinned up into the tree as easily as a cat. He climbed out along a thick limb to the place where the branch had snapped off. Bracing his legs around the bough, he pressed the damaged end of the broken limb back into the place from where it had been torn. He spoke in whispers and caressed the rough bark until the branch was once again part of the tree.

As he climbed down, he felt the first huge pang of agony flowering within his chest. When he reached the ground he sat down with his back to the great trunk and tried to regain control of his breathing.

~φ~

Jules had often thought of going back to see the old man who had healed him but his feelings for Etoile were deep and powerful. He had not felt worthy of the man's presence. Finally, though, he made his way back to the house in the small clearing to speak with him.

He took the path that led from the track this time, not needing to hide his approach. When he reached the clearing he wished he had had the courage to come earlier. He dropped to his knees in front of what was left of Etoile.

The feral cats had been chewing on the old man's legs and a

trail of ants were marching across his chest, continuing upward from his shoulder and onto the trunk of the tree. The mynah's had taken his eyes and still hung around waiting to peck once more at his unguarded flesh. Flies hummed and circled around, landing, taking off, laying their eggs. Maggots moved below his skin. There was a movement in his ruined shorts and Jules started back. A land crab sidled out onto Etoile's thigh and crept away under the layers of fallen leaves

Jules bowed his head in front of the old man and cried.

When he'd finished he noticed that the clearing was buzzing with the wings of thousands of insects eating fruit. The tree had dropped every one of its mangoes, covering most of the clearing. Jules knew they were the only tears it could shed.

Inside the hut, thieves had already taken everything of value. Most of the money the old man had made from selling fish he had never needed to spend, and that was what they'd removed. Jules saw the smashed earthenware bowl and knew it must have held thousands of rupees before they stole it. Nothing of any use was left.

Jules laid Etoile's body to rest in the place where the old fish bones and the carcass of the pig had been buried. He knew that it would keep the tree strong and encourage its magic to linger.

For a long time he sat waiting on the log outside the hut. ❧

Introscopy

*A*t dawn the chemtrails are candyfloss pink against the distant azure. Once the sun is well-established they blaze pure white, netting the sky in brilliant criss-crosses. Every sunrise is the same. There's something synthetic about its beauty; this surgically altered face of morning.

Weariness smothers my shoulders like a lead shawl; a malign intelligence perching there, crushing me. I needn't look in the mirror to know the whites of my eyes are marbled with leaking capillaries. Or that they swivel in shadowy pits. It's not the first time I've slept badly and I won't be alone in this. Not today.

At night, in the clear air, I'm able to think with lucidity – work it all out. By morning, it's impossible.

I've wasted years of sleepless nights contemplating the purpose and meaning of my existence. The matter no longer needs my attention. All will be exposed by the Eye of the Gnosis. One is either veritable or one is not. There's nothing any of us can do about it.

The Convoy of Reckoning approaches.

~φ~

"Toast or cornflakes, Alec?"

Same choice every morning.

"Toast."

"Tea or coffee?"

I believe tea goes with toast, coffee with cornflakes. Each day, she asks me, regardless. Funny how I always have to think it over.

"Uh… tea. Please."

Today all our lives will change forever and I'm having tea and toast for breakfast.

"Hold on, Suze. I'll have cornflakes... and... Tea."

~φ~

Nine years ago this was a fallen nation, the antithesis of the empire we'd once been: Family and community were forgotten ideals; respect didn't exist; the homeless crowded our streets; hospitals were understaffed and overstretched; demoralised police were corrupt and ineffectual; the coalition government was paralysed by infighting; individuals considered themselves victims and at the same time, heirs to a life of plenty; discontent and want reflected in the rising crime rates; thuggery ruled the towns.

Rising from this shameful nadir came the New Socialists and at their head, the charismatic Grant Saxon. For the first time in decades the population voted like it cared – the first act of national unity since the Oil Wars finished. New Socialists thronged the seats of parliament. And suddenly, unbelievably, things began to change for the better.

It was fast. Some kind of revolution.

Hospital queues evaporated. Employment was abundant. Street-people started lives they could be proud of. Teenagers stopped terrorising town centres. Trains and buses ran on time. The police hit the streets like the Bobbies of old. Selfishness waned in favour of community effort. Neighbours talked to each other. Free time was snatched back from the grip of workaholism. There was such a thing again as a lazy Sunday afternoon, meals eaten together at the table, family holidays.

It's the only election I remember after which disappointment and mistrust never set in. Don't misunderstand, though – it wasn't paradise. Everyone had their problems. There were still diseases, and traffic, and death, and taxes, and murder and abuse. But there was optimism. Even in the darkest, coldest winters things didn't look quite so grim.

There were other changes too: More food, more sex, more alcohol, more fun, more gratification. In the sky threads of woven cloud lingered at the break of each new happy day.

~φ~

Just as I suspected:
Cornflakes and tea are awful together.
Still, it made a change.
I already know what they're going to discover about me.
Facing it like this, knowing the truth is coming, there must be
hundreds of thousands of us having this exact revelation. We're
compelled to see ourselves honestly for the first time.

~φ~

I can imagine what they're saying over the breakfast tables
in the houses of our town this morning; sons to fathers, mothers to daughters, brothers to sisters, old men to their nurses,
widows to their pets:

"Today's the day. I can't believe it's time already."
*"Don't fret, lass. We're all God's children. This'll just confirm
it."*
"So. This is it, then."
*"I didn't fight the bloody oil wars for this. I'm telling you: They
won't get me in front of that damnable machine."*
"Time to face the facts."
"But the kids…what happens if…how will they live with it?"
*"This is no judgement. There's no scan for what they're trying to
prove. It's all a con."*
"These instruments weren't meant for the hands of men."
*"It's the things I've done, see. That's what worries me. What if
I've erased it through sin? Doomed, I am. Been a bad boy, see."*
"I can't do this. I can't go."
*"We'll be together. Positive. As a family. We're good people.
There's nothing to fear."*
*"I wish there was somewhere we could go. Live out our lives in
ignorance. I swear, we're not meant to know such things while we're
alive."*
*"Whatever they find, I'll always love you. None of this makes any
difference to us, understand?"*

Joseph D'Lacey

~φ~

It was a summons system initially. Grant Saxon and his new government believed there'd be too many screenings to cope with. To a degree they were correct. There was an initial rush of the God-fearing – not a prerequisite as it turned out – the Christian, the Jew and the Muslim. The self-righteous and the powerful. They built more Eyes to deal with the demand for truth. Shock and disappointment was widespread. Many up-standing individuals didn't receive the result they'd expected. They were separated from those that were veritable. When the first run of keen participants was over, it became clear that many of the population weren't presenting voluntarily.

That signalled the birth of the Convoy.

~φ~

"What time should we head off?" Suze asks.

She looks attractive today. I try to discern what's different. Maybe she's put on more make up than usual; outlined her lips and accentuated her cheekbones. Or am I suddenly appreciating what I ought to see – but don't – on every other day? I remember saying 'I love you' and meaning it from some undeniable place in myself. I remember being dead serious about our marriage vows. That all seems a very long time ago.

As though another person said those words.

"Sooner the better, I suppose. Might as well get it over with and get back for dinner. I fancy a roast today. Rare beef with Yorkshires and gravy. Horseradish sauce and steamed cabbage. God, I'm starving already."

It's easy to think about food.

And beer – I just fancy a few pints of ice cold lager.

And sex – I'd like to get back here quick and have Suze for an hour or so while the beef cooks.

Sport after that. Something dangerous – motorbikes or Muay Thai. Bound to be something like that on TV.

Yep, the sport'll be on whether we come back or not.

~φ~

They arrive in a ponderous column of white trucks. At their head is a stretched white limo, Gnosis flags fluttering above blazing halogen headlights. Between each truck two motorcycles ride and at the tail end a string of white Mariahs packed with mute 'staff'. They drive at seven miles per hour. It could be the funeral of some beloved saint.

This glittering motorcade of forty or more trucks slithers into town and twists towards the largest public space – usually a park or common. There, the serpent breaks into segments and rows, and each piece disgorges its cargo of staff and equipment. Queues form at the trucks, which have three doors along each side with access steps and ramps for the less able.

Meanwhile, many of the speechless staff take their maps and head to designated areas of town to ensure one hundred percent attendance. The Eye must see all.

All day the sombre queues shuffle forward, no one speaking above a whisper, and all day those who 'forgot' what day it was and those whose bruises show that they planned not to attend join the backs of the lines and no one talks to them.

All it takes is one day and your town, your village, your suburb is reckoned.

People walk into one side of the trucks in ignorance and walk out the other side with the knowledge. Those that are veritable return home. The others – the Blanks – are provided with government pamphlets on what to do next – where, when and how to report.

Blanks do not go home.

~φ~

Suze and I walk to People's Park hand in hand, smiling. I have no idea why I'm so at ease. The chemtrails are lower now, expanded and etheric like torn cheesecloth against the blue skin of the sky. There seem to be more of them today. The sun has cleared the rooftops and opens its arms to us in generosity. Families walk, laughing quietly, along the streets. Lovers press close to each other and kiss. Leafy trees nod and whisper above the pristine sidewalks of our town. Tranquillity settles over everything.

No one is afraid. I don't know where my apprehension came from. Either there's a new life waiting for me, or I get to keep this one.

"I love you, Suze."

I think I almost mean it.

~φ~

It used to be simple enough. If you were religious, Christian, when you died you took God's elevator to the penthouse or the Devil's to the basement. The Eye of the Gnosis changed all that, added a third element that made faith irrelevant. Now the agnostics and atheists and the people who believed that passing comets held the key to their salvation had the same chance as everyone else. Being the Pope was no guarantee of veritability. Being a diseased street urchin on the streets of Sao Paulo did not necessarily make you a Blank.

~φ~

Have I said this already? – my memory can be a problem.

Let me make it clear for the record. These are my beliefs based on years of nightly inner searching and desperation:

I have no doubt that this life is finite, random and ultimately without purpose. The accidents of timing and positioning that caused life on our planet are exactly that. Accidents. The vastness of space and how it came into existence will remain a mystery to us until our extinction.

In the first place, I say this because I don't believe we have the senses, the powers of perception to see things as they really are. In the second place, but equally pertinent, I don't believe our brains are big enough to understand such input even if we did. We have to see our limitations and live within them. We will destroy ourselves because power is synonymous with stupidity. Those with power will kill us all for the sake of a little more. Unfortunately, that's built into human make-up. So it goes with the lottery that is creation.

These things being the case, there is no morality but that which we invent, no philosophy that can fully explain our condition and no requirement for religion – except to appease our own terror of death and make our boring, decaying existences more bearable.

~φ~

We join the end of a queue that must already have a thousand people in it.

The silent, gesturing staff have set up their little airport barriers to concertina the lines and make them compact. Even with the huge numbers that will come today, weighted plastic poles and synthetic bands of rope are all they require to maintain order. They have other methods if necessary, but I don't think it ever comes to that. Not here anyway.

Out in the streets and the suburbs, those with a little will power will be on the wrong end of some persuasion right about now.

It's very easy not to think about that.

I check out Suze's form. She's wearing skin-tight, purple jeans and high heels. Between the tops of her thighs and the central seam of her spray-ons, there's a heart-shaped space. Her full arse juts with come-and-get-it pride. She can really fill a pair of punky drainpipes. I'm so horny my whole crotch aches. I feel myself release a bead of seminal fluid. All this prevents me thinking about the queue and the fact that we're progressing at a decent rate.

In the distance, I can see people stepping up into the white trucks again and again. The trucks rock constantly as their shock absorbers react to every entry and exit. Strung out in lines, they look like they're pulsating in the heat from the sun.

~φ~

You've got to hand it to the man who invented the Introscope. His name was Oliver Campbell.

By scanning the brains of the worst offenders in the country, Campbell discovered a connection between amorality and the orbifrontal cortex. Figuring there must be an opposite tendency too, he took his equipment on a world tour and scanned the saintliest people he could find. Throughout this time, he developed his scanning equipment with the help of a growing team of volunteer technicians.

By then, he'd developed a cult status. His published papers infuriated the establishment but were impossible to disprove. Every young technician wanted to work with him but he only took the best and most dedicated. He became a man of considerable power.

Initially, he found what he was looking for; a corresponding area in the same region of the brain. When well developed, it appeared to cause altruistic behaviour, acts of kindness and self sacrifice. Then, with a leap forward in imaging techniques, he found something new in the brain. Not a structure, but an energy trace at the centre of the pineal gland. This discovery was anomalous in terms of morality. Some criminals had it and some saintly folks had it. It didn't fit his criteria.

To give him his due, Campbell didn't change the investigation to suit his desired outcome. Instead, he went back to random testing of volunteers. For years this continued and the scientific community lost interest in him. He published no major papers. Articles were written speculating on how he'd come to the end of his career. But Campbell was far from it. With a core crew of his original groupies, he concentrated on his scanners. He needed to define his discovery.

By that time, he'd scanned hundreds of thousands of people. The odds were stacking in his favour. One day, a volunteer died whilst inside the imaging equipment. Campbell and three of his staff witnessed the energy in the pineal move upwards to the top of the head and grow *brighter*. It then appeared to exit the deceased's body.

Recreating that situation can't have been easy for Campbell, but he managed it. He took his gear to hospices and hospitals and paid families to volunteer their dying, comatose relatives for scanning. Patients with a pineal aura responded the same at the moment of death. Every single one.

Campbell wasn't satisfied. It was too early to reveal what he believed he had found. While he and the team developed an imager that would lock onto and follow the pineal energy, Campbell died very suddenly and of extremely natural causes.

That was when the New Socialists commandeered the Introscope and renamed it The Eye of the Gnosis. And, indeed, that's exactly what it was.

~φ~

Finally, a moment of apprehension. A single butterfly that flits in my stomach and is gone. Now what caused that?

True, we're nearing the head of the queue and it seems quicker now because we can see the three open doors of the truck our line leads to. It's like waiting for a free window in the bank or post office.

What occurred to me, the thing that caused the lurch in my solar plexus just now, was how incompatible this scan is with my personal theories. The very existence of the Introscope suggests that, in some people, something survives when life ends. This is inconvenient for me and I have to admit that it has made me doubt myself.

Suze squeezes close to me and offers her parted lips. I get lost in kissing her, though I'm aware we're shuffling along with the ebb of the queue. I could kiss her warm, sweet, yielding mouth forever. Then someone is tapping my shoulder with a heavy white baton and pointing to one of the doorways. I turn to Suze and try to think of something to say but she is being pointed towards another entry and is already walking away. She doesn't look back.

I take a final look around as I approach. The staff all appear to be wearing a compact breathing rig. From a slight hump on their backs an almost invisible tube comes over their shoulders, splits and penetrates both nostrils. Their mouths are sealed shut with a broad strip of flesh tone tape. You have to be this close before you notice any of it. No wonder you never hear them speak.

I'm ravenously hungry and have an equally strong craving for a mind-rocking cocktail like a Long Island ice tea. Something that really hits you between the eyes. And I want Suze badly.

The clouds have sunk to earth. A dusty mist hangs in the air and through it the sun beams its rainbow halo. There must

be fifty thousand people here in the park but I can barely hear
a murmur from them. All is peace and contentment with an
undercurrent of tense desire.

I step through the rectangular doorway. After the bright-
ness outside, the room I'm in is as dark as deep space and for all
I know could be as vast. Firm, businesslike hands impel me to
a chair. I hear the strange breathing of several intubated staff.
A blue light comes on. They shine it into my face. I can smell
roast beef and thick gravy and the crisp bitterness that comes
off an ice-cold beer. I can smell Suze's sweat and the magnetic
aroma of her sex.

The blue Eye goes off. Another door opens; a rectangle of
white light, painful after the darkness. If only it was night-time,
I know I'd understand all this. I'm pulled to my feet.

"Wait... I haven't... did you see it?"

They push me towards the light. Someone hands me a leaflet.

~φ~

I'm in a huge cordoned-off area of the park with thousands
of others. Staff have handed out prepared meals, wine and beer,
sprayed us with their cooling mist. We've spent the day in a
beautiful white haze. Some people have had sex on the grass
all afternoon. Those not involved ate and drank and watched.
Everyone's happy.

Trucks have arrived every five minutes and taken groups of
us away. They load up whoever's nearest. I don't feel like going for a ride yet and there are so many more people joining
us every minute that I doubt they'll have taken everyone away
before dusk.

The sun slips behind the trees and then the roofs of the
houses. The heat is replaced by a cool breeze. I shiver and blink,
shake my head. The trucks keep coming. Aimlessly, I saunter to
the farthest point from them. When the staff come with their
spray-guns I edge into the wind. Shadows stretch across the
park and the staff look agitated, impatient. Some of them tug at
their tubing, adjust their backpacks. The day's reckoning is not
yet complete – many people still join us from the Convoy.

I'm uneasy too. I'm praying for night to fall because I know things will be better then. I won't be hungry or horny. I won't need booze and entertainment. I won't be content.

For the twentieth time, I read my leaflet. I begin to understand. It says I have been found wanting. I am a Blank and therefore not as deserving of New Socialist benefits as The Veritable. I will be transferred to a more appropriate life, one of service to others.

The leaflet says I will be very happy in my new life and I believe it.

I shiver again. Good: I'm getting cold. My thinking feels sharper. The dusts and gases swirl at our feet leaving our heads clear. The staff have put away their spray-guns and many of them are carrying smaller, more harmful looking weapons. Over by the Convoy, the streams of participants have dried up. Doors are closing. In the twilight, some of the staff appear to pull long threads from their faces and shrug off the humps on their backs. Trucks continue to arrive. Blanks still board them.

There's a change in the air, though, like a rift between two very different types of thinking. I'm going to slip into that rift and disappear any moment now. The darker it gets, the better my chances of making it.

I've had a radical change of beliefs: Contrary to the conclusions of the Eye of the Gnosis – nothing more complex than a desk lamp with a blue light bulb in it, I expect – and to my own, I *do* have a soul. We all do; even Grant Saxon and his power-hungry cronies.

I'm going to spread the word. ⁊

Morag's Fungus

Crouching in the woods, Morag digs through papery leaf litter and into the moist black soil. The rich loam sticks to her fingers, fills in under her nails. A large moonstone like a milky, blind eye is mounted on a thick silver ring on the index finger of her left hand. This misty gem dims and glows with the movements of her hands as though its clouds might clear to reveal a long-hidden truth or secret.

She's frantic now, trying to reach a useful depth without snapping her nails or tearing her fingertips on sharp buried stones. She hears his footsteps entering the trees from the path. From the inside of her belt she draws out the black feather, black with a flash of blue when the sun catches it a certain way, and places it in the earth. Her lips move silently as she fills in the hole, interring the feather.

"Picking mushrooms now?"

"I dropped my ring."

She slips the ring off, moves one foot onto the burial site, and fumbles around through the rotting leaves.

"Want me to look?"

"No. Here it is."

She holds it up, turns to him, slipping it on again.

"I'll have to get it re-sized."

"Or eat more. Boiled potatoes at every meal. That's how they fatten up pigs, you know."

"Is that all I am? A unit of livestock?"

"For God's sake, Moz, why do you take everything as a personal insult? Pigs are a lot like people biologically. It stands to reason that what makes them put on weight would make us put on weight. I'm not calling you a sow. I'm just worried about you."

"I'm fine."

"I know. And you need broadening, woman."

He holds out his hand and she takes it. He leads her back to the path where she made him wait while she 'peed'.

Six months, the oncologist had said. She paid for a second opinion. The second opinion was four months – maximum. From the stream of his words she had sieved only a few particles before going deaf: Aggressive. Metastasised. Intractable. Palliative.

No amount of boiled potatoes is going to help.

~φ~

The back garden is really just a strip of ground that someone concreted over to avoid having to maintain it. This plan has worked only temporarily. Now, the cheap concrete – a mix with too much sand – is cracking because life rises up beneath it. Weeds sprout along each fence and through every crevice. Given time, Mother Nature will jack-hammer the concrete to pieces from below. Morag won't be here to see that.

She sits on a kitchen chair near the back door. There are real gardens all around and the trees and shrubs and flowers are very visible. She comes out here to borrow them. The sad thing is, though the flora are very much alive, the weather is only partially committed. Midsummer and the clouds still frustrate the sun. It's never warm enough but it never rains much either. Just this clammy mizzle that starts so many days. Things almost happening. Thunder in the far distance but never a storm. Shafts of sun illuminating some other part of the town. The weather upsets her because she's so much like it.

I was never really here, was I? Like someone that goes to a party but turns away before knocking on the door.

Stefan is her boyfriend. She can't abide the word partner. It implies too much commitment. It's sterile. When he's at work she misses him. When he's at her place, she wishes he was somewhere else. Stefan is her boyfriend.

She can't tell him because it will make them or break them and she can't bear either. She needs him around so that she's not utterly alone but she doesn't want him to be the one. Simply because he is *not* the one. Mortality should be shared with a soul mate, an unconditional lover. Since she is not capable of unconditional love and has not found a soul mate, she must make do with the finger-in-the-dyke that is Stefan. It doesn't matter. When she's gone there will be no more threat of flooding.

There's a crow in a poplar a few gardens away. The tree is taller than all the others and the crow is perched at the top. It takes off and glides towards her garden. It lands at the far end, inspects the cracks and then walks towards her like a professor in black gowns with his hands behind his back.

She stays motionless as it approaches. This is something. An event. An occurrence in the midst of all this blank unwinding. Suddenly the crow stops and pokes at itself with its sharp grey beak. It looks as though it has an itch. When its head reappears from under its wing, it holds a feather in its beak. It plods nearer and places the feather in front of Morag.

"I can help you," it says with a slight Black Country accent.

And she thinks, great, this is what I need: a talking fucking crow.

"Actually, I'm a rook. There are important differences."

"You're a big, black bird."

"No. Blackbirds are famously obtuse."

Some of the oncologist's words float back to her:

"…possibly some brain involvement already…"

Which oncologist said it, she can't recall. This is further proof.

And then the Rook begins to tell her a story. She listens because she has nothing better to do.

"Once there was a little girl who came from a very rich family. The family were good people and they went to church every Sunday and they gave a portion of their wealth to the needy and the sick whenever it was required. The path from their house to the church led through an ancient wood. The little girl's parents told her always to stay on the path through the wood, not because there was danger in the forest but because it was dark amongst the trees and easy to lose one's way.

"But one day, as the family walked home from church, the little

girl saw a ring of mushrooms growing not far from the path. The mushrooms were the purest white and so beautiful they were almost like flowers. Enchanted, she skipped away from her family and into the trees. She knelt down to pick one of the mushrooms but as soon as she touched it, she fell into a deep sleep. Her family walked on without her, not noticing she was gone. When they did come back and call for her, she couldn't hear them because she was so deeply asleep.

"When she woke up, it was dark and the circle of mushrooms was gone. What moonlight there was could not penetrate the canopy of the forest. The little girl was very frightened and she began to retrace her steps in the direction she thought she'd come from. But in the dark she soon became confused and before much longer she could not even find the place where she'd woken up.

"Then the little girl from the kind, rich family sat down and wept among the silent trees; trees who would have put their arms around her if only they could have moved. She cried so much her tears spilled onto the earth and where they touched it beautiful white mushrooms sprang up in their place. She was so surprised she stopped crying. She reached out to pick one of the mushrooms but as soon as she touched it, the mushroom turned black and wilted. She tried to pick another and another until soon all the mushrooms were dead, dry things that no one would ever want. Frightened and alone she sat back against one of the trees and drew her knees up to her chin. There was nothing to be done but wait until morning. Then she would find her way back to the path.

"All night she sat, too frightened to sleep. Without her seeing, the dense trees intertwined to protect her from the strange creatures of the forest; creatures that wanted to sniff and taste her. Exhausted, the little girl finally fell asleep just before dawn. Morning came but she did not wake up. The sun journeyed over the sky lighting up the forest and still the little girl slept. Then the sun sank and disappeared.

"The little girl woke to find that it was still night time. Why hadn't the sun come up she wondered? Was it because she'd tried to pick the mushrooms? All night she tried to find the path but the trees had joined their branches together. Every direction she walked in, she found a wall of woven branches too strong to penetrate, too high to climb. There was no way out. Lonely and sad, the girl returned to the tree where she had been sleeping and sat down beside it. The forest was now her prison and she did not know if it would ever let her go. She

drew her knees up to her chin and hugged herself. Just before dawn she fell asleep, still protected by the trees. The sun made its journey across the sky, giving all its light and then falling exhausted below the horizon. The little girl woke to find herself held captive by the trees. For many nights this was how it was.

"The little girl's family knew she had slipped into the forest in search of something – perhaps a flower or a toad or a sparkling crystal – and they knew there was no way they could follow the girl into the forest without getting lost themselves. All they could do was wait and pray that their little girl would come home one day. Her father became thin and weak because that is the way of time upon fathers. Her mother became bent and crabby because that is the way of time upon mothers. But the little girl's brothers and sisters became fine, strong men and women and moved away from their parents' house to have their own families.

"Meanwhile the little girl wandered each night within her cell of tangled twigs and knitted boughs. And every day the sun shone mottled light upon her as she slept.

"One night she heard terrified weeping from the forest. She heard footsteps running and the sound of paws and claws giving chase over the earth. The weeping became screaming as the forest creatures came closer to their prey. She heard the final wail of denial and defeat as the night creatures brought down their prey to sniff and taste it. And after the snuffling and crunching had stopped the forest was silent again and the little girl was so terrified she could not sleep. She sat with her back to the tree she had spent so many, many nights with – though to her it was all one very, very long night – and she cried silently once again. At least I am safe in here, she thought. At least I am not running alone through the forest at night time with its creatures chasing me.

"As she hugged herself beside that tree a strange thing began to happen. A milky light began to glow. The blackness around her faded into grey and the trees with all their branches intertwined became very, very slowly visible in the night. The little girl could not tell where the glow was coming from. All around her, she saw the way the trees had formed an in impenetrable circle around her, keeping her safe from harm. Soon she could see the wrinkles in the bark of the trees and the buds where new leaves would soon grow. Instead of black and grey, the forest became green and yellow and brown. The

*ground, covered in fallen leaves became a jigsaw carpet. She stood up
and walked into the space at the centre of the ring of trees. A shaft of
light came through the branches falling on the place where she had
slept so long her shape was in the ground. And there, in the shaft
of light, grew a single, beautiful white mushroom, bigger and more
perfect than any she'd seen. The little girl looked down at her arms
and legs and at her body and she saw she wasn't a little girl any more.
Now, as she stood in the light which she knew to be the morning, she
saw she had become a woman.*

*"She walked over to the mushroom and picked it and held it
in her hands and stroked it and admired its flawlessness. When she
looked up, she saw that the wall of branches surrounding her had un-
sewn itself. There were many ways she could walk. Not caring which
way she went because any way was better than spending another endless night in the forest, the little girl who had become a woman started
walking and after taking only a very few steps, she came onto the path
through the forest.*

"Finding her way home was easy.

*"When she arrived, the house was empty because all her brothers
and sisters had left long before to start their own families. Her mother
and father had long since been released from their husks and so she
was alone.*

*"In a pot in the garden, the woman planted her mushroom. Ev-
ery day she ate a piece of the mushroom. By the next day the missing
piece had always grown back. In this way the woman fed herself.*

*"The mushroom still grows there to this day, even though the
woman has long since been released from her husk."*

Morag sits unmoving, staring at the rook. Her cheeks are
cool and wet with tears.

"I don't know what's more upsetting," she says. "listening
to a well-delivered children's story or believing I'm hearing it
from a bird."

"It's not necessarily a children's story." The rook takes a
couple of steps closer and nudges the feather towards her with
his beak. "I do wish you wouldn't refer to me as 'a bird'. It's like
me saying 'Wow, a talking monkey."

"Sorry. It's just...oh fuck."

Morag covers her face with her hands and weeps properly.

The rook picks the feather up in his beak and pokes the quill under her sandal so that it won't blow away.

"Take this. Fill it with power. Transform it."

"What?"

She looks up to try and understand what the rook means but the rook has gone. No swooshing of wings or the tap of black claws on the decaying concrete. Just no rook.

"Oh my God," says Morag, and one hand flies up to cover her mouth but the words still fall out: "It's got to my brain." Then she looks down and sees the feather poking out from under her green Birkenstock. Expecting it to evaporate before she can touch it, she picks it up. A beautiful, silky feather; a living air-blade, so black it's blue. He gave it her, the rook, told her to do something with it. Suddenly it is a fragile, valuable object. Holding it between her palms as though praying, she takes it indoors where it will be safe.

~φ~

At night Stefan holds her making her feel more alone than if he weren't there. On the nights he doesn't stay she feels like the last, or first, woman on earth. She shares herself with no one. Who can ever understand what it means to be Morag Swain? She wonders then, as Stefan's cold fingers grip her shoulder in the darkness what the point of any of her life has been. She doesn't appear to have been present for any of it except this last – the very worst – part. Each night the pain is a little worse. She knows she's sick; really sick. Sick enough to have an appointment booked with a specialist for the following Tuesday.

No, Morag. Not a specialist. An oncologist.

She's not quite ready to start living the bad news. There's still space in each of her days for a little make-believe, a few minutes or an hour perhaps when she feels fine and can pretend to herself to be well.

Stefan, who's been 'around' for months, doesn't have a clue. She catches him looking at her in a puzzled way sometimes but she knows he's interpreting her discomfort as the feminine mystique he likes to project on her. She knows she should drop him but she can't. There isn't anyone else. Her mum and dad would be angry with her for getting sick. Yes, they'd show sympathy and send extra money in case there was anything more she 'needed' but deep down they'd blame her for depriving them of a daughter, hold her responsible for their loss. Her sister, Fay, would appear concerned, might even cry, but in reality she would be ridiculing, dismissive. *Huh*, she'd be thinking, *trust Morag to get cancer and die young. Silly tart.*

Best to keep all this to herself.

~φ~

She hasn't been quite herself for days. Maybe it's weeks if she's honest.

It's strange, when her periods stop, Morag never once thinks she might be pregnant by Stefan. Not once. Oh, it would be nice to be pregnant – not to Stefan, obviously, but to someone – but she knows her periods have stopped for a different reason. Also, she drops a dress size without any change to her diet and without taking any exercise. Also, she notices her hair seems finer, drier. Also, her skin smells different and her nails are brittle. Also, there's a dull ache from her belly right through to her back.

Also, she's lost her appetite.

"More spaghetti, Moz?"

She has now made spaghetti three times for him. He says it's his favourite.

"No thanks. I haven't finished this bit yet."

Stefan clears the pan onto his plate, plops tomato sauce on top of the Bolognese she's cooked and stirs it all up. Then he crumbles blue cheese over the mess he's created and grinds what looks like eight grams of pepper and two of salt over it. Finally, he flicks Tabasco sauce on everything.

"God, Moz, this spaghetti is wonderful. You really know how to make it exactly right."

While he slurps his pasta, she pushes pale worms in gore around her bowl and then lays down her fork.

Maybe I'm anorexic, she thinks. *Maybe I'm anaemic. Maybe it's depression.*

She's knows it's none of those things. It feels 'serious'.

Twenty-five years old and already within sight of the finish line. How very, very strange.

I wonder why I bothered coming here at all.

This thought makes her smile. Stefan shakes his head in disbelief at how good the food is, all the while making mm-mmm noises and licking his stained lips. He fills up his wine glass.

"More Chianti, Moz?"

He pronounces it chee-auntie.

"Fine for the moment, thanks."

The chee-auntie has no flavour to her and absolutely no effect on her mood. A shame, really, she'd hoped alcohol might help her see things differently, or help her to forget. It never does. Whatever's wrong, she stuck with it.

~φ~

Their first date is just before the end of the summer term. Stefan teaches science and she knows he's been watching her in the staff common room, assessing her over his coffee with a look of concentration. Perhaps he thinks she's a chemical equation – one he'd really like to have a go at. Perhaps he has a theory that needs to be proved. Stefan never strikes her as an actual man. Not a bloke, as such. More a sort of manlike plant; possibly a marble statue attempting to appear real.

In spite of this, he's bold when he asks her out, as though she wouldn't have the imagination to refuse. Or be busy. Or despise his vegetable-mineralness.

She says yes because, well… she's not sure why. It seems marginally more interesting than saying no. Besides, she's not been feeling a hundred percent recently and she could do with cheering up.

"Seven o'clock sharp in the snug at the Boar and Truffle," he says. "Drink, dinner, film. Okay? Great."

Did she only nod or did she actually say yes? She's not sure. It must have been a gesture in the affirmative. Perhaps the movement of one of her eyebrows, a micro-gesture swiftly interpreted by the interpersonally skilful scientist, Stefan.

The date is a series of precisely timed events, choreographed by Stefan, the timekeeper; Stefan, the master of ceremonies. Stefan the stud.

The actual itinerary goes: Drink, dinner, film, coffee at your place, Moz, it's probably nicer than mine, kiss for thirty seconds in living room, boy steers girl backwards into her untidy bedroom for swift and forgettable first-date fuck (forgettable even though he pushes her on top and looks disappointed about her modest breast size), sleep disrupted by his snoring and his farts, which smell of curry even though they ate Italian, wake to feel erection nudging vulva and entering before fully regaining consciousness, receive comment about low pressure in the shower followed by peck on cheek and disappearance before breakfast.

So this how people cheer themselves up, she thinks.

And then, *shit, did he even think about wearing a condom?*

~φ~

It's two weeks since she buried the feather. The pain is steady but bearable. She's stopped losing weight. This could be the respite before the final plunge. She dare not see it as anything else. Hope is such a dangerous thing.

Stefan still stays a lot. His major contribution has turned out to be the pre-full-consciousness-fuck-from-behind. Which is really just him wanking off while he happens to be inside her. She still hasn't worked out how he does it without waking her until just before he ejaculates. He's like some kind of ninja sex assassin. Except that a ninja sex assassin would be far more interesting than Stefan. He's usually out of bed before she can turn over for a hug or hello, leaving her vagina deluged with his sperm. He still hasn't used a condom and because he hasn't even mentioned it, neither has Morag. *Thank God I've already got a malignant growth in my womb,* she thinks. *That'll stop me getting pregnant. Any disease he may give me will be incidental.*

Since he discovered there was food if he stayed a little longer in the morning, Stefan has made Morag aware of his penchant for the full English. He's told her how he likes it several times.

It's a simple thing to make a full English breakfast, Stefan has told her. He doesn't know why she can't get it right. The tomatoes must be grilled. The bacon must be fried about half-way through frying the sausages. The baked beans must not be allowed to boil. The eggs should be fried in the fat from the meats plus a little oil, using a spoon to baste their tops instead of flipping them and risking a broken yolk. Broken yolks are not part of a full English breakfast. The toast should be made at the same time as the eggs so that it is served hot. The eggs should be laid carefully on the toast beside mushrooms that have been cooked in unsalted butter. The mushrooms must not be rubbery. All the items must be arranged harmoniously on the warmed plate in a manner pleasing to recently opened eyes. Once this dish is placed before him, Stefan annihilates it with condiments. Tomato ketchup and English mustard for the sausages. Brown sauce for the bacon. Tabasco and mayonnaise for the eggs. Mango chutney for whatever's left. Morag wonders about Stefan's full English breakfast fetish. Where does it come from? Stefan is half Dutch and half Scottish.

She makes a start while he's in the shower. She'll have to wait to clean herself of his gloop properly. For now a swipe around with a tissue and a wet wipe will have to suffice.

In the kitchen she creates a meatless breakfast she's been imagining for some time. Mushrooms cooked in soy sauce and garlic, potatoes diced and fried with onions, thyme and paprika, baked beans with cheese grated into them, eggs poached until they're almost solid, a type of vegetarian sausage she's never tried before, tinned tomatoes with a little fresh basil, cold toast with thickly-spread butter. She usually waits for Stefan to come to the table but today she's hungry. Rumbly, cramp-in-the-tum hungry. Breakfast tastes inspiring, she can feel her body absorbing the nourishment from it, turning it into energy.

Stefan arrives scrubbed, combed and dressed. He points.

"What is this?"

"That, Stefan, is breakfast."

"It's not the full English."

You're a sausage shy of a breakfast yourself, she thinks.

"No. It's not. It's something different."

"What's that smell?"

She shrugs.

"Garlic? Spices?"

"I can't eat stuff like that first thing in the morning."

"You eat mustard and mango chutney."

"That's not the same kind of thing." He sits down, hungry but uninspired. "Can I have some tea?"

"Of course you can," says Morag. "You don't have to ask."

She continues to eat. She feels like she could eat this breakfast and then eat another one exactly the same. It's all she can do to prevent herself from making mm-mmm noises like Stefan.

He sits there, blinking as though seeing her for the first time. Or perhaps he thinks he's woken up in the wrong house. Or the wrong life. She knows how that feels; she's been doing it as long as she can remember. Except for today. Today she's in the right life. It appears to have had a displacing effect on Stefan. Over in the wrong life, Stefan has sprayed himself with water whilst filling the kettle. Now he's searching for a mug. A little self-consciously, it appears. Then the milk. Then the sugar. Then a tea spoon. Then a tea bag. Finally he returns to the cooling mass he refuses to accept is his breakfast.

"Are you all right?" he says.

Morag is chewing. She nods with enthusiasm.

"Mm Hmm."

He pokes around at his food, takes a few small bites, sighs and lays down his fork. He has a sip of tea and grimaces.

"Ugh."

"What's wrong?"

"It's revolting."

"Is the milk off?"

"God knows. Look, I've got to go. I'll... I'll call you."

"Okay." She smiles. "Great."

When he's gone she tastes his tea. He's put salt in it. She laughs out loud. She makes two more rounds of toast, waits for them to cool, butters them and then loads what's left from the pans on top. When she's finished, her plate is so clean it might have come right out of the cupboard. Every few minutes she thinks of Stefan's face as he drank his salty tea. It makes her laugh every time.

~φ~

It's a beautiful day. She can't remember a day like it. The sky is optimistically blue, there are clouds but they're the fluffy kind that never seem to get in the way of the sun and would never dream of raining on anyone. It's actually warm; properly warm and dry. As she laces her boots up, the sun soaks into her the way her food soaked into her. She absorbs it and feels like she's expanding.

In the wood it's darker but she can still see the sun up there through the trees. She follows the path until she comes to a place she recognises. She looks in both directions but there's no one around. She slips off the path and pushes into the trees. It's more overgrown than she remembers and much darker too but she knows where she's going – it's only a few yards away. Funny how it seems to take a lot longer than she remembers. Why she's come she doesn't really know, nor what she'll do once she finds the place.

And then she's there. She remembers the particular tree now although she had no recollection of it before arriving. There, near the base of the tree where she buried the feather, grows a pristine white mushroom. A shaft of sunlight has fallen on it. It reflects this as though the light is coming from inside.

The mushroom probably came up the night before. In a day or so it will be gone, fallen prey to hungry slugs and beetles. But right now it is perfection.

She knows better than to try and pick it. ◣

The Quiet Ones

*A*t dawn on a granite outcrop you lie on your belly in the soft cold powder. You set up a tripod to rest the rifle on. A flat stone tamped into the snow makes a good sturdy base for it. You unclip the lens covers and scope out the village.

You can see chickens wandering free and goats tethered near most of the bare timber houses. There are geese too, which means you will have to be careful not to get too close. At the first sign of a stranger they'll make a hellish noise and you'll be discovered. Some of the people are up already attending to various chores. They move with a considered yet easy grace. They are deliberate and unhurried. Until now you have only ever seen men such as yourself move in that way under similarly unobserved scrutiny. But these people are different; there is a lightness to their demeanours. Theirs is not the grim routine of cold, measured gestures. These people are easy of spirit and carefree. After watching for an hour or so you realise that they do not talk to each other but only nod or smile their acknowledgements. Can it be that they never speak?

The crosshairs of your sight fall on two children milking a goat. One of them holds the goat's head gently in its hands and the other one squirts the milk into a wooden pail. They too, even though they cannot be more than seven years old, never open their mouths to speak. You zoom in on one of the children's heads and refocus. She is a beautiful child with fine blond hair that radiates under the reflected morning light. Her face is serene and open, her cheeks rosy in the frosty air. Even at this distance you can see the strands of flyaway hair moving in an invisible breeze.

You zero the crosshairs on her temple and let your finger rest on the trigger. Death is a moment away.

You are the keeper of that moment.

You release the trigger and scope the other child. He looks almost exactly the same but his hair is a fraction coarser. Perhaps they are twins.

Through a shuttered window you see a man sitting cross-legged in meditation. You watch to see how long he will practise for. Two hours later he has not moved. You begin to get a sense of what these people are like.

In truth, your understanding started in that soundless moment when you stopped among the trees on the other side of the pass. Now you are seeing the effect of letting that silence grow. You are like these people. You have the potential for peace within you in spite of your calling, in spite of everything you have learned to the contrary.

Yes, death is close but peace is close as well.

~φ~

Some days earlier you left the grinding clamour of civilisation and trekked into the foothills of this merciless range. The influence of urbanity fell away from you in successive snakeskin layers with each crunch of your boots on the rock and later with each pulsing sigh of the skis. A few hours brought you among the evergreen sentinels of the vast mountain pine forests.

You stopped for a moment and your cross-country skis sank into the virgin snow. You were fit but that was by sea-level standards. Up here you could feel your heart and hear it too. Your lungs ached to keep you oxygenated. You recovered quickly, though, ignoring the insistent complaint from your calves and thighs. That was the benefit of training, it made discomfort bearable by the sheer fact of familiarity.

Soon both your breathing and heartbeat were normal and inaudible. You listened for anything unusual. For perhaps the first time in your life you heard no sound at all. The forest was in total silence and you were unwilling to break that peace in any way.

No sound. No movement. It implied death but the stillness was alive. The air itself seemed charged with a vital force. You wanted to breathe such air forever, spend your life listening to that living silence. The notion was sudden; impulsive but undeniable. It was also impossible to fulfil. You had tasted a strange moment of peace. In that instant, you had become as still as the forest around you. You wondered how you would handle the inevitable loss of such a feeling. How would you live on knowing such a world existed and only being able to visit that world in your memory? As if the forest could hear you and respond to your inner prompts the silence was broken.

A few yards behind, you heard a whisper and a soft thump and, twisting to face it, you reached for the pistol. Flakes of snow were sifting down through the branches of a nearby tree. One of the higher branches had shed its thick load of powder and was still swaying gently having been released from its burden. You listened once more, turning your ears to each direction but heard nothing. The silence was everywhere, but the peace was gone.

Fled, you suspected, now that it knew your heart.

~φ~

You skied on, cresting ridges with effort and slipping easily into their subsequent valleys, but all the time you climbed upwards. Soon there were no more crests and dips, only a steepening gradient. The trees began to thin out in the higher altitude but you doubted that you would be seen at that stage. The zebra camouflage made you almost invisible even over short distances. It would be after you crossed the pass that you would have to slow the pace and be more careful. Your employers didn't tolerate mistakes and, were you to be discovered they would deny your existence. Were you to fail, they would send another and your own disappearance would be in the new set of orders. You had only one option, but you were used to that option. You had lived in the shadow of its compelling discipline for many years.

The pass was the highest altitude you would reach during your journey and the effort of continuing became great. It was just high enough for a person to become sick from the low pressure and lack of oxygen. You began to notice a pain at the base of your skull and subsequent dizziness and nausea. You decided to pitch a camp for a couple of days knowing you would acclimatise.

You doubted that anyone else would be making the crossing at this time of the year but you couldn't take the chance of being wrong. Just a few metres higher, hidden behind a giant bulb of deformed rock, you erected your tent and took stock of your situation. You had enough condensed food to last another twenty-seven days. It was easily twice what you required to get in, get the job done and get out. Melted snow would serve as water for the whole trip and you had plenty of gas for your stove. Wraith operative issue was state of the art, your clothes super warm and highly breathable, your weapons and instruments second to none. Your movements were being tracked by satellite and your GPS was accurate to within two metres. You could relax, gather your strength and become part of the environment.

Being unseen, blending with the world around you no matter where you might be; that was your skill. You were a chameleon, an expert in mutability. You could be invisible anywhere, be it a jungle or a crowded street. No one ever saw you coming.

As night swept into the mountains you made coffee on the tiny stove and sucked some food from an already opened tube, disregarding the synthetic flavour. The hiss of the stove was the only sound and you snuffed that as soon as the water boiled. A very light snow was falling in the dusky whiteness and occasionally a flake would fall into your mug and melt. The trance-like feeling that you had experienced in the tree-line took hold of you once more, but it was different this time. You were tired, your senses weren't as sharp. As you stared into the middle distance with your hands wrapped around your coffee your eyes defocused and you drifted away from the moment. Into remembered data.

Government called them "The Quiet Ones". They had moved in small numbers away from the swollen cities and into a remote part of the mountains where no infrastructure existed and where total commitment to a simple way of life was essential just for survival.

They had made no advertisement of their passing from one another. They had not evangelised or recruited. They merely disappeared. Among their number were educated and uneducated alike. Individuals from every background. No one with the will to survive the journey and the establishment of the community was turned away.

Between them they had all the skills they needed to make a start. Rumours of their existence were infrequently passed around like an urban myth. Occasionally, the impact of such stories would prompt other individuals to give up the ways of modern society and strike a path for that remote destination, not even really knowing if the rumour was true. Such people, after a difficult probationary period and initiation process that demonstrated their commitment, would be accepted. The journey itself killed those who did not have what it took to survive. Those who lacked the faith to complete the trek turned back to save their own lives and rejoined the masses. Because of this, The Quiet Ones became a truly secret society. Had they been less perfect in their lifestyles, if their experiment had not worked, perhaps the government would have left them alone.

The fact was that The Quiet Ones had thrived. In the fifty years since the colony had been founded they had taken root and stabilised. Children had been born; elderly founders had passed away. It wasn't that the population was growing at a threatening rate, it was only the fact that after half a century The Quiet Ones still existed.

You took a sip of coffee and found it hardly had any warmth left in it. Either you had been musing for longer than you realised or the temperature was dropping rapidly. You checked your GPS which also showed accurate forecasts, barometer and thermometer readings. The temperature was twenty below and you hadn't even noticed. If the sky had been clear, the moon and starlight would have lit up the landscape but with snow falling heavier now there was no light and the darkness was almost complete.

Somewhere behind your tent a noise snapped you back on like an interrogator's lamp. It was not the sound of falling snow. There were no trees up here. You listened hard but there was nothing. You replayed the noise in your mind over and over, trying to recognise or imagine what it might have been. Something slipping in the snow perhaps. Fox? No, too small. Bear?

Probably would have made more noise and would still be making it. Wolf? Yes, wolf. Up here in the winter there was not much sustenance. It was not inconceivable that a wolf would check you out with a view to supper. It was the logical explanation.

Of course, the illogical explanation nagged and irritated like a splinter in your mind; someone or something was aware of you. Either forewarned, lucky or very clever to have discovered you. You found the pistol in your hand before your thoughts had even taken shape. You mated the silencer with the muzzle as you cocked your ears into the darkness. You knew there would be no sleep that night.

A night awake anywhere can seem two days long but in nature, and in the mountains particularly, where there are less hours of sun, it is endless. The mind flicks in and out of true consciousness and becomes part of the sunless shift. Eyes open or closed, the darkness is the same; cold, deep velvet.

Without vision, the other senses come into play. Your hearing was stretched out like web in all directions until you were imagining sounds on the edge of your perception. Careful to make no sound yourself, you sniffed constantly for a hint of any scent, but all you could smell was the coldness of the air until it numbed the membranes of your nostrils. You tried to sense movement with the skin of your face but it too lost all sensitivity to the cold.

There is no training that can make the night shorter.

You listened.

You waited.

The shock of waking suddenly and jerking upright was dreadful each time. You would wonder how long you had been asleep for and hope that in waking or sleeping you had made no sound. The fear that the unseen stalker might have crept closer in those moments would then keep you awake until the strain exhausted you once more and the whole cycle would begin again. There are some who, in such a situation, would pray but you could not. There is no God who would listen.

Not to you.

When the greyness of dawn seeped into your vision you had already dreamed its arrival a dozen times. As soon as you were certain that the sun was truly shedding light once more, you stood and began to look around for signs of an observer. Your entire body was stiff with cold and lack of movement. It had snowed all night and any tracks that there might have been were invisible. Your tent had six-inches of fresh powder on it.

You spent the day watching the pass from your vantage point but saw nothing move across the land. In the sky however, an eagle circled and once or twice let out its penetrating shriek to ricochet across the many slopes and faces of the mountains. The sound brought you back to the silence you had felt in the pines far below. The contrast of the eagle's cry and the stillness which multiplied in its passing became a physical presence in your body. You felt it in your chest as sure as a blade. As simple. The stillness grew in you like a seed drawing nourishment in a wasteland. It was impossible – it was inevitable.

This time, it took an effort to put your mind back on The Quiet Ones. The space cradled by those mountains continued to draw you away.

They had a simple life, if a rugged and unluxurious one. Why the government should show a shred of nervousness about their existence was beyond you until you extrapolated the possibilities. They had no communication with the outside world; no phones or transport. They had neither wealth nor currency. They did not elect leaders. They paid no taxes and had no streets or addresses. They did not marry in order to prove commitment. They were good for their own sakes and in their in own eyes. Yet they had no religion.

They tended sparse crops and kept small livestock. When someone was sick they used western medical techniques alongside the wisdom of ancient traditions. They were not luddites by any means; they employed any technology they had or could develop to great advantage. However, it did not rule them as it did the world outside. They had no identifiable political or power system but undertook the highest degree of personal responsibility. Each individual looked after his own health and needs and would try to learn the skills of the others in order to attain a maximum level of self-sufficiency.

Their sense of community was lent great strength by a total respect for the freedom of the individual. One could argue that they had become the first self-realised community on Earth. Or one could argue, as the government did, covertly and behind closed doors, that they were anarchists and had to be eliminated. The fact that anarchy could work scared the hell out of them. Anarchy meant no more government.

Most interesting of all was the development of what was rumoured to be called the "Non-fighting mind". This was a way of keeping the peace between The Quiet Ones without any need for an organised system of law or any kind of police force. The imperfect nature of humanity had achieved perfection. Whether the files on The Quiet Ones were accurate or not you admired them deeply for what they had achieved.

~φ~

You spent the next night in the same spot but found no evidence that anyone or anything was nearby. You managed a few hours of sleep, albeit light, and set off over the rest of the pass just after dawn. You felt high and healthy as you skied away from your camp. You had become a part of the mountains.

Two days of skiing through more pine forest brought you within a few miles of The Quiet Ones. You entered the most crucial part of your journey. Your map showed the view from satellite. You decided to give the community a wide berth.

They had situated their loosely knit village in a clearing about a third of the way up a valley where the gradient wasn't too steep. They were on the west side of a river nine miles from your position. Studies of satellite film had shown them collecting water from a small reservoir which collected clean mountain spring water. The river was not usually used except as a hydro power source. From the photos the facilities looked primitive but effective. Several dwellings were scattered through the clearing.

You planned to watch them for a while from a ridge on the east side of the river before making a move. You stayed as far away as you could without leaving the valley completely and after another half day of skiing you attained your observation point. It was a granite rock formation but this time surrounded by dense pine. The top of the rocks looked out to the opposite side of the valley and with mounted sights you would be able to see the people as if they were only a few feet away.

You made your camp as unobtrusively as possible near the base of the protruding rocks, hidden by the dense firs and pines. You ate and turned in as soon as night fell. You needed to be fresh the following day. Birds began singing long before the light came back and you rose and prepared your rifle and tripod before heading up to the vantage point. You didn't eat, as it would cloud your thinking to do so.

~φ~

From your mounted tripod you watched them for two days, taking note of patterns of movement and behaviour. On the third day you were ready. It was always best to travel light at this stage, so you packed up your tent and everything non-essential and hid it in the snow. Skiing was easier with less on your shoulders and you moved swiftly round the valley to a place where crossing the river would be easy. You forded the river about five miles upstream from the village as the snow began to fall again. It seemed auspicious that your tracks would be covered.

Before noon that day you reached the ridge above the village and skied down towards it. Your senses were strung like tripwires and the animal stealth deep within you was surfacing. Half a mile above the village you stopped and removed your skis. If anything went wrong now you would need a different kind of agility. You could hear no human voices as you crept from tree to tree. But the sounds of clucking chickens and tools being wielded seemed incredibly loud after days of emptiness. You hoped that your direction would bring you out right beside the reservoir of spring water.

Some minutes later you were looking through a gap in the trees at the top end of the reservoir, perfectly situated. They had built it with stones from the river and some kind of rough mortar. It seemed to hold the water very well. Beyond the reservoir, parts of the village were in plain view. You drew your pistol – you were near enough to use it if necessary – re-attached the silencer and continued to use trees as cover for as long as you could.

You were almost at your goal when you heard running footsteps coming towards you from the right. You crouched and froze. It was the girl you had seen milking the goat with her brother but she was headed for the reservoir and had not seen you. No one else seemed to be with her. If she discovered you, everything would change. There would be blood. You doubted that even with the silencer you could shoot her without someone detecting you – it was just too quiet for no one to hear it. You watched with the muzzle trained on her. If she so much as looked your way the plan would alter. But all she did was dip her hand to the icy water and take a drink. When she had had enough she ran off again. Twice she had been a twitch from death. Twice she had walked free. But for her and for the rest of The Quiet Ones there would be no more reprieves.

You slid on your stomach the last few yards to the reservoir and reached into your pocket. Inside was a gel vial, slightly green when held against the white background of snow. Sure to make no sound, you placed it into the water and slid away. If they continued to draw water from the lower end of the reservoir they would probably not see your tracks. You could now be ninety percent certain of success.

The snow was falling harder and was even covering the route you had taken after removing your skis. You had no problem finding them, however, and headed back the way you had come to your hidden camp on the opposite side of the valley. Once there, you re-packed everything and took a last look through your scope at The Quiet Ones and their village. Everything seemed normal. For a while that was how it would be.

You left then and headed back towards the pass.

~φ~

There is no hurry but still it seems that you need to push the pace. Perhaps it's just the training; never letting yourself ease up, never letting down your guard. Or maybe it's that other feeling, the feeling that once again something has discovered the scent of your trail and is pursuing you. You don't want to spend any extra time in the pass but the weather closes in on you and you are forced to stop. It's mid afternoon on the day you hoped to have cleared the pass and left it behind. As before, you move away from the main trail to pitch camp. You take refuge from the blizzard inside your tent but make coffee often, both to warm your insides and to keep your senses sharp.

You hear sounds again deep into the night while half dozing and come awake with your heart loud and strong in your chest. You don't sleep for the rest of the night, such is your fear. The blizzard rages for several days and your rations dwindle. Every night a presence is there with you in the heavy darkness. Never quite approaching. Never quite leaving.

As you are beginning to doubt your supplies, the storm withdraws and after the insistence of the wind, the silence followed once more; the silence you do not want to leave behind. Through the virgin snow you ski over the rest of the pass and back down into the expanse of pine forest on the far side. Part of you stays in those mountains. That quiet part, you believe, cut from you like a tender spring bud. And somewhere, hidden by trees or high on a ledge, something watches you.

Something has you in its sights. ❁

BEV VINCENT is the Bram Stoker and Edgar Award nominated author of two books, *The Road to the Dark Tower* (NAL, 2004) and *The Stephen King Illustrated Companion* (Fall River Press, 2009). Since 2001 he has been a contributing editor with *Cemetery Dance* magazine, where he writes "News from the Dead Zone."

He has published over 50 short stories, including appearances in *Ellery Queen's Mystery Magazine*, *Borderlands 5*, *Tesseracts Thirteen*, *Cemetery Dance*, and *Doctor Who: Destination Prague*. He is a member of the Storytellers Unplugged blogging community and writes reviews for *Onyx Reviews*.

Originally from eastern Canada, he has lived in Texas for the past twenty years.

His website is www.bevvincent.com.

Bev Vincent

Silvery Moon

*E*d is basking in the silvery light of the full moon when he hears the distinctive sound of a tent zipper nearby. He crouches behind a cluster of bushes and watches. In his present condition, it makes little difference which of his traveling companions appears. Any of them will satisfy his bloodlust better than the rabbits and deer he's been stalking.

The man who clambers out of the red two-person tent might as well be an elephant for all the noise he makes. He rises to his feet, stretches, scratches his crotch and staggers toward the nearby trees, presumably to relieve himself.

A low growl forms in the back of Ed's throat. He tilts his head back a few degrees to catch a hint of his prey among the other delectable scents that permeate the mountain air. The matted hair covering his arms prickles as he flexes his curled fingers in anticipation.

He bides his time until the man lumbers into the shadows before emerging from cover to take up pursuit. In the daylight, his prey towers over Ed by several inches and outweighs him by at least fifty pounds, but the night is Ed's domain, especially when the moon is full. His movements are fluid, efficient. His feet make no sound, even though the ground is covered with twigs and nettles. His heart rate accelerates and his eyes focus on his target to the exclusion of all else.

Once he has closed the distance between them, he leaps.

The man grunts when Ed knocks him to the ground, rolls him onto his back and pins him. His eyes widen when Ed's face looms before him, transformed as it is into a snarling mask of abject fury and raw hunger. He opens his mouth, but only a strangled gasp comes out.

He struggles beneath Ed, but to no avail. Ed rakes his right hand down the man's face, clawing through flesh and muscle.

The man cries out. The horror Ed senses in his victim sends adrenaline coursing through his veins. He shows the terrified man a mouth full of teeth before lowering his head. Blood splashes his face and squirts between his lips when he opens an artery in his victim's neck.

The man squirms as the realization of impending doom kicks in. He wrests one hand free and scratches at his attacker, but Ed is prepared – he's been through this many times before. He recaptures the flailing arm and howls in triumph, feeling his victim's strength ebb. Blood jets out in diminishing spurts that reflect the slowing of the man's heart.

When it's all over, the man's eyes remain fixed open and glassy, forevermore astonished by the final sight they registered.

Ed claws at the ground and pushes around dead leaves and fallen branches to cover the evidence of his kill before dragging the carcass into the woods.

Then he feeds.

~φ~

When the morning sun crests the Beartooth Mountains, illuminating the interior of his blue nylon pup tent, Ed's consciousness drifts gradually to the surface. His entire body aches – more than two days of hiking can account for. He rolls onto his stomach, grasping at the remnants of a dream that flashes through his mind like scenes captured by a strobe light, but the details elude him. Eventually he gives up. At least he's in his tent and not huddled on the ground beneath a stand of pine trees. Stranger things have happened.

He unzips his sleeping bag and throws back the flap, letting the crisp morning air embrace his naked body. He becomes aware of a burning sensation on his left forearm. He probes the spot and winces when his fingers encounter a raw wound. Sucking air through clenched teeth, he raises his arm before his face and gapes. Clotted blood surrounds a quartet of shallow scratches about three inches long.

Hindered by the tent's close confines, he rolls onto his side and fumbles for his clothing, locating first his boots, then his jeans, socks and underwear. After donning them, he searches for his t-shirt. There aren't many places it could be. Eventually it turns up, wadded at the bottom of his sleeping bag.

The blood staining the white shirt didn't come from the scratches on his arm – there's too much of it. The shoulder features a vivid splatter. Several hand-shaped splotches, still damp to the touch, obscure the image on the front: Opus the Penguin. He can't tell if the blood is from an animal or a person. If it's human, then to whom does it belong? One of his companions, or someone else he encountered in the woods last night?

Ed scrutinizes his fingers. They're clean, except for a small crimson stain on one fingernail, which he licks away. He must have cleaned up before returning to the tent. There's no way to wash the blood out of his shirt, though, not out here in the wilderness. He'll have to dispose of it when the others are distracted. He puts on a denim shirt that he normally wears in the evenings when the air turns cool. Its long sleeves cover the scratches on his arm.

He runs his fingers through his hair before performing a closer examination of the clothing he wore the previous day. He detects bloodstains on his jeans that he overlooked at first, and finds another splatter mark on one of his new hiking boots. Wetting the tail of his bloodstained t-shirt with water from his canteen, he wipes off his boot and does his best with his jeans. The damp stains look like chocolate or coffee when he's finished. A couple of days on the trail have left the hikers looking scruffy, so he doubts anyone will notice.

Someone outside the tent calls his name. He crams the soiled shirt into a side compartment of his backpack, where he can get at it quickly if the opportunity arises. Then he unzips the tent door and sticks his head out into the bright morning.

Three people are gathered in front of his tent. Mike's brow is furrowed. Krista has her arm wrapped around Jill's waist as if she's afraid her friend might collapse.

"Have you seen Paul?" Mike asks. "We thought he might be with you."

He frowns in an attempt to mimic the right blend of concern and confusion. "What? In here?" He hopes the wave of elation that washes over him doesn't show. Paul, his nemesis...

"He's gone," Jill says, her voice thin and unsteady. "When I woke up a while ago, he wasn't there. I thought he went out to, you know, take a leak or something, but then he didn't come back."

She's wearing a thin tank top and flowered pajama bottoms. Nothing else. Ed studiously maintains eye contact, resisting the urge to ogle her body. "How long since you noticed he was gone?"

Jill's hair caresses her neck when she shakes her head. "Almost an hour."

"And you thought he might be with me?" The words come out sharper than he intends.

"Well," Jill starts. "Out getting firewood or something. I woke Krista first, and then we got Mike up."

Ed hears what Jill isn't saying: He's their last resort. Even before this trip he and Paul didn't get along. Dealing with rugged terrain, persistent flies, and half-cooked food hasn't improved matters. For the past two days, they sniped at each other constantly until the others pleaded with them to call a truce, at least until they got home. When they shook – a pretense everyone recognized for what it was – holding back a sneer wasn't easy. How a troglodyte like Paul ended up with Jill defies explanation.

"What should we do?" Krista asks.

"He can't have gone far," Mike says.

They fan out and search the area near their campground. About twenty yards to the east, Ed sees faint signs of a struggle and drag marks leading into the woods, but his traveling companions don't notice. When he feels like he can break free for a few moments, he returns to the spot and scuffs the ground with his feet, completing the task he obviously started during the night. Then he catches up with the others again.

When Mark sees Ed approaching, he asks, "You don't think he just left, do you? Got pissed about something and took off?"

Ed resists the urge to criticize Paul. Instead he just says, "Maybe."

Jill calls out Paul's name every few minutes, but all that does is scare the birds, which take flight from the bushes and trees. Her voice grows hoarse. "What happened to him?" she asks of no one in particular.

"Maybe a wild animal got him," Mike says. Krista swats him. "What?"

Jill bursts into tears and Krista goes to console her while Mike rubs his shoulder and shakes his head at Ed, as if to ask: *What did I do?*

Ed conceals a grin. Mike is right. A wild animal did get Paul. He could offer alternate explanations, though. People disappear out here all the time. There are deep ravines and water-slick rocks. Moose have been known to gore people, and grizzly bears and cougars stalk the forests. Searchers with dog teams do steady business seeking out missing hikers, a process akin to looking for a person hiding in a closet somewhere in Denver. Their success rate at finding missing hikers alive is low. Paul's disappearance will be written off as just another of the many mishaps for which the area is known.

The group spreads out as they expand their search. Once the others are out of sight, Ed heads back to their campsite, nestled in a wide clearing beside the trail. He builds a small fire in the rock-lined circle around which their tents are clustered. Once the flames take hold, he sets his t-shirt on fire and watches its ashes merge with those from the previous night's bonfire.

He tries again to remember his nocturnal activities. Did he stalk Paul or did fate deliver the man into his hands? If Jill had emerged from the tent instead of her insipid lover, would Ed have dragged her into the underbrush instead, tearing her lovely, delicate flesh, ripping into her firm, succulent breasts? He shudders at the thought, but he doesn't know how his mind works when he's under the moon's influence.

The day is getting warmer, so Ed swaps his long-sleeved shirt for a fresh t-shirt. He carefully washes the dried blood from the marks on his arm, applies peroxide from his first aid kit and covers the wound with a bandage. Then he puts out the fire and heads back into the woods.

With Paul gone, Ed might stand a chance with Jill. Though she apparently favors the muscle-bound, oafish type, she might turn to him for comfort. He would hold her in his arms and let her hands rest on his chest…

"What kind of name is that anyway?" Paul said to him the previous day when they were halfway up a steep climb. "Ed Wynn. It's like in Ed McBain's books, you know, the guy with the same first and last name?"

"What do you mean?" Krista asked.

"Don't you see? Ed Wynn – Edwin. You take Ed and put it with his last name and you get Edwin, his first name." He explained this in the patronizing tone geeks use with people who can't understand relativity or string theory, even though Paul would never be mistaken for a rocket scientist himself.

At that moment, Ed's loathing for Paul deepened to hatred. Not for making fun of his name – that was just childish – but for how he spoke to Krista. She isn't the brightest bulb in the candelabra, but she's sweet and doesn't deserve to be treated with disrespect – especially by someone like Paul. He's not sorry Paul is dead. He just wishes he could remember the last moments of the man's pitiful life. His look of terror. The taste of his flesh.

"What happened to your arm?" Jill asks after he rejoins the group. She looks drained, and her eyes are red.

"It's nothing." Ed touches the bandages. "Scratched myself on a branch while I was searching in a thicket."

"Maybe this isn't safe," Jill says, "stomping around in the woods like this. What if it was a bear?"

"Bears don't like people," Ed says. "We're making plenty of noise. We're fine. If it was a wild animal, like Mike said, I'm sure Paul startled it in the dark." Ed knows a lot about animals and what they do to their prey, but he keeps that information to himself.

"I don't see any place where he could have fallen," Krista adds. "It must have been an animal." Mike pretends to swat her arm, but his attempt at humor earns him a steely glare from his girlfriend. Jill notices the interaction, though, and winks at Ed. His heart thrills at the sight. Jill seems to have perked up. Now they share a secret. Another bond.

The scratches on Ed's arm itch under the bandage, so he distracts himself by focusing on other things. Jill's unfettered body, primarily, which he glances at discreetly as they comb through the woods. For a while he falls into step beside her, hoping to chat, but mostly they walk in silence, probing into the underbrush as if they know what they're doing.

Eventually, they decide to halt the search and return to the camp. On the way back, something pale catches Ed's eye, contrasted against the dark brown and lush green vegetation. A man's leg. He stops and crouches, pretending to tie his bootlace, blocking the view from the others. He can hardly breathe, but his companions aren't looking around any more. They've given up.

After they pass, he peers into the bushes, admiring his handiwork. A broken bone protrudes through the calf. Vicious wounds and gashes adorn the limb, and the toes are missing. It looks as if they've been chewed off. Without digging into the brush, he can't tell if the leg is still attached to the rest of the body or not.

He hears someone approaching. Out of the corner of his eye he sees Jill shuffling toward him. She can't see this. He rises quickly from his crouch and deliberately collides with her, knocking her off balance. He grabs her by the shoulders to steady her. For a long moment, they are almost embracing. Then Ed releases her and steps back, mumbling an apology. "Didn't see you. Sorry."

"It's okay," Jill says. "No harm done." She offers a crooked smile as Ed leads her away from the clump of bushes and its gruesome prize.

"What's that?" she asks, pointing to the other side of the trail.

"What? Where?" he replies. His heartbeat accelerates.

"There. It looks like…" Jill crouches and rises. In her hands she holds a hiking boot. Its laces are loose and its tongue flops like a leaf in the wind. A distinctive red stain defaces the tan material on one side.

"Is it… ?"

"It looks like Paul's," she says, clutching it to her chest. "What does this mean?"

They continue on to the camp in silence. Once there, Jill shows the boot to Mike and Krista.

"It could be anyone's," Ed says.

"It hasn't been outside long," Mike says. Krista glares at him. "Still… you're right. It could belong to anyone."

Ed rebuilds the fire and puts on the kettle for coffee. When it's ready he pours a cup – Jill takes two sugars, he knows – and carries it to her. He rests one hand on her shoulder and is pleased when she doesn't pull away. He leads her to a wind-fallen tree and urges her to sit. He extracts the hiking boot from her hands and sets it on the ground beside her.

They sip coffee and eat granola bars while discussing their course of action. Krista keeps trying to get a signal on her cell phone, but Ed knows that's a waste of time. They're a long way from civilization.

"Let's pack up camp and head back to town," Mike says.

"Is that wise?" Ed asks. "What if Paul's hurt? We can't just leave him here."

Going back to town makes perfect sense, but Ed knows that emotion trumps logic. Jill rewards him with a look of gratitude, and nods her agreement. *Ah, yes, this might work out fine*, he thinks. Slow and steady, that's how it has to go, especially during the next couple of days.

"We've already looked everywhere. Why stay?" Mike asks. "We need help, and the Carbon County Sheriff's office in Red Lodge is the closest place to get that." He doesn't mention the boot, but they all seem to know what it means.

Jill doesn't look at Mike. Instead she turns to Ed. The pleading look on her face is easy to read.

"Let's stay tonight," Ed says. "Get a fresh start in the morning. That way we can be absolutely sure he's not somewhere close by, hurt, waiting for us… " He lets his voice trail off and watches Jill out of the corner of his eye. He knows the matter is settled in her mind, no matter what anyone else says. After further debate, Mike agrees, reluctantly, to wait until morning.

"Besides," Ed says, "another group of hikers might come by and we could get them to ask for help when they reach town." He has other arguments ready in case someone suggests that two of them stay behind while the others go down the mountain, but no one comes up with that idea. He refills Jill's cup from the pot brewing on the campfire. Their fingers touch briefly when he passes her the sugar.

"This trip was a bad idea," Krista says.

"It was Paul's," Mike says. "All I did was research the trail."

"I wasn't blaming you." The hurt look on Mike's face softens.

"Paul always felt like he needed to prove something," Jill says. Her voice is soft and distant, as if she's recounting a dream. "He thought we should climb Granite Peak. I had to talk him out of that. It might look easy from the trailhead, but a lot of people die there every year."

The sun starts its descent behind the Absaroka Mountains to the west, turning the massive granite plateaus above the timberline into eerie lunar plains. At the same time, the full moon emerges from behind the Beartooth Mountains. Croaking toads begin to replace the wall of sound generated by birds and insects during the daytime. The texture of the air changes as it cools and grows darker. They're crossing from one territory into another.

Though technically the moon is completely full for only an instant in time, Ed is vulnerable to its influence over three consecutive nights. Tonight it will be stronger, with the moon in full bloom.

Ed wonders what Paul had planned for him up here in the mountains. There was something behind the unexpected invitation from his co-workers to join them on their outing. Some prank, no doubt, that would have made Ed the butt of their jokes for weeks to come. He saw Paul and Mike whispering in Mike's office and could tell from the way Paul behaved that he had something up his sleeve.

Despite this, Ed accepted their invitation because it afforded him the chance to spend a few days with Jill away from the office. There was a brief discussion about fixing him up with a woman from accounting, but Ed said he didn't mind going by himself so long as the others didn't mind having a fifth wheel along for the trip.

"Glad to have you, Eddie boy," Paul said.

Glad to have you, Ed thinks now. The joke was on Paul. The timing couldn't have been better. There was a chance that nothing would happen during this full moon – his affliction didn't always control him and he sometimes went for months immune to its effects – but being in the open enhanced the likelihood of a reaction. He loves the feeling of power that accompanies a night abroad, even though he never remembers what transpired. The next day he is always exhausted but euphoric. It's better than meditation. Maybe even better than sex.

As darkness falls, they stoke up the fire and heat some food, though none of them have much interest in eating. Ed is hungry, but he will forage later. After their rudimentary meal, they sit in silence around the blazing campfire, sipping cocoa from tin mugs. The moon is enormous, bathing them in its silvery night. It won't be long now.

"Let's turn in early so we can get under way at first light," Ed says. The others agree. After they clean up, he hangs their food from the highest limb he can reach to keep it away from animals, then retreats to his tent.

And waits.

He checks his watch. Nearly 10 o'clock.

The seconds tick past. Deadwood crackles as an animal of some size lumbers past. Owls hoot in the distance. From the tent to his left, the muted but unmistakable sounds of lovemaking emanate. Two people seeking comfort in the face of despair. When he closes his eyes, he imagines Jill lying in the third tent, alone and awake, staring into the darkness.

He can already feel the change beginning, even though midnight is over an hour away. He wishes he could control his impulses – that he could imagine a specific victim while lucid and then act upon it later. However, he has no more influence over his nocturnal excursions than he does over his dreams. Whatever will happen will happen. It won't be his fault. Not really.

Nevertheless, he lies on his back and chants silently: Not Jill. Not Jill. Anyone but Jill. Not Jill. The blood coursing through his veins feels warmer. His skin feels matted with hair. His jaw aches. It's as if his very skeleton is transforming and his musculature is adapting to these changes. His hands flex. His breathing grows shallow and rapid. His eyes narrow. The sounds of the night grow louder and more distinct. He can tell exactly where every bird is and what kind. The rustling he hears in the distance – that's a raccoon, attracted by the scent of their recent meal. Mike and Krista are finished with their earnest fumbling and Mike is now snoring. The world is so much more alive when he's like this.

A tent flap zips open nearby. Seconds later, the amber glow of a flashlight beam sweeps across Ed's tent. Tentative footsteps approach, scraping through the leaves and branches. He freezes, like a predator suddenly detecting new prey.

The footsteps stop outside his tent. The beam dips and sways erratically. The zipper tab at the bottom of his tent door rattles. A voice mumbles something that he can't make out. Then the zipper is drawn upward. A shadowy figure is framed in the moonlight.

It's Jill.

The neck of her loose shirt billows open as she stoops to peer inside. Ed's vision is sharp enough to make out every detail of her body. His breath catches in his throat. What is she doing here? She's in great danger. Entering a lion's den. His muscles are coiled like springs, ready to pounce or flee.

"Ed?" Jill's voice is a harsh whisper. "You awake?" Without waiting for an answer, she clambers inside and closes the zipper.

He can feel her presence as she approaches on hands and knees. She can't be in here.

In his tent.

With him.

Like this.

"Ed?"

His response is more of a growl than a word.

"Do you mind if I sleep in here tonight? I'm… it's so… I'm…" She pauses. "He's gone. I know it. That boot."

She interprets his second growl as affirmation. When she crawls onto his inflatable mattress, he's jostled up and down and side to side. He wants to puts one hand down against the ground to steady himself but he's paralyzed. This can't be. It's the worst possible scenario and yet it's something he has fantasized about for months. He can smell the hint of days-old perfume and sweat mingled with her natural female aroma. His hands continue to flex, the only part of his body that he dare move.

He hears another zipper, this one very close, as Jill opens his sleeping bag and stretches out beside him, wrapping one arm across his body and nuzzling her face into his neck.

"Thank you," she says.

Ed makes no sound in response.

A few moments later, her respiration deepens. Her breath is warm and moist against his neck. Her arm weighs heavy on his chest.

Conflicting thoughts and emotions cloud Ed's mind. In a second, he could roll Jill onto her back and have his way with her. His own, special way, ripping his teeth into her soft, pink neck and feeling her lifeblood spurt into his mouth. He could sink his clawed hands into the firm breasts that ride high on her chest. He could suck her fingers into his mouth one at a time, licking and caressing them before biting them off and swallowing them.

But the moon doesn't yet have him completely in its thrall... yet. There must be another way. Maybe he doesn't have to let the moon take control. He's allowed it in the past, but only because it gives him an excuse to give rein to his bloodlust.

He doesn't need to let the moon take over.

He is in charge.

He's the master of his own destiny.

To deal with a brute like Paul, Ed channeled his inner wolf. He pretended that fur grew out to cover his face and limbs. He imagined claws extending from his fingers. The teeth that sank into Paul's flesh were his own, but in his mind's eye they were the curved lupine fangs of a predatory carnivore.

With Jill, he can take a different approach, allowing his power to manifest itself in another form. Clearly Jill was drawn here by his irresistible allure. She has offered herself up to him, yielding to his seductive charm. She wants to be taken by him, claimed by an infamous, invincible creature of the night.

Ed looks at her sleeping form with eyes accustomed to staring in the darkness. He notes the tiny lines at the corners of her eyes that appear when she offers one of her dazzling smiles. He sees her full lips, slightly parted as she breathes deeply. He is mesmerized by the pulse beating in her neck; so young, so strong.

In his mind, he imagines himself transformed into a dashing, handsome nosferatu. When he smiles, he envisions his incisors extending beyond his other teeth, ready to plunge into Jill's succulent neck. He has the power to give her everlasting life. She will join him forever and, as master and mistress of the darkness, they will rule the night together. As he imagines this, he grows harder than ever before.

In the morning, he won't remember much of what happens from this moment forward. He never does.

Perhaps that's for the best, he thinks, as he lifts himself up on his elbows, turns, and lowers himself onto the warm-blooded woman at his side. ❧

Knock 'Em Dead

A man died immediately before Simon Gilliam's book signing. Not just anyone, either: the bookstore's Community Relations Manager, the man who had organized the event.

Who should have organized it, that is.

Simon was hideously early that Saturday afternoon because this was his first-ever signing for his debut novel, *No Longer Dead*, and he'd heard all about demanding authors with no regard for the people responsible for their success – like the clerks who hand-sold their books, generating the valuable word of mouth that could create a bestseller. Simon vowed he'd never be one of those divas, never forget where he came from and the "little people" who helped along the way. Assuming, of course, that there would be little people who'd help him and that his way was up.

When Simon introduced himself and explained why he was there, the CRM – his name was Edward Meyers – froze, his mouth agape. His face lost all color. Instead of shaking Simon's proffered hand, Meyers turned and made a beeline for an office near the restrooms without uttering a word. Simon trailed behind, wondering if he'd somehow offended the man.

A few minutes later, Meyers emerged, red-faced and contrite. Simon's appearance had fallen off his calendar. He'd been out sick for a few days and someone else had been handling things. Not to worry, he assured Simon. An announcement had run in the local newspaper and the store's monthly newsletter contained the correct information. A box of books from the publisher was sitting in the warehouse. There was even a poster for the event in the side window. Setting up the reading area would take no time at all. A table, a podium, a microphone, some chairs, and they'd be good to go. He apologized for the mix-up and sent Simon to the café near the front of the store, promising everything would be ready on schedule.

Simon had almost finished a venti chocolate brownie Frappuccino, which cost more than any meager royalties he stood to earn from book sales that afternoon, when two EMTs bearing the countenances of men on a mission rushed through the main entrance pushing a gurney. Simon followed them to the back corner where his reading was slated to start in twenty minutes.

The moment he saw Meyers on the floor beside an overturned stack of chairs, one arm sticking straight out like a football blocker, he knew the man was dead. The paramedics poked, pumped and shocked to no avail. Finally, they lifted him onto the gurney and rushed him into the awaiting ambulance. That was the last Simon saw of Edward Meyers.

However, his ordeal wasn't over yet. A young man who looked about twenty took Simon aside and said they'd be ready in a few minutes.

"But," Simon started, then paused, not wanting to appear difficult. "The manager."

"I'm the manager. Mr. Meyers was the Community Relations Manager."

"He died."

The manager's face took on the studious look of a high school student trying to field a complex math question. He nodded and raised one eyebrow.

"You're sure we should go ahead?" Simon asked.

The manager tilted his head toward the group of people in the reading area. "Some of them drove nearly an hour to get here," he said.

Despite concerns about the propriety of reading from a horror novel in the wake of what had happened, Simon agreed. The show must go on. Besides, word of Mr. Meyers' misfortune had created a stir of interest, even if many of the people gathering had no idea who Simon was. Publishing was tough, and you took the breaks when they came – however they came.

While the manager read from a promotional letter sent to bookstores with advanced copies of his novel, Simon rifled through *No Longer Dead* in search of a suitable passage. *What does one read in the wake of a fatal heart attack?* he wondered.

He settled for a scene where the protagonist discovers an empty drawer in the morgue and, shortly thereafter, the drawer's former occupant, unceremoniously raised from the dead and pissed off. The further he got into it, the more inappropriate it seemed. He kept flashing back to Meyers sprawled on the floor, and felt like he was telling off-color jokes at a funeral.

For a wonder, though, people chuckled in all the right places. By the end, the audience had grown to over forty people. Most lingered after he finished, asking questions and bringing forward books to be signed. Some purchased multiple copies. He'd covered the cost of his venti chocolate brownie Frappuccino after all.

After relating the episode to Stephanie, his publicist, by phone the next morning, he was shocked into silence when she responded, "I knew you'd slay them." She snorted at her own joke. A few seconds later, Simon laughed, too. It was pretty funny when he thought about it.

~φ~

The next person to drop dead had the decency to wait until after Simon's reading.

As his target listener, Simon picked a young woman in the front row with long dark hair, entrancing green eyes, full lips, and perky boobs straining the buttons of her powder blue shirt. Having a target listener was supposed to help quell his nerves. The woman returned his gaze with interest, Simon thought, and laughed out loud at the funny parts during his reading. While the CRM opened the floor to questions, he entertained a brief fantasy where the woman caught up with him afterward and invited him back to her place for a drink.

He shook his head at this flight of fancy. Writers didn't attract groupies. Besides, he had at least ten years on her. Maybe fifteen. He was the kind of guy people rarely looked at twice. He doubted anyone in the audience would recognize him on the street thirty minutes later.

Still, the woman asked several questions during the Q&A. Her voice was low and sultry, and she played with her hair when she spoke. Later, their hands touched when she presented his book for a signature. He learned that her name was Melissa, but resisted the temptation to write a suggestive inscription. Something like that might come back to haunt him when he was famous.

While he signed the rest of the store's stock of *No Longer Dead*, he kept watch to see if she'd stayed behind. No such luck. It looked like another night alone in a hotel, eating pizza and watching mindless drivel on television. First thing tomorrow, he'd be on a plane to his next destination.

He pushed through a crowd that had formed outside the main entrance. A siren wailed in the distance. After he broke through, Simon saw two men kneeling beside someone on the sidewalk. The young woman in the powder blue blouse was sprawled on her back, legs curled, arms spread. Her emerald eyes were wide open but unseeing. A copy of *No Longer Dead* lay at her side.

After the ambulance departed, Simon returned to his hotel but he'd lost his appetite.

According to the newspaper he read the next morning en route to Midway airport, a brain embolism was the suspected cause of death. The grainy photograph accompanying the article didn't do Melissa justice.

He called Stephanie. "You're never going to believe this."

"A success?"

"I guess. A bigger crowd than in Silver Springs. They sold over a hundred copies."

"Excellent. A few more stops like that and you'll be ready for the big times."

"Meaning?"

"Are you willing to extend your trip? We're working on Seattle, San Francisco and L.A and then back to the East Coast."

"Sure."

"You don't sound thrilled."

"I am. Don't get me wrong. I appreciate all your work and support. It's just that…"

"What?"

"It happened again."

"The Community Relations Manager died?"

"No, no, that would be too freaky. But someone did die

afterward."

"Really?"

Simon heard gears churning in Stephanie's mind as she looked for a way to spin this development.

"Brain embolism, they say."

"Hmmm."

"She was young. Thirty-two, according to the paper. Looked younger. Pretty."

"And she was at your reading?"

"Uh-huh. She even asked questions. Good ones."

"Wow."

"Yeah."

"Who's that guy?" Stephanie asked. "You know who I mean. Funny name. A few years ago he was all the rage because his stories were so gross that people passed out at his readings."

"I thought that was just a publicity stunt," Simon said.

"Wish I'd thought of it. His next short story was published in *Playboy*. *The New Yorker* after that."

"You're not going to make a big deal out of this, are you?"

"No-o-o-o," she said, but Simon heard those gears grinding again.

~φ~

The first leg of Simon's book tour was a test drive. *No Longer Dead* had garnered favorable advanced reviews in the trade magazines and orders by the big chains were encouraging, so his publisher decided, to his delight, to finance a five-city tour to places where the orders had been strongest. Suburban D.C., Chicago, southeast Texas, Nebraska of all places, and finally to Reno. Several weeks ago, Stephanie said they would track the numbers and, if things went well, they'd consider adding more cities. At the end he would return home to a triumphant appearance in New Hampshire.

His third signing was in a suburb north of Houston. He arrived in the mid-afternoon and had an early dinner at an outdoor bistro at the upscale shopping mall near his hotel. The event organizer, a middle-aged woman named Alicia, introduced him to the staff, and escorted him up the escalator to the reading area, which was the nicest one yet, a glassed-in octagonal nook overlooking an artificial waterway complete with gondoliers and water taxis. Awaiting him were two chilled bottles of water, a pitcher of iced tea, several plastic cups, sandwiches and other snacks, and impressive stacks of books beside a poster featuring the cover of *No Longer Dead* and his publicity photo. At least thirty people were loitering nearby, many of them paging through his book.

Simon hadn't yet gotten used to seeing his novel, the physical manifestation of his imagination and labors, in such quantities. Dozens and dozens of pristine copies. He'd framed the dust jacket his editor sent him before the book was printed, had fawned over the galleys and advanced review copies, and cleared out a shelf above his desk for the first hardcover copies.

He checked his watch: ten minutes until he was scheduled to begin. He excused himself to the restroom, where he splashed water in his face and patted down his hair. He was at the urinal, wringing out the last drops, when a man standing next to him spoke. "You're that guy aren't you?"

"Excuse me?"

"The writer. The fellow what wrote that scary book."

"Scary but funny, I hope."

"I read about it in the paper."

"Uh-huh." Conversing with a stranger at a urinal seemed creepy. Simon zipped up and retreated to the sink to wash his hands.

"You reading from it tonight?" the man called out.

"That's right."

"Good on you. I respect a man who can make shit up. I tried once, but never got past 'Once upon a time.'"

Simon wasn't sure what to say, so he glanced over, averted his eyes, and nodded.

"I'll be picking up a copy. Knock 'em dead out there."

Simon uttered a hasty word of thanks, dried his hands and left the man to his business.

The turnout was impressive. Standing room only. As he was about to start reading, he noticed the man from the restroom standing among the overflow at the back. Simon didn't pick him as his target listener, though. Instead he found a grandmotherly woman in the front row who sat with her back arrow-straight, a copy of *No Longer Dead* on her lap beneath folded hands. To his delight, she guffawed when the reanimated corpse chased the mortician around the room with a scalpel. After three consecutive successful performances, Simon allowed himself to believe that people actually liked his book. The stacks on the table at the entrance to the reading area had dwindled. So many people willing to fork out twenty-five bucks to read it – he couldn't help feeling good. He finished the passage to polite applause and said that he'd be happy to answer any questions they might have. People asked whether he planned to write a sequel, if he based his characters on people he knew, and where he got his ideas from.

Simon was about to call on an audience member waving her hand in the air when a commotion distracted him. The man from the bathroom had fallen to the floor next to the table of books. He seemed to be suffering some sort of seizure. Simon was inappropriately reminded of a "dance" he and his buddies did in high school called the worm where they would lie down on the floor and thrash around.

The Community Relations Manager barked into her walkie-talkie. A security guard showed up a few minutes later, a man of about sixty whose belt buckle bore the dual burdens of an oversized radio and a belly that belied a love for food. He did his best to restrain the man on the floor, but the seizure continued unchecked. The guard whipped off his belt and tried to force it between the man's lips, something he probably learned from a television show, Simon thought.

By the time the paramedics arrived, the man had stopped moving and the crowd in the reading area had doubled in size. Simon noted in passing that the table of books was now empty.

~φ~

"It looked like he touched a live wire," Simon told Stephanie the next morning.

"Wow," she said. "The store sold every copy?"

"Uh, yeah," Simon said, disoriented by the question. "People still wanted me to sign their books, despite that poor man dying. I didn't get out of there until nearly ten o'clock. The police showed up and everything."

"Impressive. We sent a hundred and fifty copies." Stephanie said she didn't want to get his hopes up but there was a good chance *No Longer Dead* would debut on the *New York Times* bestseller list. She was trying to book him on one of the morning shows. "And Letterman's people have expressed interest."

"All these people dying… it's starting to freak me out."

"It's just a coincidence," Stephanie said. "Let's milk it for all it's worth."

"Yeah, but I spoke to all three of them. And then they died."

~φ~

On the day of his Nebraska appearance, national newspapers picked up an AP wire article about the curious spate of deaths at his signings. The story led with a strained joke based on his book's title. He had an inkling that Stephanie was behind it.

The line at the bookstore in Omaha ran out the door and down the sidewalk. Two lines, actually – one for people to buy his book and the other where they queued after making their purchase, according to large signs posted outside the building. The only time Simon had ever seen anything like it was for a Stephen King appearance he'd attended in Vermont years earlier.

Several people were wearing t-shirts that featured his publicity photo and book cover on the front, but he couldn't make out the accompanying text. "What's the deal with the shirts?" he asked his escort, a bubbly young woman named Andrea who had shuttled him from the airport to his hotel and again between hotel and signing.

"No idea," she answered. "That's your picture on the front, isn't it?"

Simon nodded. It was indeed.

Inside the store, a solid wall of copies of *No Longer Dead* greeted him. Several boxes of books were stacked near the shelves. "We had them trucked in from our other branches in town," the event organizer told him. "From Lincoln, too. People have been calling all day to reserve copies. They've been lining up since noon."

Simon realized that his mouth was hanging open. His teeth clicked together when he closed it. His head was swimming.

"We can't handle this many people for a reading. How would you feel about just signing? If we start exactly on time I think we can get everyone through before closing."

All he could do was nod and take his place at the long table that had been set up on a makeshift dais. To speed things along, a bookstore employee greeted each person in line and tucked the dust jacket flap in at the title page. Camera flashes blinded him as he scrawled inscription after inscription, barely taking time to glance up from the open books that a second employee slid in front of him. Two burly security guards lurked over his shoulder, encouraging his fans – his *fans*! – to move along quickly.

A young woman moved into position before Simon. What caught his attention wasn't the shapely thrust of her chest so much as his own face smiling back at him. The slogan on the t-shirt said: *I survived Simon Gilliam's book signing*. He stared at the woman's chest for several seconds before he realized what he was doing. "Where'd you get that?" he said at last.

The security guard shooed the woman along before she had a chance to answer. A guy with a shaggy beard stepped into place. In his case it was a beer belly that distorted Simon's publicity photograph. "Dude's selling them out of his trunk down the street," he said. "Only ten bucks. Awesome, right?" He pointed at the book in front of Simon. "Make it out to my good buddy, Dan."

Simon wasn't sure it was awesome. Supposedly there was no such thing as bad publicity, but this seemed in questionable taste. Still, he couldn't complain. *No Longer Dead* was flying off the shelves, at least in the telemarketing capital of the world. Without a gimmick, he could toil in obscurity for years, hoping for a break. Wondering if he was selling a piece of his soul, he decided to follow Stephanie's advice to take full advantage of the situation. Who knew how long it would last?

"Do me a favor, will you?" he asked the guy as he pulled

out his wallet. "Dan? Here's twenty bucks. Get me a large and keep the change." He shook his wrist a few times to ward off a cramp and wrote: *To my good buddy, Dan, who survived one of my signings. Thanks for the shirt!* He added his signature, an unintelligible flourish, at the bottom.

"Awesome, dude," Dan said. "I'll be right back."

Simon didn't think about Dan again until he took a bathroom break thirty minutes later. He could see where the line ended, but it would be at least another hour before the last person reached the table. "Prick stole my money," he muttered. Then he noticed red and blue flashing lights reflecting off the store's front window. He pressed his nose against the glass and watched paramedics load a stretcher into a waiting ambulance. The police were talking to a teenager who was waving his arms and pointing repeatedly at the ground.

~φ~

"He was carrying the t-shirt I asked him to get," Simon told Stephanie that evening. By now he had her private cell phone number and an invitation to call her any time, day or night. "It was on the sidewalk with my book after they put him in the ambulance. An allergic reaction to an insect sting, they think."

"I don't know what to say," she answered. "It's like bad karma, except —"

"Except it's good for sales. Right?"

"Well…"

"I'm nervous about Reno. All I can hear is *Folsom Prison Blues*."

"Huh?"

"You know, the part about shooting a man just to watch him die." He wondered how old she was. From the sound of her voice, he figured she had a few years to go before she reached thirty. "Johnny Cash?"

"Oh, right. Listen, Simon."

"Yeah?"

"Think you could get me one of those shirts?"

~φ~

Nobody was shot in Reno, much to Simon's relief. In fact, he thought he was getting away from Nevada free and clear until he received word that his driver had died at the wheel of his Escalade on the way to take Simon to the airport.

While he waited for a cab to take him, he scrawled ideas in a small notebook he always carried. How much of what was happening could he use in his next novel, he wondered, without being considered an insensitive, exploitive clod?

For her part, Stephanie milked the tragedies for everything she could manage. She sent Simon an iPhone and encouraged him to update his Twitter account frequently. A man in green scrubs and a white lab coat, a stethoscope dangling from his neck, was posted beside Simon's table at his Seattle signing. When a woman waiting in line suffered a stroke, the man turned out to be an actor, as helpless to assist the dying woman as everyone else in the Book Barn. A local news crew on hand captured the whole thing for their evening report. The video went viral, garnering over a million hits in the next twenty-four hours.

When he saw the crowd outside the store in San Francisco, Simon wondered how many people were interested in the book and how many were merely attending to say they were there... and survived. This time they had a real doctor on hand, who was summoned to the alley behind the store about an hour into the signing. Simon found out later that a guy had asked a friend to hold his place in line while he stepped out back to have a smoke. The cigarette was still dangling from the man's lips when the doctor arrived. When he saw the man's picture on CNN that night, Simon was sure he'd spoken to him on his way into the bookstore. He never did find out why the man died.

Simon met Stephanie for the first time when she flew out to L.A. to handle publicity. If he'd known what she looked like when he was talking to her on the phone as he sprawled on various hotel beds over the past week, his mind might have been preoccupied with other thoughts besides dead fans and book sales. She was only about an inch shorter than his six feet, thin but shapely, willowy and formidable. A tangible presence in any room. She greeted him with a friendly hug in the bar of his hotel.

She'd tried to book the Hollywood Bowl, but settled for the largest stadium theater at a multiplex cinema because of the short notice. She hired a local company to manufacture t-shirts, which were sold at the theater's ticket booth. Amateur vendors were served with cease and desist letters and security guards made sure no one sold unauthorized merchandise near the venue. A full medical staff was on hand and an ambulance was stationed near the main entrance with its lights flashing.

Neither Leno nor Conan O'Brien could fit Simon into their schedules, Stephanie told him over drinks, but Letterman was starting to look like a real possibility once they got back East. "And Larry King wants you. That's big. Almost as good as Oprah." Her enthusiasm was contagious. Simon's mind filled with visions of paparazzi and red carpets with Stephanie on his arm, and appearances on C-SPAN where academics quizzed him about the subtexts in his novel.

The theater was packed to capacity when Simon strolled from the wings at six o'clock. Over half the people in the audience were wearing the new t-shirts. Stephanie had changed into one backstage, too. He blushed when she caught him staring at her chest, but she just grinned at him and gave him the thumbs up.

Standing in front of the enormous white screen, he felt like George C. Scott in *Patton*. He opened with a joke about the ambulances and medical staff, which was received with polite laughter. When questioned about the trail of dead bodies he was leaving in his wake, though, he shrugged them off as an unfortunate coincidence. He saw Stephanie frown when he also dismissed the suggestion that his tour was cursed. At the end of the three-hour signing, his wrist ached but he couldn't imagine being happier.

Later, Stephanie took him to dinner at Spago. She was so pumped up he could barely get a word in. "You've got to play up the curse," she said as she drained her second glass of wine. "Controversy sells. You could be the next Dan Brown." She refilled her glass and topped off Simon's. "The publisher has authorized a second printing. A hundred thousand copies. Hold on to any first editions you've got – some day they're going to be worth a lot." She pushed pasta around her plate without eating anything. "Not that you'll need it. I think you're going to be very, very rich."

Exhausted from all the travel and publicity events, the wine went straight to Simon's head. Emboldened when Stephanie's leg brushed against his under the table, he tried to feed her chocolate mousse and missed, then wiped the dessert from her upper lip. She grabbed his hand and licked his fingers. He barely noticed her pay for their dinner, he was so eager to get her into the back of the limo. She pushed a button to close the privacy window. After that, everything was a blur.

~φ~

His head throbbed when he awoke the next morning. Too much light filled the room, so he closed his eyes again. Someone nearby was talking, but he couldn't figure out who it was or what was being said. Every syllable hurt.

He pried his eyes open and squinted. Stephanie was sitting up in bed next to him, TV remote in hand, the covers draped casually across her lap. He could have counted every bone in her spine if his eyes would focus. From the solemn voices, it sounded like she was watching a newscast.

"Look at this," she said.

"What?" His throat was so dry the word came out in a croak.

"After everyone left last night, they found a woman dead in the back row of the theater. Looks like natural causes."

Simon closed his eyes and filled his lungs with air, trying to keep his stomach from churning up its contents.

"Wouldn't normally be news, but all the networks are running it. Cable, too. Because of you."

Simon cradled his aching head in his hands. "For all I know, the last thing that poor woman ever heard on this earth was me reading from *No Longer Dead*."

"We leave for Atlanta at ten. You're on *Larry King* tonight. I'll prep you on the way."

"Okay." After a few moments, his stomach settled and he was able to focus on the vision of beauty that presented itself when he opened his eyes again.

Stephanie clicked off the television. When Simon looked up from her bare breasts, she was grinning. "Well, we do have a *little* extra time." She crawled on top of him and reached between her legs. He sprang to life faster than a teenager. After years of struggling for a break, everything seemed to be going his way. He tried not to think about the trail of dead bodies. That wasn't his fault. All he had to do was lie back and enjoy the ride.

When Stephanie started moaning a few minutes later, he figured she was enjoying the ride as much as he was.

~φ~

The makeup felt strange on Simon's face. He sat on the tail of his jacket and leaned forward, as Stephanie had coached him. He ignored the cameras, maintaining eye contact with the man across the desk, comforted by Stephanie's presence at his side.

The host turned to the camera. "Tonight, Simon Gilliam speaks out in his first interview about what's been happening during the publicity tour for his new book. People are showing up for his signings wearing shirts that read, 'I survived Simon Gilliam's book signing.' Not everyone does. One person has died at each of his eight appearances so far. Some people believe his book tour is cursed. *No Longer Dead* enters the *New York Times* bestseller list at number three this weekend. Simon Gilliam is in our studio to tell us what he thinks about all this and more, and we'll be taking your calls. It's all next on *Larry King Live*."

~φ~

Stephanie got Simon up the morning after his Atlanta signing the same way she'd awakened him the previous morning and the morning before that. She was insatiable. He remembered how hard she'd been to reach a few months earlier when he wanted to know what was planned for *No Longer Dead*. Nothing succeeds like success, he mused, responding to her kisses and caresses.

Naked and sweaty, they checked the papers and the morning news programs. They found reports of three homicides and numerous accidental deaths, but none could be linked to Simon's reading. The news crawl at the bottom of the screen on Fox featured a blurb speculating that the curse had been broken.

Simon and Stephanie sat around in glum silence. "There must be something," Stephanie said, running through the channels again while Simon leafed through the newspapers.

"Maybe someone died during *Larry King*," Simon suggested. He felt like a ghoul.

Stephanie got up and went into the bathroom. A few seconds later, the shower started.

~φ~

Miami and Boston were similarly death free. Simon was no longer front-page news, having been replaced overnight by the peccadilloes of a celebrity athlete. The turnout in Boston was the smallest since Texas, and only a handful of people sprang for the distinctive black t-shirts being sold in the lobby. His New York appearance was relocated from Radio City Music Hall to a bookstore in Manhattan.

At La Guardia, Stephanie waved goodbye near the luggage carousel and said she might see him at the signing that evening. Simon dragged his suitcase out to the curb and hailed a cab, no longer certain where he stood with his publisher. Preliminary sales were solid, and *No Longer Dead* was a debut bestseller, but they wouldn't know for a week if the bubble had burst. If something didn't happen soon, the second printing might end up being a costly mistake.

Simon sat in his cramped hotel wondering what had gone wrong. He'd briefly ridden the crest of a wave and, just as quickly, had plummeted to the bottom. Would his editor be interested in another Simon Gilliam novel? It looked like he wasn't going to be the next Dan Brown. Unless...

He called Stephanie and, after waiting on hold for nearly

fifteen minutes, invited her to lunch. "On me," he said, when she claimed she was busy.

She greeted him with a cool kiss on the cheek and sat across from him at the little table in the bistro with her hands folded in her lap.

Simon hesitated. They had shared some intimate moments, so he felt like he could broach this outlandish idea. He'd seen the greed in her eyes before and had observed how quickly she'd been able to turn tragedy into publicity. He thought she would be open to it, but had no idea if such a thing was even possible, or feasible.

He waited until the waiter was out of earshot and laid it out for her. It didn't take long. The best ideas seldom do.

Her eyes widened. At first he was sure he'd crossed a line, but then he saw the old Stephanie again. She became a dervish, juggling her cell phone, her PDA and a glass of herbal tea. Simon leaned back in his chair and watched her at work. She was glowing. Her face looked almost exactly the same as it did when he was on top of her, hitting all the right spots.

Finally she put down her phone and PDA and said that she'd found a guy who knew a guy who, for the right price, could make it happen. It wouldn't be cheap, but she could bury the expense in the marketing budget. "You're a genius," she said. "We make a terrific team." She battered her eyelids at him. "Wanna skip lunch?"

~φ~

That evening, on the upper level of the Manhattan bookstore, sixty people gathered in the reading area, though there was room for twice as many. Simon stumbled over the familiar words of the morgue scene from *No Longer Dead*. Stephanie winked at him. He resisted the urge to wink back – someone might remember that later – and concentrated on his reading. His voice was thin and reedy. His hand shook. Adrenaline flooded his body. Every sound in the room seemed magnified. He didn't pay undue attention to anyone in the audience. That might cause trouble. Instead he let his gaze flicker from person to person while he did his best to keep his place.

Out of the corner of his eye, he detected a furtive movement. He ignored it and plowed on. The words felt like blocks of lead, weighing down his tongue as he forced them over his lips.

Then he heard a gasp. He looked up and saw a young man slumped over in his chair. He did not appear to be breathing. The woman beside him shook him. The man tumbled to the floor. The woman shrieked and crouched at his side, shaking him as she blubbered.

A man slipped from the crowd and headed toward the escalator. Simon made a point of looking elsewhere in case the man looked back. He didn't want to be able to describe the man, if it should ever come to that.

Though Simon didn't make it onto Letterman that night, the comedian's top ten list was about the things that could go wrong during a Simon Gilliam book signing. Overnight, *No Longer Dead* rocketed to the number one position on Amazon's bestseller list. Almost everyone who showed up at his New Hampshire appearance two nights later bought a black t-shirt. Simon's agent reported that the publisher had reopened discussions about a multi-book deal.

Everything was back the way it should be, Simon thought as he surveyed the crowd, wondering who would feel something pinch the back of his or her neck or her leg or shoulder, and, a moment later, would feel his or her heart seize up.

It would make a great plot for a crime novel, he mused as he opened the reading copy of his novel that had been with him from the beginning. But who would believe it?

Something In Store

Kim called to me from the top of the stairs as I stomped snow from my boots, trying not to spill my coffee in the process. "Check this out, Harv." He descended slowly, counting each step. "Eleven, twelve, thirteen, fourteen. Is that cool, or what?"

I shrugged. The coffee hadn't kicked in yet.

"Don't you get it? Fourteen."

I shook my head.

"Until this morning, there were only twelve."

"Twelve what?"

"Twelve steps, silly. Yesterday there was an even dozen. Today, fourteen."

I chuffed a weak laugh, my breath forming a hazy cloud in the cold. I wasn't sure if Kim was serious. I had no idea how many steps there were, though I had climbed them every day – most days more than once – for over a year and a half.

The steps in question led to the second story of the old Victorian house on Queen Street we both called home. The door inside the front entrance opened into my second-hand bookstore, Back Pages, which occupied the lower half of the house. Kim and I each had a small apartment upstairs.

"You think I'm joking." Kim peered at me with intense blue eyes.

"All I can think about right now is putting out the shingle, getting out of the cold and drinking my coffee. You're on for two o'clock?"

"Yeah, okay. See you at two." He trudged upstairs, disappointment dragging in every step.

~φ~

Two years ago, Karen and I were still married, living south of the border in a much warmer climate than Halifax offered on such blustery, wintry days. We'd been together for eight mostly good years. She'd always been prone to dark moods but usually she rebounded within a day or two. Eventually, though, the frequency of her fugues increased and she stopped talking to me about what was happening inside her head.

Ultimately she descended into a morass from which she never emerged. I don't know why, and I still wonder if there wasn't something I could have done to help her.

After she left, things got ugly, with lawyers doing all the talking. We had no kids so, once things were settled, I quit my job and retreated to Halifax, the city where I'd attended university. The city where I had transformed from a diffident adolescent into a more self-assured adult.

Halifax was only vaguely as I remembered her. Many of the qualities that had made me want to move back still existed – her somewhat European aura, the pedestrian-friendly downtown, street musicians, the waterfront, the parks – but after fifteen years I no longer knew anyone. It took a while to readjust.

When I was in university, I spent every Saturday morning in my favorite used bookstore, finding treasures in its quasi-organized stacks. The store intrigued me as much as its contents. The guy who ran it back then – I knew him only as Mike – had gutted the ground floor of the Victorian house and filled it with shelves. I envied him his life of leisure, sauntering into the store each morning, casually dressed, looking like a holdover from the sixties. He was always reading, surrounded by the endless stacks of dreams that were his trade.

Each downstairs room featured a different subject and even the halls were lined with shelves. Inside a glass-paneled case that served as the checkout counter rare editions beckoned, though all were beyond my budget.

On my first Saturday back in the city, I fell into my old routine, leaving my hotel room early to wander down Spring Garden Road, drawn irresistibly toward the short side-spur of Queen Street leading to Back Pages. The building was still there, but it was for sale.

The following Monday, on a whim, I called the realtor, who told me the house had been on the market for over a year. Not many people were interested in managing a used bookstore these days, and major renovations would be required to restore the building to a private residence. Back Pages had made its mark.

What I really wanted to do was write. The complexities of life with Karen and a high-pressure job had left me little time to indulge this fantasy. With an assistant helping me run the store, I'd have plenty of free time to work on the stories and novels burning inside me. Living upstairs was a bonus. All those books below would provide inspiration. Maybe sitting on the shoulders of those giants would let me see farther.

After the deal was finalized, I took stock of my new home and business. The storage room was full of boxed books, none the worse for their prolonged imprisonment, but the empty shelves demanded more. I ran ads, attended estate sales and auctions, and bought inventories, stretching my finances to the limit. Soon Back Pages was operating near its former glory. More advertisements, a grand opening, and people slowly began to rediscover the magic of spending an hour or two among the stacks of books. Business wasn't exactly booming, but it was a start.

I advertised for an assistant and found Kim Foltyn, an English major in need of both a job and a place to live. For the first six months, Kim entertained – very loudly – a steady stream of men in his apartment. We shared a bedroom wall, so I became uncomfortably familiar with the details of his intimate life. He probably never realized how audible his passionate interludes were, since there was nothing for him to hear in return.

The parade of men dried up after a while and Kim's focus changed. He became attentive to me, bringing me coffee during my shift, complimenting my appearance. I wasn't offended but I wasn't interested either. I did my best to deflect his attentions, pointing out potential candidates to him from among our customers, cracking him up with ribald fantasies concerning their private lives.

"Keep your mind open to possibilities," he called to me when he reached the top of the staircase that winter morning. I counted the steps before turning to open the store. Fourteen. Surely there had always been fourteen.

~φ~

Cat emerged from among the stacks to greet me when I entered the store. She pushed between my legs in welcome before retreating to a dark corner. I put out food and water after I took off my jacket. I never saw her eat, but the dishes were always empty each morning.

There had been a cat in Back Pages twenty years earlier, too, usually found reclining atop a row of books or on the only window ledge in the store, behind the checkout counter. It had given the place a homey feeling.

Not long after I dragged the freestanding Open sign out to the sidewalk for the first time ("We have something in store for you," it advertised – a corny sentiment, but one I remembered fondly) a grayish-black cat crept into the store on the heels of a customer. No one responded to the posters I distributed in the neighborhood, so Cat became a fixture of Back Pages. She allowed customers to stroke and scratch her, purring contentedly at the attention. She came and went according to her own schedule, but she was always back before closing.

Saturday mornings usually start slowly, the domain of some of my regulars: a few college students, and a retiree who usually arrived with a shopping bag crammed with books to sell. It's a comfortable time, especially on mornings when flurries dance outside the window and a gentle but penetrating wind swirls around the corner from Spring Garden Road. I enjoy my coffee while reading the newspaper, raising my head to greet people as they come and go.

One of my regulars arrived around ten-thirty. She had been coming in most weekends since classes began in September, and I had her pegged as a sophomore. Twenty, tops. Long brown hair framed high cheekbones, crystal-clear eyes and a mouth that pouted seductively when she wasn't smiling. She had a killer body, ripe with the barely restrained sexuality of someone who hasn't yet realized she is beautiful. This day, however, her luscious curves were hidden beneath a heavy parka with a fur-lined hood.

If she hadn't been less than half my age, I might have asked her out. She was definitely my type, with those penetrating hazel eyes and a mysterious aura tinged with intelligence. Sexy as hell. And she liked books. She flashed a quick, self-conscious smile in my direction before retreating to the back room, the one that contained fantasy, science fiction and horror. The genre room, I call it.

I know very little about my customers beyond their reading habits. We exchange pleasantries as I make change or wait for the credit card machine to churn out a signature slip. The only names I know come from charge cards, and I forget those almost as quickly as I read them. I would have bet that most of my customers didn't know my name, either.

Which is why I was surprised to hear someone say, "Mr. Stewart?" I looked up from the newspaper to find the attractive brunette standing before the counter with an armload of books. Her brow was furrowed, her mouth turned down slightly at the corners.

"Can I help you find something?"

She bit her upper lip before answering, a simple gesture of vulnerability that endeared her to me. "No, I found everything. I was surprised to see the new room at the back. I didn't know you were expanding."

I smiled vaguely as I tried to make sense of what she was saying. Clearly I hadn't had nearly enough coffee yet.

"I mean, you did it so fast. I didn't see any sign of construction last week."

~φ~

Lewis Carroll said we should try to believe six impossible things before breakfast. It was almost lunchtime, but already two people had said things to me that were, on the surface, impossible.

I didn't know how to respond without making one or both of us seem crazy, which isn't an approach recommended for building good customer relations. I half-smiled and settled for a noncommittal "Thanks." At the best of times, I was tongue-tied speaking with her. Her dynamic features and intense good looks robbed my lungs of air, making speech difficult.

Her eyes narrowed further, but she didn't pursue the matter. I rang up the books and made change from her twenty. Those dark eyes riveted me as if she were trying to see inside my skull. The room's temperature rose perceptibly.

Uncomfortable with her scrutiny, I busied myself filling a plastic grocery sack with her purchases and wished her a nice day. On her way out, she looked over her shoulder at me, and then glanced toward the back room.

The store was empty except for Cat and me, though Cat was hiding in whatever dark corner she secreted herself when she wasn't feeling sociable. I strolled past the shelves, running my hands along the familiar spines. So far, the rows of books had not been the literary inspiration I had hoped for, but I was enjoying working for myself, even though I made barely enough each month to balance accounts.

I came to a standstill when I passed through the doorway into the genre room. The pretty coed hadn't been hallucinating. A door directly opposite me led into a book-filled room I had never seen before. I checked my watch, perhaps to reestablish contact with reality. It didn't say fourteen o'clock and it wasn't running backwards. It was a few minutes past eleven a.m. The second hand marched forward toward noon.

When I looked up, the new room was still there. I had to detour around a few rows of books to reach it and – just for a second – the new doorway vanished from sight. My pulse raced. I was sure the doorway would be gone when I got to the other side of the racks. Part of me hoped it would be gone.

~φ~

No one else came in before Kim relieved me at two o'clock. I was sitting behind the counter staring out at the falling snow, trying hard not to think about what was happening to my store.

Kim enters a room like a tornado even when he isn't accompanied by a gusty, frigid wind. I don't know how he manages it, or why.

"Fourteen steps, man. Fucking awesome," he announced as he blew in.

"Still?" I said.

He looked at me with one eyebrow raised, as if trying to gauge my mood.

"These came in for the horror shelf," I said, pushing a paper bag across the counter. "Rack 'em up, would you?"

He looked at the sack with studied indifference. "Sure, I'll take care of it."

"Now, please."

Kim's eyes widened. He wasn't used to being given such direct orders. I was normally fairly easy-going as a boss. He grabbed the bag and plodded to the back of the store, the sack of books cradled under one arm. As I waited, I thrummed a rapid beat on the countertop with my fingers.

"Fuck me silly," he shouted from the genre room. The paper bag crashed to the floor. "Harv, you've got to see this."

Kim's head tilted back to take in the surroundings like someone watching for incoming aircraft. He rushed toward me when he heard me approach. "You did that on purpose, you bastard." He punched my shoulder. "You knew all along." He looked at me fondly – wild excitement bubbled in his eyes – and for a moment I thought he was going to kiss me. "Where did all this shit come from?" he asked, louder than necessary.

I smiled wryly and shrugged. "Must have come with the new steps."

He nodded as if that made perfect sense. "This is just too cool for words. Hang on – I'll be right back."

I heard the front door close a few seconds later. I stayed in the new room, browsing the titles on the shelves lining the walls. When I discovered the addition to my store, I had a sinking feeling that the shelves would contain strange, ancient tomes with arcane titles about magic and demons. Instead, I found row after row of first editions hardcovers, all in as-new condition. All were signed and dated without inscription, a bookseller's fantasy. Many of the books were rare enough to be worth several hundred dollars apiece unsigned. A quick survey revealed that my inventory had suddenly increased in value by over fifty grand based on original cover price alone. It would take weeks to catalog and price them according to current market value. There could easily be a half million dollars' worth. No wonder my customer had been amazed by the addition.

A few minutes later Kim was back, out of breath. Snowflakes melted on his dark eyebrows. "Check it out, man. The building's the same size. Do you get it? It's the same bloody size."

I nodded – I had confirmed this earlier. The new room should have taken up most of our postage-stamp backyard but, from the outside, nothing had changed.

He pulled one of the books from the shelf, flipping to the copyright page, then to the back to verify the date code in the gutter. "Shit! This is a first. You know what this thing's worth?"

"At least twenty-five hundred, last time I checked," I said. "More since it's a flat signed and dated the week it was released."

"Woo-hoo," he yelled. He carefully returned the book and slipped an arm casually around my shoulder, pulling me close. Then, realizing what he'd done, he released me and stepped away. "Uh, man, these books, they gotta be worth…" his stammer trailed away.

I put my hand on his shoulder, my heart pounding. Cat arrived on the scene, demanding attention as she twined between our legs, defusing the tension. She looked up at the new shelves and meowed plaintively. I ushered her back into the genre room. "No perching in here, Cat. Your claws could cost me thousands."

~φ~

That night, I lay awake trying to sort out the day's events. Was it possible the room had always been there without us noticing it? If that was true, what had happened to the shelf of books that used to be where the new doorway now appeared? And what about Kim's extra steps? Were they real, too? I could make no sense of it. No one would sell a used bookstore and leave behind hundreds of thousands of dollars' worth of inventory. Besides, some of the books had been published after the store closed.

Business picked up appreciably when news of our magnificent inventory spread. Collectors called from across the continent to survey our current holdings. None of our customers commented on the mystery of how the new "first edition" room fit into the framework of the house. Perhaps if they had access to our backyard and could see the overall shape of the house, they might have been disturbed by it.

Adding to the mystery, I never had to restock the new room. Every time I shipped or sold a flat-signed first edition Grisham or Clancy or King, something new and equally valuable appeared in its place by the next morning.

I could easily have stopped buying books from the regulars who lugged in grocery sacks overflowing with old treasures and relics, but I didn't. People who brought me books weren't simply clearing out shelf space for themselves. They felt like they were contributing to my business and passing on treasures for others to enjoy.

~φ~

The next change at Back Pages occurred about six weeks later, on a stormy March morning after my daily trek to Tim Hortons for coffee and the newspaper. The weather was brutal. I almost turned back when I opened the front door but I needed coffee. Flush with cash for the first time in years, I splurged for a jelly-filled donut, too.

Shivering, relishing the first sip of hot coffee after I had the store opened, I flicked on the light switch with an elbow and eased the door closed behind me. Heavy, gray, snow-laden clouds cast a pall over the morning, so the strangely subdued lighting in the store didn't surprise me at first.

Only after I hung up my parka did I notice that the shop's solitary window – behind the now-redundant glass-covered rarities display at the checkout counter – was gone, replaced by an ornate, book-filled cabinet. The only light in the room came from the array of bare bulbs that hung between each row of shelves.

I stared at the apparition, my mouth agape. I'd grown to accept the mysteriously replenishing room of first editions. I was even willing to grant Kim his two extra steps, but the level of strangeness at Back Pages had remained constant for a while. I wasn't sure I was ready for this turn of events. For one thing, I was going to miss my window. During long hours alone in the store, or when browsers loitered among the stacks, I often passed the time watching the pedestrians pass by on Queen Street.

Still, the new book cabinet, ornately exquisite, added to the store's eclectic ambiance. The doors were carved with intricate figures. Glass panels revealed four shelves of volumes. Unlike the new arrivals in the first edition room, these appeared more exotic. I placed a hand on the knurled knob and drew the door open, breath bated, wondering what mysteries lie within. Cat sprang out from the bottom shelf, startling me, and tore around the corner, disappearing into the back of the store.

The books in the cabinet, both modern and ancient, were filled with sexually explicit drawings, photographs, and stories. They covered the entire repertoire of human sexual experience. Every fetish imaginable – and more – was represented on these shelves.

Time passed in a haze as I perused the pages, transfixed. Customers came and went, but I barely noticed them. I do remember blushing furiously when the gorgeous coed brought her weekly stack of fantasy novels to the checkout. Acutely aware of the volume lying open to an etching of six people entangled in an acrobatic display of sexual ardor, I was scarcely able to meet her eyes. I couldn't tell if she noticed my erection, prominent at counter level, or the flush in my face. Heat enveloped me. My breathing deepened. The room felt close – she felt closer.

Our eyes met briefly, then I looked away. I felt her intense scrutiny again. I wanted her. My chest rose and fell in exaggerated rhythm. Afraid to touch her hand, I fumbled her change. She had to ask me for a bag for her purchase.

I watched her leave, torn between returning to the pages and the need to see if she would look back at me.

She pulled the door open. *Look back*, I urged. Her free

hand flicked her long brown hair over her shoulder. She turned briefly… our eyes met. Everything stopped.

Then she was gone, her absence accentuated by a blast of cold air.

I returned to the books, their images and words filling my mind with possibilities.

~φ~

Kim arrived at two p.m., but I didn't hear him come in. Everything I saw on the pages riveted me; nothing repelled me. Sexual practices I had never before considered titillated me. I could imagine myself engaging in any and all of the fascinating fetishes. When Kim approached, I had a coffee-table book filled with graphic photographs of homosexual rapture spread open on the countertop.

"Oh, man, I knew it," he said, his voice a soft whisper.

Our eyes met. The erection I had previously thought reserved only for the lovely coed raged anew. When Kim came around the counter, his condition was similar.

I stood upright, unashamed of my prominent bulge. Wordless, Kim took me in his arms, a tentative hug that surged with intensity when our bodies came into full contact.

Back Pages closed early that day. We climbed the fourteen steps to Kim's apartment in silence. Arctic wind made the walls creak. My mind swam with anticipation. I remembered listening to Kim's lovemaking through our shared apartment wall. This time no one would be on the other side to hear. It would be us, alone.

The next morning, Kim awoke me with a kiss. I was wrung out, drained; we had slept less than two hours.

"We can do this any time you like," he said, his lips less than an inch from my ear.

I was still groggy, my eyes struggling to focus.

He wet his lips. "I know you probably don't love me. This is just about sex, right?" His face was wide-open and innocent as he awaited my response.

I nodded, unable to lie. I liked Kim, and his body held pleasures I'd never before sampled, but I didn't feel anything more than the bond of friendship. I didn't think I could love any man in the passionate way I had loved my ex-wife.

"That's okay. We can still do this any time you want." He had me in his hand, then in his mouth, and I lay back and let him do whatever he wanted with me.

Then it was my turn.

It took away some of the loneliness, I think. For both of us. I knew Kim's feelings for me were stronger than mine for him, but there was nothing either of us could do about that. When I realized that Kim was probably the same age as the young coed – slightly less than half my age – I started thinking about possibilities.

I felt no shame about our relationship. I had never been with a man before, but I had fantasized about it when I was younger. Probably all men do, if they are honest with themselves. Fear of exposure and ridicule is what stops most from doing anything about it. That and AIDS, of course.

We didn't flaunt it, though people probably noticed how Kim touched me at every opportunity. Gentle caresses, pats on the back. Nothing overtly sexual, but obviously tender. I felt bad for him. I know what it's like to be in a relationship where feelings aren't reciprocated. It's a subtly desperate life; always hoping the other person will wake up and realize what they have in their grasp.

After we started sleeping together, Kim spent most of his free time in the store with me. He would bring in a textbook and work on his studies at the end of the counter while I read or did paperwork for the store. His touches – his very presence – never failed to turn me on. I was like a teenager again, hiding an ever-present boner. Every now and then he would give me one of those looks and we would put out the 'Closed For Lunch' sign and careen upstairs to his room.

Sometimes we didn't bother going upstairs.

Kim was my first lover since the divorce, after a sabbatical of two long years. I had buried myself in Back Pages, living a life of lonely frustration. Our affair woke me from my trance.

Or maybe it was the new books. I browsed through them from time to time, though never again with the rapt, overwhelming awe I did that first day. I never sold any of them, either. Whenever anyone inquired about the contents of the new bookcase, I deflected them by saying it was a private collection, not for sale.

~φ~

One Saturday in late April, before opening the store, I went for a stroll up Spring Garden toward the Public Gardens, taking in the fresh air. I felt at peace, but I also felt a burning urge within me. The call of the wild, perhaps.

When the coed came in for her weekly visit, I turned on my friendliest smile. I was genuinely happy to see her and I wanted her to know. She was dressed in jeans and a form-fitting white T-shirt, with a light jacket tied around her waist. She returned my smile with a fifty-thousand-watt beam that lit up the dreary store.

Kim was at a daylong seminar on the campus, so I had the place to myself. From my perch behind the counter, I could barely see her in the back rooms. Every now and then I caught a glimpse of her long brown hair or her white shirt. My mind conjured images from the books behind me, substituting her and me into the erotic pictures.

She emerged half an hour later with six paperbacks nestled in the crook of her left arm. I envied their position, hugged close against her soft, plump breast. In her right hand she clutched a hardcover, holding it like a trophy. She set it down first, being careful to not damage the dust jacket. Then she released the pile of paperbacks in a flood beside it.

I realized I was staring at her, drinking down her beauty in huge gulps. Blinking several times to escape the trance, I looked down at her acquisitions. Never before had she bought a hardcover. This one came from the first edition room. It was Stephen R. Donaldson's *Lord Foul's Bane*. Flat-signed, of course. His "Chronicles of Thomas Covenant" series had been a favorite of mine when I was an undergrad.

"A nice copy," I said.

"I decided to treat myself," she replied, her gaze meeting mine without wavering. "No more exams."

I beamed, inexplicably proud of her. "Congratulations!" I

picked up the volume, treating it with the same respect she had. I pulled out the pricing card stuck inside the front cover. Four hundred and fifty dollars. Handling only the edges, I leafed to the title page. Donaldson's flourish covered most of the white space beneath the title. "Tell you what. No charge, as a token of appreciation for one of my most loyal customers."

Her eyes opened in amazement. She repeated the lip-biting gesture that had captivated me earlier. "Oh, but I couldn't! It's so much."

"Things have been good lately. Besides," I began, feeling my pulse race, my face flush, "I always look forward to seeing you on Saturday mornings." My voice broke and a light sweat beaded on my forehead. I busied myself searching for packing material for the first edition. Sweat trickled from my armpits down my sides.

"Thank you, Mr. Stewart. Gosh!"

"Call me Harv." I wet my lips. "Going back home for the summer?"

Her smile brightened. "Nah, I got a job in the lab, so you'll be seeing me around just like always."

"Great! Would you ever consider, I mean, you don't really know me or anything, but, sometime, maybe..." Words tripped and tumbled over my tongue like comic characters falling down a staircase.

"Are you asking me out, Mr. Stewart? Harv, I mean?"

I nodded, unwilling to trust my tongue with a simple yes. My Adam's apple bobbed as I swallowed.

"I'd like that a lot. How about tonight?"

I couldn't believe my ears. A vision of us walking arm-in-arm through the Historic Properties on the waterfront flashed into my mind. I realized she was still waiting for my answer.

"I'm free," I managed, grateful to get two simple words out intact. I tried for a third. "Dinner?"

"You bet." Her enthusiasm seemed genuine. Had I been stupid all this time? Maybe her weekly visits hadn't been about stocking her bookshelf.

"Where should we meet?"

"You close at six, right?"

I nodded.

"I'll come by at a quarter to and help you close up."

"Terrific!" I finished wrapping her books and passed the package to her. Our hands met in an electric jolt. Hers lingered, extending the contact.

Finally she turned, reluctantly it seemed, and headed for the door.

"Wait!" I called, almost in panic.

Distress creased her face when she turned to look back at me.

"I don't know your name!"

She beamed. "Diane. Diane Landry."

I rolled the words around in my mouth and in my mind for the rest of the afternoon.

Kim returned from his seminar at shortly after five. I'd slipped upstairs to change into something more appropriate for my date that evening and was busy tidying up when he arrived.

He cast a suspicious eye at my apparel. "Hey," he said, his voice tinged with forced enthusiasm. "Wanna go see the new Merchant-Ivory?"

I wasn't thinking clearly when I answered. It was all I could do to not hover two feet off the ground. "Can't. I'm going out to dinner."

"Since when?"

I pulled up short. Even swept up in euphoria I recognized the green-eyed monster. "Since a while ago. This morning."

"I see." His eyes narrowed to slits as he grabbed a sack of new acquisitions from the counter and stormed to the rear of the store.

I didn't want to get into an argument with him, so I didn't pursue it. I'd let him handle it in his own way. Nothing was going to spoil my evening.

He was still out back when Diane arrived fifteen minutes later. "I'm locking up," I called out as we left.

~φ~

Later that night, Diane followed me up the narrow staircase to my apartment. For a moment, in the magical silence after we made love the first time, I wondered if Kim was listening through the paper-thin walls. I pushed the thought from my mind and allowed myself to be fully present. It wasn't difficult.

"So, what's with you and that guy you work with?" she asked me the next morning.

"What do you mean?"

"He's in love with you, in case you hadn't noticed." Her voice was soft in my ear.

I nodded, though she couldn't see me in the still-dark room. "He'll be all right."

~φ~

On Sundays, Kim opened up and I relieved him at two. I didn't know how to talk to him about Diane. I didn't feel like I should apologize – we both understood that for me our relationship had been purely physical. A romp.

I left Diane in the apartment curled up naked on my ragged bachelor-couch surrounded by a stack of paperback fantasy novels. She seemed perfectly content to stay alone until closing. I invited her to sit with me in the store, but she said she didn't want to get dressed. The sight of her gorgeous figure in my modest apartment sent a thrill-rush of adrenaline through me.

Back Pages was unlocked when I went downstairs, but Kim wasn't at the counter. Cat greeted me at the door and meowed. I filled the food dish and replenished her water. She lapped as I poured – a first – then disappeared among the shelves.

I wandered through the aisles, returning a few paperbacks to their places on the shelves. The store appeared empty. It felt empty. I stuck my head in the first edition room for a quick look. Shortly after discovering the addition, I had considered camping out one night to see if I could witness the miracle of the replenishing shelves, but I was afraid I might jinx the magic. Some things are better left alone.

I was so focused on looking for Kim that I almost overlooked the most recent change in the bookstore: A dark patch halfway along the wall to the right of the new room's entrance.

A staircase.

In an ordinary universe, this staircase would have broken through the wall into the genre room; however, that part of the store was unchanged. The steps – like the first edition room itself – defied explanation. On one side of the wall they led up to some unknown chamber. On the other side, normalcy persisted.

I stepped into the room and approached the foot of the murky staircase. "Kim?"

A charcoal blob materialized in the darkness and resolved itself into Cat, who was strolling languidly down the stairs. When she reached the bottom, she brushed past me. There was no other response to my call.

I climbed the steps slowly, testing each one, certain they would fade into nothingness and I'd fall into a bottomless abyss. That Cat had descended them comforted me only slightly.

The top stair – the fourteenth, of course – gave way to a dim room. Dust and mildew assailed my nostrils. By my best estimate, I should have been standing in Kim's apartment, but this room was empty and devoid of windows. There was a second room at the back, revealed by a flickering yellow light within. I smelled smoke, but it wasn't the alarming scent of a house fire. It was oily, like kerosene.

I eased my way into the room, approaching the small arch at the far end of the wall. The oily smell grew stronger the closer I got. I paused. What was waiting for me on the other side?

I took a deep breath and passed through the archway.

Two torches protruding from wall holders lit the inner chamber. Their flickering illumination made the scene seem ominous. Kim sat on the floor, his back against the far wall, ancient books stacked around him and a large tome spread across his lap. His lips moved as his finger traveled across the page, but I didn't hear anything at first. A moment later I realized he was reading aloud, but I couldn't make out the words. He looked up briefly then returned his attention to the book on his lap without acknowledging my presence.

"What's this?" I asked, my voice weak and unsteady in the unfamiliar surroundings.

He held his finger on the page to keep his place. "Only everything I ever dreamed about," he said. "You got your room of riches and your little armoire of sexual fantasies. I got all this."

I was about to take a step closer to see what the books were, but something in Kim's look made me hold back. Torch flickers reflected in his glassy eyes, giving him a demonic aura.

"Fuck off, Harv. Leave me alone. You've got what you want. Now, so do I." Tangible energy emanated from him, pushing me away.

Stunned, I retreated from the room, stumbling down the staircase. Kim's voice grew louder. Unintelligible words and chants followed me until I reached the bottom step. It seemed like more than just Kim's voice, but that wasn't possible. Was it?

I closed the shop early that day. As I carried the sign in from the street, the slogan struck me as oddly appropriate. There was certainly something in store for us. I didn't know what, and I wasn't sure I wanted to know.

I brought take-out Chinese back to the apartment and Diane stayed over. I didn't tell her about the new upstairs chamber in the store, or about Kim's strange behavior. There would be plenty of time to deal with that matter later. We fed each other egg rolls and chicken chow mein with chopsticks and giggled like teenagers when I licked duck sauce from her breasts. We made love with the lights on, and again later with the lights off, long after I thought I was too worn out to rise to the occasion. We talked and bantered, discussed our favorite authors and our favorite positions. I tried my best not to think about anything but the delights of a newfound relationship.

When morning arrived, I reluctantly crawled out of bed. I'd listened for the sounds of Kim returning to his apartment, but they never came. Diane finally drifted off to sleep around six a.m. I quietly got dressed and went downstairs.

The entrance to Back Pages, a solid wooden door with a single thick and opaque window, seemed to want me to stay away. It was tempting to declare a holiday. I could certainly afford it.

Still, I had to know what was going on inside. I wasn't going to let Kim scare me out of my own store. The bell tinkled when I pushed the door open. Otherwise the shop was silent.

Cat didn't appear. I looked behind the counter; her food dish was untouched from the day before.

All I had for a weapon was a baseball bat. A horrible cliché, but no one robs bookstores, even reasonably profitable ones. I kept it behind the counter more as a conversation piece than as serious protection. This morning, I was glad of its heft. Resting across my left shoulder, it was in perfect position to lash out at a moment's notice.

A trace of bitterness tainted the air, reminiscent of burnt sulfur. As I detoured around the rows of bookshelves to reach the first edition room, I remembered how dark and daunting the staircase had been. My only flashlight was upstairs in my apartment. Having gotten this far, I didn't want to go back.

If the staircase still existed, it was hidden behind a new, ornate door. It looked like something out of an old estate, with intricate scrollwork set into thick mahogany panels. There was a pair of hinges along one side, but no doorknob. It reminded me of a mystery novel I'd read as a teenager about a house where every door was opened by solving a puzzle involving the decorative design work. I searched my memory for details as I toyed with the engravings. When I squeezed the opposite sides of a flowerlike motif, a panel clicked open and a handle popped out.

The staircase seemed the same as the night before. The light from the bare bulbs in the first edition room penetrated only a few inches beyond the doorframe. I took a deep breath and braced myself to plunge into the darkness again. "Should have brought a light," I muttered.

Crack!

The baseball bat jolted against my shoulder. A blast of heat warmed the back of my head. I yanked the bat away from my body to find it transformed into a flaming torch. Its shape was essentially unchanged. The Louisville Slugger seal still appeared on the shaft.

Don't ask, I thought. *There are no answers, only more questions.*

The torch helped, but the staircase was still a daunting, shadowy tunnel. I ascended slowly, straining to hear anything from the room above. At the sixth step, something swooped overhead. Something large.

I jabbed the torch up as high as my arm would reach, but whatever had lunged at me remained out of view. For a second I imagined pterodactyls, then forced the thought from my mind, remembering the way the torch had appeared in response to my wish. "There's nothing there, nothing at all," I repeated, like a mantra.

I climbed the remaining eight steps. In the illumination provided by the bat-torch I saw the antechamber in its entirety for the first time. The walls were intricately patterned, decorated with weird, unnatural tableaus depicting otherworldly scenes. The flickering torchlight made them seem to writhe. I touched a figurine to convince myself it was only an optical illusion. The demonic shape, half female-half beast, squirmed against my fingers.

The creepy sensation lingered long after I snatched my hand away. When I continued toward the arch, a shadowy figure appeared, blocking the way.

Kim.

Backlit by torches from the inner chamber, his long hair flamed. He looked bigger than I remembered. Both taller and more substantial. "I thought I told you to fuck off. You have everything you need. Why can't you let me be?"

"What's this all about, Kim? Is it Diane?"

"Spare me the speech about how what we had was just about sex, please," Kim said. "You can't be that simple."

"I'm sorry. That's really all it was for me. You said you understood."

"And my feelings don't matter?"

"I never pretended it was anything else. You knew it could never be more." The torch was growing heavy in my hand, but there was nowhere to put it down.

"A guy can hope," he responded. "He can dream. Look where dreaming got you. All the money you'll ever need. Any sexual fantasy you ever had… fulfilled. Lust after some sexy little morsel and – hey! – before you know it she's sharing your bed."

I didn't know how to answer. Things *had* gone well for me lately. After nearly hitting bottom when Karen left me, I had rebounded. I hadn't done anything to deserve it, but I wasn't going to apologize for it, either. "What do you want?"

"I wanted you. Nothing more. For a while I had you, even though it was only on loan. Now all I want is this." He indicated the inner chamber.

"What's in there?" Bizarre images played against the wall behind him. They could have been shadows from the flickering torch flames, but I wasn't convinced. Goosebumps rose on my arms, raised by a chill emanating from the walls.

"Nothing you'd ever understand, Harv. Now go away and leave me here. I'm happy. Close the door behind you on the way out."

I stepped forward but Kim blocked me from going any farther. He seemed to loom over me. A bolt of flames erupted from his eyes, scorching the floor inches in front of my feet. The unexpected burst blinded me momentarily.

"Stay back, Harv. You don't want to come in here, I promise you. Take what you have and be happy with it. Leave me be."

The bitterness in his voice pierced me, and I hung my head. Nodding to myself, I retreated to the stairs. I must have lost count on the way down, because it seemed like there were only thirteen steps. I wasn't going back to check, though.

In the first edition room, I pushed the carved door shut. With a metallic click the latch retreated into the recess. The wooden panel merged into the rest of the door seamlessly.

"I don't need this," I said. "I don't need any of this in my store. In my life."

The hinges smoothed out and vanished. The intricate wooden designs faded into flatness. A rush of warm air forced me back a step. The bare spot in the wall transformed into a bookshelf filled with valuable first edition hardcovers.

Something brushed against my legs. My heart leapt as I stepped back in panic. It was only Cat, yowling at me. I picked her up and listened to her purr contentedly. She seemed as happy as I was to see the abominable room gone.

What had become of Kim? Had he faded into nothingness along with the room and its contents? Crossed over to some other dimension, like in an H.P. Lovecraft story, following his Elder Gods? Was he trapped in purgatory, forever condemned by my selfishness? I would never know. And, in time, maybe I wouldn't think about it very often.

Looking around the room, I wondered why I had been blessed with such good fortune. Had Mike, the previous owner, tapped into this, too? Had he ended up trapped in some chamber of his own dreams, like Kim? Or had he found the key to happiness?

As I surveyed shelf after shelf filled with first editions but – more importantly – filled with imagination, with stories and ideas set in this world and others, I knew my place was here, among these books. Not necessarily among the valuable first editions, but maybe in the other rooms, with the well-read hardcovers or the dog-eared paperbacks.

The overwhelming urge to write swept over me. I had been marking time, finding excuses not to put down the words swimming in my head. Living on autopilot.

I wandered out of the mystically replenishing room into the main store. The stories in here were just as valuable as the ones in the back room, even if the price of admission was only fifty cents for a third-hand copy of a sci-fi epic. Yes, I belonged here, not only among these rows of shelves, but some day on these shelves, cover-to-cover with the authors who had stirred my imagination and made me want to create as they had created. To conjure worlds out of whole cloth.

I set Cat down as I left the genre room. Sunlight greeted me, streaming in through the window that once again looked out onto Queen Street from behind the checkout counter. Another rush of warm air blew past me. Without turning to look, I knew the entrance to the first edition room had been replaced by another bookshelf. I didn't mind. As Kim said, I certainly had enough money to live comfortably a good, long time.

It wasn't going to be easy to come up with an explanation for the suddenly missing room of treasures. I thought I was up to the task, though. Telling stories was going to be an important part of my life from now on.

I didn't put the Open sign out that morning. I rechecked Cat's food dishes, turned out the lights, and locked up. I needn't have bothered with the food – I never saw Cat again after that day.

Upstairs, two things awaited me. One was Diane, her vibrant body and fresh young mind both ready to engage me. I wasn't sure how long we would last. The novelty of an older man might wear off when the new semester began in the fall. We had opened each other up to new possibilities and if she decided to move on, well, I would survive.

But maybe we did have a future together. Lately, my wishes seemed to have a way of coming true. Maybe there was enough magic left in the old place for another wish or two.

The other thing that waited for me in my little apartment at the top of the stairs was the computer, a doorway into new worlds. I felt ready to sit down in front of the keyboard and let my mind guide my fingers. The possibilities were endless.

I climbed the twelve steps to the landing and opened the door to my apartment. ⬊

Purgatory Noir

I was sitting in my office, staring at the ceiling and contemplating the sorry state of my existence when she barged in. Once upon a time, I had a receptionist who was easy on the eyes and ran interference between me and the rest of the world, but those days have been over for a long time.

She swept in like a force of nature, this dame, moving fast on long, good-looking legs. Her curly dark hair bounced like tightly coiled springs and her slinky dress adored her body. I closed my eyes, trying in vain to catch a hint of the perfume someone like her would have worn once. Before.

"Someone's got to do something," she said by way of introduction.

I took my time responding, hoping that my cool demeanor would slow her down. I didn't want her getting hysterical. "By 'someone' I assume you mean me."

She gave me a look that would have withered a lesser man. For a moment, I thought I recognized the look and the face that wore it. Sure, I'd seen her around, but it was more than that. When it didn't come to me, I pushed the thought aside.

"All right, doll," I said. "What's got you in such a tizzy."

The look grew darker. "You're not very nice."

I shrugged. "Do you blame me?"

"Look, I know it's difficult, but we have to make do the best we can." Her pause was as loud as her words. "All of us."

I sighed. "If you say so. What's on your mind?" I didn't call her sweetheart, though it was tempting, just to see how she'd react. She struck me as the kind of woman who had an extensive repertoire of scathing looks.

"It's Mrs. Parker."

I searched my mind until I came up with a hazy image of an elderly woman with blue hair who wore a flowery dress and too much costume jewelry. "What about her?"

"She's gone."

"It happens," I said, not liking where this conversation was headed. Not one little bit.

"Hardly ever, and you know it. Until… recently."

I understood this pause, too. We all had problems trying to describe the passage of time.

"No one has left in ages, but now all of a sudden five people go. Just like that." She snapped her fingers.

I hadn't realized there were that many, but I hadn't given it much thought. I leaned back in my chair and conducted a mental census. McGinty's departure had a lot of people talking, that much I remembered. He was such a cantankerous bastard, we were sure he would be around forever.

After him there was Noonan. I never understood why he was Here in the first place, but that was the big question, wasn't it? Why were any of us Here?

Then Yolanda went. She was sweet and shy and could sit for what seemed like hours without saying a word. I liked that in a woman. So quiet that she left without saying a word. I guess when you finally figure out how to get away, you don't want to waste a second.

Who else was there? The dizzy dame had said that Mrs. Parker made five. Before I had a chance to itemize them, she beat me to the punch, holding up her fist and extending one finger at a time as she counted them off. "Joe, Marty, Yolanda, Greg and now Mrs. Parker." When she was finished she looked like she wanted to slap me. Maybe she did.

Greg. Now I remembered. Kept to himself. Not that any of us really tried to fit in. We just put in our time and hoped that someday we'd figure out how to move on to whatever came next.

"What do you want me to do?" I asked. Her name finally came to me – Eve something. Like Mrs. Parker – I doubted anyone knew the rest of her name. She might even have forgotten it herself. "I mean, isn't this what we all want? To get away from this place?"

"Somebody's doing something," she said again.

"And you want me to figure out who."

"It's what you used to do, isn't it? Besides, who else is there?"

Who else, indeed?

~φ~

I didn't get out of the office very much. People left me alone there. Like most everyone Here, I had constructed a comfortable cocoon to remind me of what things were like back when I was alive. Maybe I hadn't had the most luxurious life, but I'd been reasonably content. Plenty of work, plenty of women, plenty of booze. The formula for happiness.

As Eve implied, I used to be a detective before I stuck my nose where someone thought it didn't belong and I ended up swallowing a load of lead. I always used to joke that domestic cases would be the death of me. The naked broad who pointed the .357 Magnum at me after she caught me taking pictures of her and her lover in the sack screamed that she hoped I'd rot in hell as she pulled the trigger.

She almost got her wish.

None of us believed Here was hell, but it was definitely the next best thing. Near as we could figure, we were in some remote corner of purgatory reserved for people who had a lot to make up for. Every so often someone new joined us, which created a bit of excitement, but it was a rare occasion when someone left. The dame was right. Something unusual was going on. I didn't really care that people were disappearing – except, maybe for Yolanda – but if they were figuring out how to move on, perhaps there was a chance for me.

Here was constructed in a shallow bowl, like a meteor crater. My office building was about halfway down the gradual slope. Once we were out on the street, Eve led me past an odd assortment of buildings and then across a sandy beach lined with palm trees. A few steps later, a skyscraper jutted from the pavement next to a log cabin in the woods. Even the most corrupt zoning committee would never have approved of the layout of our crazy reality. It seemed to be cobbled together out of random pieces, part memory of the places we used to know and part fantasy of places we always dreamt of living. After a while I stopped being amazed by how strange it all looked.

Until it got stranger, that is. Mrs. Parker's corner of Here wasn't there any more. It was as if someone had reached down from the sky with a huge eraser and rubbed everything out. Where there used to be a gingerbread house with a white picket fence, a neatly manicured lawn, a garden, and swing sets, now there was nothing. Literally. For a moment I wondered what would happen if I stepped into the void, but I wasn't brave enough to try. I had no doubt that there were worse fates than being Here. Far worse.

"She's gone, all right," I said.

Eve didn't dignify that with a response.

Someone called out from behind us. "Nothing much to look at, is there?"

I turned to see a grizzled man wearing a wife-beater under an unbuttoned Hawaiian shirt. He had on cutoff jeans so faded they were almost white. His feet were bare. He was sitting on a folding lawn chair under the awning of a doublewide trailer. Was this the best he could dream up? Or all he ever knew?

"Came out the door a while back and everything was just plumb gone. Her included."

There was no point in asking him how long she'd been gone. Some of our fantasy houses may have had clocks on the walls, but they all run at different speeds, if they run at all. There was no sun to rise or set, just a perpetual, flickering twilight that cast a pall over everything, caused by the glow from the wall of fire at the edge of the crater that prevented us from venturing beyond it.

"She didn't say anything?"

"Oh, she said lots of things. That woman could talk. I didn't mind, most of the time. Better'n just sitting here and stewing in my thoughts. Can't say I actually took in most of what she said, but if you're asking whether she mentioned anything about leaving, then I guess the answer's no."

"Did you notice anything different?"

"Ha," he said without any humor. "When's the last time anything changed around here?" He jerked his head toward the void. "Other'n that. You're that guy that used to be a detective, right?"

I nodded.

"Got yourself a real mystery to solve, then. Lucky you." He focused on Eve for several seconds. "This your assistant?"

"His client," she answered before I had the chance to say anything inappropriate.

"The game is afoot," the old geezer said and grinned.

"Did she have any visitors?"

He was still staring at Eve. Can't say I blamed him. She was definitely easy on the eyes. Not that either of us could have done anything about it, even if the spirit was willing. Beyond the obvious fact of no longer being alive, being dead had some distinct disadvantages.

"Oh, people used to come by from time to time," he said. "Like I said, she was a talker."

"But you haven't noticed anything strange going on lately?"

He stretched his legs out and clasped his hands behind his head. "What's your interest?"

"She's the fifth person to vanish…" I stopped myself before I added the word "recently."

"Really?" he said. "Maybe there's hope for us after all."

~φ~

In the beforetimes, everyone had hopes and dreams, even if it was as simple as wishing for enough to eat or a man wanting his children to have a better life than his. Critically ill people hoped the end would come quickly to put them out of their misery. I used to wish a rich, grateful client would die and leave me a ton of cash in his will. As far as I could tell, none of that wishing and hoping ever paid off for anyone.

Besides, it was hard to figure out what to hope for Here. Oblivion? Paradise? No one knew what became of those who found their way out. They didn't send us postcards from wherever they ended up. For all we knew, we might have been preparing ourselves for eternal damnation and this was just the softening-up stage.

The old geezer wished us well and returned to whatever it was he was doing when we got there. Staring into the void to see if it stared back, perhaps. He told Eve to drop by and see him anytime she wanted to, and she said that she just might. He didn't make me the same offer, I noticed.

We moved on from Mrs. Parker's former corner of Here to the other "crime scenes." Some of them had started to readjust. The voids were shrinking. Eventually they would disappear altogether. Either that or some new soul would arrive to take up residence and remodel the grounds in his or her image.

Everyone we encountered along the way called me "the detective." I hadn't realized I had such a reputation. They all seemed eager to talk, but none of them had observed any changes in the "victims" before they vanished without a proverbial trace. If this had been a real case from back when I was alive, I would have told my client that it was going nowhere and she was wasting her money. Unless I was hard up for dough, in which case I would have dragged it out a little longer before giving up.

I figured the same rules applied Here. "This is going nowhere," I told Eve when we reached her place at the bottom of the crater. It was a tidy little bungalow with a two-car garage. Big enough for two or three kids, from the look of it, but there were no children Here.

She forgot herself for a moment and reached out to grab me. When her hand passed right through mine, she sighed. Who knows – maybe if she had been able to touch me, she would have invited me inside her comfortable little house. It had happened to me often enough in the beforetimes. Any port in a storm for a lonely person. Instead she said, "Promise me you'll keep looking into this."

I had nothing to lose by making an empty promise, so I did.

I climbed the slope to my office building, mounted the stairs to the second floor, lowered myself into my comfortable chair and leaned back to contemplate the ceiling tiles. A bottle of bourbon in my bottom desk drawer would have helped, but no matter how much we fantasized about things like that – food, drink, sex – none of it ever materialized.

Sometime later – who knows how long? – Eve barged into my office again, those long legs propelling across the room in two quick strides. "Bernard's gone," she said, pointing her thumb over her shoulder.

"Who was he again?"

"Mrs. Parker's neighbor. The guy in the trailer."

I nodded to let her know that I remembered him. I didn't want her to start losing confidence in my detecting skills. I sort of liked having her around. She was a breath of fresh air and a beam of light in a place where the wind never blew and the sun never shone.

I didn't really care about Bernard – not in the way Eve seemed to. I was, however, intrigued to learn that he had gotten away. He hadn't seemed particularly interested in leaving Here when we talked to him – other than his general comment about there being hope for us all. And yet he had somehow managed to solve the mystery.

I didn't like feeling left out. I was also vaguely curious about what would happen if the void he had left behind merged with Mrs. Parker's in the adjacent lot. I had a brief vision of a swirling vortex appearing at their interface that drained away everything around it until we, too, were sucked in. The notion had a certain appeal. I used to think that when the end came, I would close my eyes and then there would be nothing. Seemed like a good alternative to this place.

"Are you coming?" She didn't say it like a question. I wondered what she had been like in the beforetimes. She might have been a knockout, but I was willing to bet she had been a shrew, too. The kind of woman who could get a guy to do anything and gave him nothing in return. I'd known a lot of women like that. Almost married one once, before I wised up.

I didn't have anything better to do, so I followed her out into the street, past a mansion and a university dorm, across thirty feet of beach, past the skyscraper and the log cabin in the woods before we re-entered suburbia. We found no spiraling vortex, just two voids, one on either side of the street. Crossing the ribbon of asphalt between them felt like walking a balancing beam. There goes the neighborhood, I thought. At the rate people were disappearing, soon there would be nothing left.

I had no idea why we were here – just like I had no idea why we were Here. Bernard was simply gone, same as Mrs. Parker.

He wasn't coming back, no matter what I did. Besides, I didn't want him to come back. I wouldn't wish this place on my worst enemy. Bernard was gone – good for him. I put my hands on my hips and sighed. I'd been sighing a lot since I died.

"Aren't you at all concerned?" Eve asked. Based on her tone of voice, I knew what answer I was supposed to give.

I shrugged instead. "I don't get what you're so worked up about," I said. "We should be happy for him, right?"

She gave me another one of those looks, the kind that said she would have slapped me if only she could. A piece of the puzzle suddenly fell into place. A void was filled. I knew where I had seen that look before. I hadn't been focusing much on her face at the time because she had been naked and pointing a .357 Magnum at my chest.

"You," I said. Not my snappiest line, but my mind was reeling. "You're the bitch who shot me." It sounded like a line out of a movie. Even dead, my life was a cliché.

I thought she would at least blush or look away, but she held my gaze without blinking. "Took you long enough," she said. "Some detective."

"I didn't recognize you with your clothes on," I said. That was better. I was starting to get my groove back. Still no blush, though. "And without a big gun in your hands. Pointed at me."

"A bad day for everyone," she said.

Curiosity got the best of me. "What happened after you shot me?"

She finally looked away. "The guy I was with – Greg – you remember Greg, right? Anyway, after I shot you, he sort of freaked out. Grabbed the gun. Still had it when the cops arrived. He shot one of them – McGinty. So the cops shot back. We were a regular Bonnie and Clyde, gunned down in a blaze of glory. The first bullet did the trick. Got me here." She placed her hand over her left breast.

"McGinty?" I said. "The grouchy old bastard?"

She nodded.

"And Greg?" It seemed like one hell of a coincidence – to be stuck in purgatory with, what, three other people she knew from when she was alive. "Next you're going to tell me that Mrs. Parker was…"

"My mother."

"Huh. Who else? Noonan? Yolanda? The old guy – Bernard?"

She just smiled.

I stabbed my index finger at her. "You killed me. You. I'm here because of you."

"No – I'm here because of you."

I shook my head. "That doesn't make any sense," I said. "Did the others recognize you?"

"Not at first," she said. "You remember getting shot, though, right?"

"I remember *you* shooting me, yes," I said. It seemed important to make sure that that little detail didn't get overlooked.

"But you didn't recognize me until now."

"I guess I didn't expect to see you here – or anyone I knew from before, for that matter."

"Don't feel bad. Even my own mother didn't know me."

"But you knew her. And me."

She nodded. "From the very beginning."

"Why didn't you say anything before?" The pull of the two voids, one on either side of us, seemed to be growing stronger. Though we were standing in the middle of the road, I was so disoriented that I felt that at any moment I might suddenly stumble and fall into one of them.

"I had to put things right. One step at a time. Make amends to all the people I hurt in life."

I slipped a hand under my shirt and found the little divot on my chest where her bullet had begun its journey toward my heart. It was in almost the same place she had indicated on her chest.

"So all these people who disappeared —"

"They left because they let me go. They went back to where they belong."

"You knew that when you came to see me."

"I couldn't just drop this on you all at once. It's a process. I had some things to work out – with the others, too. You'll see."

"What do you mean?"

She was looking me straight in the eyes again. "This isn't the end for you. I have a suspicion you'll be back Here someday, or in a place very much like this."

"And you?"

"I still have more to do Here. More sins to confess. More forgiveness to seek." She reached out for my hand, and this time she made contact. The unexpected touch took my breath away. I almost stepped back, but that would have meant losing contact with the only person who had been able to touch me since I arrived Here. Her hand was warm.

"Benjamin. I am terribly sorry that I tried to take away your life. I was a selfish, thoughtless person. I regret most of the choices I made while alive." She raised my hand and clasped it against her chest. I could feel her heart beating. Her heart!

I inhaled deeply – it wasn't a sigh. I needed air. I hadn't been aware of breathing the whole time I'd been Here, but suddenly I needed to feel air rushing into my lungs. And it did. Real air. What had she meant – *tried* to take away my life? The divot on my chest throbbed and burned. To feel her warmth, her skin against my skin, her heart beating an inch below the place where my hand touched her…

"I forgive you," I said, and I did. She had deliberately aimed her gun at me and pulled the trigger, but I forgave her.

"Thank you," she said. "Have a wonderful life. Be good to people. Do good things."

"What – ?"

She faded from view, along with everything around her. It took me a second to realize that it was actually *me* who was fading, disappearing from Here the same way McGinty, Greg, Mrs. Parker and all the others had. Leaving behind my own void in Eve's purgatory.

And then I was flat on my back, in a sterile room surrounded by beeping equipment and anxious-looking people in scrubs. The man who was holding the shock paddles smiled when he realized I was awake.

"Welcome back, Mr. Kane. We almost lost you."

I took another deep breath. This one hurt. I felt like I'd been run over by a transport. My chest burned. I'd never felt better in my life. I nodded at the doctor to let him know I'd heard him, then closed my eyes again and drifted off to sleep. ⊠

BOB WEINBERG is the author of 17 novels, two short story collections, and 16 non-fiction books. He has also edited over 150 anthologies. His most popular novels are the three books that make up the trilogy known as the *Masquerade of the Red Death*, published by White Wolf Books.

His most popular character is detective, Sid Taine, nicknamed "the psychic detective" who appears in the novel, *The Black Lodge*. Taine also stars in a series of short horror-mystery stories, many of which were collected in the book, *The Occult Detective*.

In non-fiction he's best known for *The Weird Tales Story; A Biographical Dictionary of SF/Fantasy Authors*; and *Horror of the Twentieth Century*. Bob has also collaborated with the talented Lois H. Gresh on a series of pop-science books including the best-selling *The Science of James Bond*. In 2000, Bob began scripting comic book stories for Marvel Comics. He later worked for DC/Wildstorm and Moonstone Comics.

Bob is a two-time winner of the Bram Stoker Award; a two-time winner of the World Fantasy Award; and a winner of the Lifetime Achievement Award from the Horror Writers Association. In 2005, Bob was Guest of Honor at the World Fantasy Convention in Madison, Wisconsin. He served as Chairman of the 1983 and 1990 World Fantasy Conventions and was co-chairman of the Chicago Comicon from 1976-1996.

Robert E. Weinberg

Elevator Girls

*Any resemblance between characters in
This story and real people and publishers
is, of course, purely coincidental.*

1.

Brian Cassidy encountered his first elevator girl at the 1989 World Fantasy Convention in Seattle.

A quiet, introspective writer, Brian disliked science fiction conventions and usually turned down any invitations he received to attend them. Not that he was often asked. Horror writers, except for the few biggest names, were considered nonentities by most fantasy fans. And, though both of Brian's novels had received excellent reviews in the mainstream press, neither of his books had been plugged by the horror critics in either of the monthly science fiction newsletters. Which, by fan standards, meant he was not a "Hot New Author."

His agent, Milt Gross, was determined to change that perception. He had insisted that Brian leave his comfortable Chicago apartment and travel to Seattle over the Halloween weekend to attend the convention and "network" with the right people. Going against all of his convictions, Brian reluctantly agreed. He had poured his heart and soul into his novels and their lack of success hurt him, both financially and emotionally.

The gathering so far had proven somewhat of a surprise. The fantasy convention was a limited membership weekend with a high admission price and no events catering to science fiction media fans. Costumes were not allowed and with only 750 people in attendance, there was not the usual crush of humanity that made socializing at such affairs impossible. Though he hated admitting it, Brian was actually having a pretty good time.

He had participated on two panels that afternoon – one dealing with the use of black magic in horror stories; the other on why horror protagonists acted so foolishly in most novels. Each of the discussions had been well attended, and the audiences were attentive and appreciative. Their questions at the end of each panel indicated real interest in the subjects, and they had actually applauded when the panelists had left the podium.

Afterwards, Brian had been astonished to have more than two dozen people approach him to autograph *Dead Kisses* and *Grave Shadows*. For an author whose best signing in Chicago bookstores had attracted three people, it was heady stuff.

That feeling of euphoria was starting to wear off by the time he and Milt made it to the Lion Books party that evening. Introverted by nature, Brian disliked loud gatherings in suites stuffed with people he didn't know. He felt isolated and alone, especially when Milt wandered off looking for free refreshments and never returned.

The air in the room stank, and it was hot as hell.

Feeling slightly faint, Brian tugged the neck of his shirt open wider. When they had entered the suite around midnight, Milt had told him the party was just beginning and that it usually lasted all night. Brian doubted that he could spend five minutes more there, despite Milt's admonition for him to "network, network, network."

Brian took a swallow of soda pop to clear his throat. The atmosphere was so befouled by smoke that his lungs burned just from breathing. Not accustomed to smoke-filled rooms and large crowds, he found the party overpowering. There were several hundred people squeezed into the suite that normally held fifty or sixty comfortably. The din of conversation was overwhelming. It was impossible to hear anything said in less than a shout.

"They say the air on the U.S. space station smells like this after a few weeks," declared someone dryly on Brian's right. "But they don't permit smoking there."

"No surprise," replied another person. "You'd kill all the

plants on board with this much carbon dioxide. Not to mention the crew."

Brian smiled, then grunted in pain. An unexpected elbow caught him in the side as a big burly man smoking a pipe pushed his way past. Brian knew better than to expect an apology. Manners didn't exist when this many people crowded into a party.

Sighing, Brian stood on his toes and tried to catch a glimpse of his agent. For all of his talk of making new contacts and conducting important business at these parties, Milt spent most of his time at the bar or refreshment spread. At times, it seemed to Brian that his agent lived on the largesse of others. In fact, he could not remember seeing Milt pay for a meal during the convention.

It wasn't a thought that pleased Brian. Milt represented him in dealing with editors and publishers. If his agent was regarded as a grifter, it reflected worse on him.

He had signed with Gross when he first started writing. Few agents expressed any interest in his early work. Milt had taken him on at standard rates while others had asked for reading fees merely to look at his stories. Gross had been the one who steered him away from writing short stories and into novels. And, though neither deal had been of earthshaking proportions, it was Milt who had sold his first two books to Paperback Library. Brian felt he owed what little he had accomplished so far in the horror field to his agent. Still, the thought hadn't stopped him from thinking about finding someone else to handle his work.

"Hey, Brian," a voice called from behind him, breaking his train of thought. "How you been?"

Smiling, he turned. The speaker's accent was unmistakably Texan. It could only be Jack Landers.

A stocky middle-aged writer with jet black hair and a perpetual grin, Landers had been one of the convention's most pleasant surprises. He had been a member of Brian's first panel and afterwards had made the point to come over and introduce himself. Jack had long been one of Brian's favorite writers, and the Texan had caught him totally by his high praise of *Grave Shadows*.

"Kicked me in the head like a mule," Landers had declared

in his own unique vernacular. "Damned book showed a lot of talent, Brian. A lot of talent."

It was heady praise, coming from one of the most successful writers attending the show. Landers had recently made the leap from horror to mainstream suspense with an ambitious, long novel about serial killers. Rumors of his most recent deal with Green Dragon Books pegged his advance in the six-figure column.

"Enjoying yourself at this wingding?" Jack asked with a chuckle. Wearing a black shirt with metal buttons and a hand-made string tie, he looked much more a cowboy than an author. "These parties ain't exactly my cup of tea."

"Mine either," admitted Brian. "My agent insisted I come and circulate. He wanted me to network."

Landers shrugged. "Nothing wrong with that. Too many anthologies these days get filled by the editor's friends. It ain't what you know, but who. Not fair, but it's no different any place you work. Man's got to deal with the bullshit if he's going to work in the pasture."

Brian nodded. "So I've discovered. I always thought quality counted. Now, I'm not so sure."

"It matters," said Landers, unconsciously fiddling with the decoration on his tie. Constructed of tiny bits of wood, string and beads, it resembled a tiny human figure. "Trouble is, there's a lot of good writers out there, all capable of producing salable fiction. An editor can only print so many stories in a book. Time and economics dictate that he invites only a small number of authors to contribute. Business sense tells him to select the ones who he feels will do the best job and deliver their work on time. Being human, he tries to include those writers he knows and likes. Like I said, it ain't fair, but that's the way it happens."

Landers noticed Brian staring at his tie. "Like it?" he asked, grinning. "My wife gave it to me when I first started attending these conventions. She's half-Cherokee. Little lady insisted I wear this thing for the weekend. It's a charm to keep away evil spirits." Landers' voice sunk to a conspiratorial whisper. "Not that I believe in such stuff, mind you. But, I know better than to risk offending my better half. She can be pretty evil when she's mad."

The Texan chuckled. "Besides, I like the fella. Makes me feel right comfortable. Not like most of the stuffed shirts attending this here party."

Brian tugged at his shirt again. He could feel the droplets of sweat trickling down his back. "There doesn't seem to be much actual socializing taking place. Everyone appears to be talking to people they already know."

"Right you are," said Landers. "It's just like real life. Nobody is looking to meet anyone new. Especially newcomers. You got an agent? He's the one who should be running interference for you here, making all the introductions and such."

"I lost Milt a half-hour ago," admitted Brian. "For all I know, he's left for the hospitality suite."

"Tempting food there," said Landers, laughing. "Lots of salmon. In years to come, they'll remember this show as the Salmon Con."

The Texan frowned. "Milt? You ain't hooked up with Milt Gross, are you?"

Brian nodded. "That's right. Why? Is there something wrong with him?"

No longer smiling, Landers took Brian by an elbow and steered him to the rear of the suite. He stopped by an open window, away from most of the crowd. The Texan leaned close so that he couldn't be overheard.

"There's two types of agents, son," said Landers. "A writer's agent and a publisher's agent. A writer's agent works for his client, getting him the best deal possible. It makes sense, don't it? Agents get paid a slice of your earnings, so the better deal you get, the more they collect as well. A good agent earns every penny, cutting deals, retaining rights, stuff like that."

"That ain't the case with a publisher's agent. They're the lazy ones, the prairie dogs with a foot in the door of a certain company or two. They're primarily interested in making sales, lots of sales, and so they don't fight so hard for their clients. Usually, they take what's offered, or do a little adjusting in the contracts so it looks like they're doing a good job. Instead of struggling for the writers they represent, they work keeping the publishers happy. It's the old case of you scratch my back and

I'll scratch yours. And the authors get the shaft."

The muscles tightened in Brian's chest, signaling the on-slaught of a tension attack. "And you're saying Milt...?"

"He's a publisher's agent all the way," replied Landers, nodding. "What'd you get for that second book of yours?"

"Five thousand," said Brian.

"You should have gotten ten," said Landers. "Lancer Books would have paid that, easy. They're always looking for new horror talent. And you're good, son. You're real good."

"But Milt took me on when no one else would even look at my work," said Brian. "I felt I owed him..."

"Bullshit," interrupted Landers. "You don't owe your agent nothing. Good ones or bad ones – remember they work for you, not the other way around. Without you, they're nothing. Don't ever forget that, Brian. Agents, even the best of them, are parasites. They're like vampires. They live off your blood, your creativity. Gross ain't your friend, he's your employee."

Brian drew in a deep breath, trying to steady his nerves. "I appreciate your honesty," he said to Landers, his voice shaking. "It's not that you're saying anything I haven't suspected already. Confirmation is just a bit difficult to accept."

"You okay?" asked Landers, sounding concerned. "I didn't mean to lay it on too heavy. But you're too good a writer, Brian, to be stuck with the likes of Milt Gross."

"I'm all right," said Brian, feeling somewhat shaky. "The smoke in here is making me dizzy."

"Hey, Landers," screamed someone from across the room. "Come on over here and tell these fools how your wife hired a stripper to deliver your birthday card last year."

The Texan grinned and shook his head. "I'll never live that one down. Sorry, Brian, gotta run. My public calls." Lander's voice grew serious. "You take it easy now. Ever need some help, give me a call. That's what friends are for."

"Thanks," said Brian, as Jack was swallowed up in the crowd.

2.

Deciding a drink would clear his head, or at least make his problem less pressing, Brian headed for the bar. Located near the front of the room, it was staffed by two attractive women, in their early thirties, dressed conservatively. Brian recognized them both from a panel that afternoon as editors for Lion Books.

"I didn't know editorial duties included tending bar," he said to the nearer of the two, a brunette with long hair and piercing gray eyes. "Can I have a Coke? Easy ice."

"You'd be surprised at what editors have to do to earn a living," the woman replied, her tone indicating she was only half joking. She handed Brian his soda pop. "Brian Cassidy, right?"

"That's me," he admitted. "I'm sorry, but I don't remember your name."

"No reason you should," said the woman. "We've never met. I'm Sarah Milhouse."

They shook hands. "I'm horror editor for Lion. I've read both your novels," said Sarah. "They're strong stuff. If you ever consider switching houses, I'd be happy to see your next book."

"Why... thanks," said Brian, overwhelmed. Sarah Milhouse had the reputation for being one of the most savvy editors in the field. "I've just started working on a new book. Needless to say, I think its my best one yet."

"You're with Milt Gross," said Sarah. It was not a question but a statement of fact.

"Right," said Brian, immediately feeling defensive. "Though I have to admit, I'm starting to have second thoughts."

"Good idea," said Sarah. She leaned forward across the bar, so she could speak softer. "You...."

Whatever wisdom the editor was about to impart was drowned out by the arrival of another writer at the bar. "How about some service," the man bellowed, his tone belligerent. He stared at Brian for an instant, as if trying to place his face. Then, with a shrug of dismissal, the man focused his attention entirely on Sarah. "I need a drink, babe. Now."

Sarah grimaced at Brian then turned to the speaker. A smile that went no further than the edges of her mouth blossomed. "What would you like, Amos?" she asked sweetly. "Nothing's too good for one of Lion Books' best."

"Damned right," said the author. A big burly man with a ruddy red face and bloodshot eyes the size of saucers, he hung onto the edge of the bar like a life preserver. Brian recognized him as Amos Sawell, known in the field as the master of quiet horror. The author of more than twenty novels, Sawell had been writing dark fantasy for more than a decade.

"Give me scotch on the rocks. Straight up, none of that fuckin' ice to water it down."

"Whatever you say," declared Sarah, pouring the author a tumbler full of liquor. "Your wish is my command."

The sarcasm so evident in the editor's voice was completely lost on Sawell. Eyeing Brian, he sneered as if in contempt. Manhandling the glass, he disappeared into the crowd.

"Is he always so…" began Brian, searching for the right word, as Sarah wandered back to him.

"Angry. Obnoxious. Drunk?" replied the editor, smiling. "Yes, to all three. Don't let his attitude bother you. Amos treats everyone he perceives less important than himself like dirt. And that includes just about everyone in the world."

"He seems rather bitter," said Brian.

"You might act the same if you wrote twenty novels and not one of them ever made the best seller list – any best seller list – despite wonderful quotes from all of your buddies in the field. Friends, by and large, who have passed you by and left you standing in the dust."

Brian's eyes bulged at Sarah's casual, almost offhand remarks. "But, he's one of your top authors."

"Sawell?" she declared with a nasty laugh. "He's a coaster. Nothing more, nothing less. We publish him to fill up the slots in our list."

"A coaster?" repeated Brian, puzzled by her choice of words.

"You are a naïve one," said Sarah, pouring herself a drink. "You sure I can't get you something stronger?"

"Coke is fine," said Brian. "It helps me stay alert with all you wolves around. You were going to explain coasters?"

The editor laughed. "A coaster is someone who survives on his or her past accomplishments, Brian. They've lost their creative spark but know enough to keep afloat in their chosen profession. It's not just true in the writing field. Every profession is filled with coasters.

"Ever watch Hollywood Squares? Or any of a dozen other celebrity quiz shows on afternoon television. Few, if any, of the participants have made a film in years. They're coasting, living off their reputation." Sarah grinned. "Tell me one thing Zsa Zsa Gabor's done lately other than get arrested for slapping a police officer. One project? Get what I mean?"

"But Amos Sawell," protested Brian. "He's a big name."

"Only in his own mind," replied Sarah. "His agent put his last novel up for auction. Sawell proclaimed it was his best book ever, his breakthrough novel. The one that would finally vault him into the mainstream horror market." Sarah lowered her voice to a whisper. "By my count, it's the fifth breakthrough book he's written. Needless to say, they never caused a ripple. This time, none of the other publishers even bothered to enter a bid. We got it for the floor. The lack of interest shook Amos up pretty bad. I haven't seen him sober since."

Brian shook his head, not knowing what to say. Swallowing his coke, he handed the glass back to Sarah. "Another please."

"Going for a caffeine jag," she laughed as she poured him more pop. "Half the authors in this room are coasters, my naïve young friend. They haven't had a new idea in years. They merely re-circulate old concepts again and again, packaging them in slightly different ways. Fortunately for them, most publishers, mine included, don't care. They're not looking for new, innovative books. They want novels that sell. And, most fans aren't looking to be challenged either. They enjoy reading the same familiar stuff they've read time and time again. Look at the popularity of series books. I don't have to mention names because you know who I'm talking about. Some of the people who write them haven't had an original thought in years. But they keep on selling books. Lots of books."

Brian sighed. "It's not the way I envisioned the field. Not the way at all. I thought creativity meant something."

"It does," said Sarah. "The best and the brightest still turn out smart, elegantly written books filled with ideas. Take Jack Landers. Or Drake Kresin. Or half-a-dozen other writers who treat their work seriously. They're the ones to admire. Not people like Sawell."

Sarah paused. "Trouble is, that except for Landers and one or two others, the top authors rarely attend conventions any more. It's almost as if they keep away on purpose. Maybe they feel they'd lose their inspiration if they start making the rounds. It often seems to me that the only writers at these shows are the newer, ambitious ones, anxious to make their mark on the world, and the coasters."

The editor smiled. "There's a story idea in that, somewhere, Brian. Oops, gotta go. That's my boss over there. I need to suck up to him for a while. See you around. And remember me with that next book."

"I will," said Brian, downing the rest of his drink. He still felt a little dizzy. Plus the one-two punch of Landers and Milhouse had overwhelmed his sensibilities. He needed a little time to sort things out in his mind. A short walk outside the hotel, he decided, would help immeasurably.

3.

The Lion party was located on the twentieth floor of the hotel. Not in the mood for company, Brian was relieved when he found only one other person, a slender old man with a white goatee, waiting for the elevator.

Though the corridor was still too warm, at least it didn't stink of tobacco smoke. Sighing with relief, Brian removed his name badge and put it into his pants pocket. For a few hours, he preferred not to be associated with the convention. Closing his eyes, he leaned against the wall. After the constant din of the party, the quiet was a pleasant novelty.

"Excuse me." It was the old man with the goatee. Up close, he appeared frail, not slender. Skin drawn so tight across his face gave him an almost skeletal look. Bright blue eyes stared directly at Brian. "Are you taking the elevator to the ground floor?"

"Yes," answered Brian, trying to sound polite but distant. It did no good.

"Would you mind if I accompany you?" The slender man's

mouth bent into a slight smile. "An odd request, you are think-ing. With good reason. The explanation is quite simple. I am somewhat claustrophobic. Riding the car all the way to the bot-tom on my own would be a great strain. Normally, there's al-ways a crowd going down. But, tonight, no such luck."

"No problem," said Brian, glancing at the older man's name tag. Startled, he looked again. "Why, you're Gene Macklin! I've read all of your books. Some of them many times."

The slender man's smile broadened. "Thank you. No au-thor tires of hearing words like that. It's always a thrill."

Brian flushed. "You're one of the guests of honor. I should have recognized you."

"Nonsense," said Macklin. "My last novel was published fifteen years ago. In the horror field, that's several generations. I haven't been at a convention of this sort in more than a de-cade. The committee invited me as a courtesy. I'm the old-timer guest. I doubt if more than a few attendees have any idea who I am or what I wrote."

"That's not true," said Brian, knowing it was but not want-ing to admit it. "*Call Me Legion* is an acknowledged classic werewolf novel. As is *My Soul Is Darkness*."

"Perhaps," murmured Macklin. "Which perhaps explains why both books have remained out of print for the last ten years."

The old man stiffened, all the blood draining from his face. "Here's our elevator. My personal horror story."

They entered together. Brian couldn't help but notice how Macklin's entire body shook with fear. The old man's hands clenched tightly into fists as he stepped into the car. Blue eyes wide with terror, the author turned and faced front, as if trying to ignore his surroundings.

Surprisingly, there was another person standing in the el-evator. Surprising since they were on the top floor of the build-ing. She, for the other rider was a young and very attractive woman, showed no signs of exiting. Brian surmised she had boarded the car not realizing it was heading up, not down. It was none of his business. He punched the button for the lobby. The door slid closed.

Macklin stood frozen in place, his gaze fixed on the door

indicator. He never once looked around, remaining absolutely motionless as the car hurtled downward. Only the shallow rise and fall of his chest indicated he was alive.

Arms folded across his chest, Brian waited patiently as the elevator descended. Trying not to be too obvious, he studied the other passenger with more than idle curiosity. She was definitely worth a second, even third look.

Tall, dark, and very sexy were his first impressions. The young woman, he estimated her age no more than twenty-one or twenty-two, wore a short black leather dress that hugged her body like a second skin. Her hair, cut short, was jet-black as were her eyes. She wore black fishnet stockings and five-inch heels. Her skin had a slightly yellowish hue, leading Brian to guess she was Asian. Not unusual, with Seattle's large Japanese community. Her small mouth was painted with bright red lipstick and her cheeks showed just a touch of makeup.

Brian immediately pegged her for a hooker. He had heard stories that this hotel attracted a number of high-class call girls. Then, he noted that the girl was wearing a fantasy convention badge and held a copy of *Science Fiction Times* in one hand.

He shook his head in mock dismay. The first really attractive girl he spotted at the entire show and he mistook her for a prostitute. Grinning, he turned back to the front of the elevator. With the barest whisper, the door slid open. They had reached the lobby.

Macklin hurried out of the car, eyes straight ahead. "Bye, bye, Gene," said the girl, catching Brian by surprise. "Nice to see you again."

The old man didn't stop or give any indication he heard the young woman's words. Brian, feeling slightly embarrassed by his companion's actions, pressed one arm against the recessed elevator door. He gestured with his other hand. "After you."

"Thank you," said the girl. There was a faint trace of an accent in her voice, but Brian couldn't place it. "But I'm not getting off here."

"Uh, sure," said Brian, puzzled. The girl had ridden the elevator from the top of the building to the lobby. There weren't any more floors. "Whatever you say."

"Nice meeting you, Mr. Cassidy," the young lady said unexpectedly as he stepped out of the car. "I'm sure we'll bump into each other again."

"I hope so," said Brian, but the door to the elevator had already closed.

Frowning, he wondered how she knew his name. He no longer wore his badge and the girl had definitely not attended either of his panels. He would not have forgotten someone who looked like her.

Macklin waited for him a few feet away, an unreadable expression on his face. "Sorry for my rudeness," he said. "I can't help myself. Care to join me for a drink. I'd consider it repaying a favor."

"My pleasure," said Brian. "Should we go to the bar?"

"There's table service in the lobby," said Macklin. "Let's sit there. The chairs are much more comfortable."

They found a small cocktail table located in the far corner of the huge atrium, away from the hustle and bustle of the front desk. Their drinks were delivered by an attractive blonde cocktail waitress whose eyes lit up with pleasure when Macklin paid her with a twenty and told her to keep the change.

A touch of color returned to Macklin's cheeks as he slowly sipped from a glass of white wine. Still, there was a disquieting, almost haunted look in his face that Brian found troublesome.

"Attractive girl in the elevator," said the older writer, his eyes staring directly at Brian. "Almost too good for this type of show, don't you think?"

Brian chuckled. "She caught me by surprise. I've never seen anyone like her at any of my panels or signings. Do you know her very well?"

"We've met at previous shows," said Macklin. He offered no explanation how he knew a girl in her early twenties if he had not been to a convention in more than a decade. Brian assumed that Macklin must have forgotten attending the more recent cons. "Her name is Talia Van. I'm surprised to see her here on her own. Usually she attends conventions with several of her girlfriends. They're a wild group."

"I'll bet," said Brian. "Are her friends as good-looking as she is?"

"Better, depending on your taste of course," said Macklin.

"I've never seen her or anyone like her at any of the small shows I've attended," said Brian.

"Nor will you," said Macklin, softly. "They only go to those affairs that attract the biggest names in the field. And then, only to the parties."

"Science fiction groupies?" asked Brian, trying not to sound naïve. "That's hard to believe."

"Perhaps," said Macklin, "but the world is filled with unbelievable things."

"What do you mean?" asked Brian. There was a subtle note of menace in the old man's voice. As if trying to warn him of something without stating it outright.

"Nothing," said Macklin, "nothing at all."

He took another sip of wine. "Ever read Ray Bradbury's short story, 'The Crowd'?" he inquired. " Or Poe's 'The Man in the Crowd'?"

"I read them both," answered Brian. "Each describes how people seem to show up from nowhere whenever an accident takes place. The implication in each is that the onlookers are anything but innocent bystanders."

"A wonderful concept," said Macklin, sipping his drink. "Over the years, I've developed my own variation of the idea based on my personal observations at conventions. Haven't you ever wondered why so few people at the publisher's parties look familiar? There always seem to be many more of them there than ever in attendance during the daytime activities. Party people, I call them, because they only appear at night at the parties. That's the reason those events are so unbelievably crowded."

"Party people," repeated Brian. "It almost sounds like a story title."

"It is," said Macklin, with a chuckle. "I've been working on the novel for twenty years. One of these days, I hope to finally finish it."

"It's a mystery?" asked Brian. "Or a psychological suspense story?"

"No, no, no," said Macklin, chuckling. "Straight supernatural fantasy. A modern day horror story. These hangers-on aren't human. Though they appear absolutely normal to anyone who meets them, they're vampiric in nature. Succubi actually. They live on human emotions. In this case, they suck out the creative spark in artists."

Macklin's eyes glowed feverishly, all humor gone from his voice. "They prey on writers, draining them little by little, of their imagination. Physically, their victims remain unchanged. But, mentally, that's another story."

The old man grimaced and drained his wine glass. "Another story entirely. Traveling from convention to convention, using their issues of *SF Times* as directories, these party people slowly devour every shred of talent from their unsuspecting quarry."

"How?" asked Brian. Somehow he got the impression Macklin was no longer discussing a book concept.

"Through sex, of course," said the old man, smiling as if from some secret joke. "Each seduction takes a little more from their prey. After all, Brian, they are succubi. Beautiful women, they always dress in black."

Macklin chuckled dryly. "Enough of this yarn-spinning. Forget my party people. Someday, you'll know the whole story."

Know the story, Brian thought to himself. Not read it, but actually know it. He wondered again, if Macklin hadn't attended a convention in more than ten years, how he knew Talia Van who looked young enough to be his granddaughter?

"I've heard your name mentioned several times at this convention by people whose opinions I respect," said Macklin. "I've rambled on long enough with my wild tales. Tell me about yourself and your work."

Brian couldn't help but obey. When one of the most famous authors ever to write in the genre asked about your career, you spoke. And afterwards, you answered honestly his very perceptive questions.

Thirty minutes and several drinks later, Brian concluded his autobiography, finishing with his recent conversations with Jack Landers and Sarah Milhouse. With a sigh of relief, he settled back in his chair. Usually quiet and introspective, it felt strange and yet exhilarating to spill his doubts and fears to a near complete stranger.

"There are three rules, Brian," said Macklin, "necessary to

survive as a writer. Would you like to hear them?"

"Of course," replied Brian.

"Almost all editors are scum," declared the old man solemnly. "Almost all publishers are scum. And almost all agents are scum. Remember that advice and you can't go wrong."

"What you're saying in other words, is that you can't trust anybody," said Brian.

"Exactly," replied Macklin. Reaching into his wallet, the old man pulled out a business card. "That's my agent's name and phone number. Laura Armstrong. She's one of the best in the business. Laura isn't taking on new clients. But, mention my name and she'll look at your work. If you're as good as everyone say, she'll do right by you. A lot better, for damned sure, than that sleaze, Milt Gross."

"Thanks," said Brian. "I don't know what to say."

"Then don't say anything," advised Macklin. He raised his wine glass as if in a toast. "Here's to big advances, honest royalty statements, and to beautiful young girls wearing black leather in elevators."

"Agreed," said Brian, finishing his drink. He couldn't help but notice the fear in the old writer's eyes. The fear and more than a hint of remorse.

4.

The next six months passed in a blur of activity.

Brian finished his new novel, *We Are the Dark* in January and sent it off to Milt Gross with high expectations. Two months later, the agent reported back that he had an offer of $7,500 for the book from Paperback Library, with a slightly higher royalty rate. As usual, Milt urged Brian to accept the deal, saying it was the best they could expect in a weak market.

Restraining his anger, Brian called Gross and told him to submit the book elsewhere. Milt objected, again stating that the market for vampire novels was dying and they dared not risk offending the one publisher who was interested in Brian's work.

Brian's reply was short and to the point. "Milt," he said, no longer feeling the slightest trace of guilt. "*You're fired.* As of this moment, you no longer represent me or my work. I'll expect you to return my manuscripts within a week. Or you'll hear from my lawyer. Goodbye."

Five minutes later he was on the phone with Laura Armstrong. The agent recognized his name immediately. "Gene Macklin mentioned you might call. He urged me to read your books. I was extremely impressed. If your new work is as good as the others, I think with me acting as your agent, we can generate some real money. Maybe even a movie deal. Vampires are hot these days in Hollywood."

Flushed with excitement, Brian didn't know what to say. He wasn't prepared for such enthusiasm. "How's Mr. Macklin doing?" he finally managed to ask, trying to stay calm.

Laura Armstrong didn't answer for a minute, her silence chilling Brian. "Gene died last week," she said quietly.

Brian was stunned. "But, but, he looked fine at the Fantasy Convention."

"Gene suffered from incurable cancer for the last three years," said Laura. Her voice cracked with emotion as she spoke. "He kept it secret from everyone but a few close friends. That was his style. That convention was the last one he ever attended. One of the committee members knew about Gene's condition and wanted to honor him before he died."

"I'm sorry," said Brian, feeling terrible. "I truly am."

Then, another thought struck him. "His last novel? The one about the party people? Did he ever finish it? From what he told me about it, the book sounded like a classic. It would be a fitting tribute to his life to see it published."

"Manuscript?" said Laura, her voice sounding odd. "Gene never mentioned anything to me about another novel. The pain made writing impossible. It's been years since he put a word on paper.

The breath caught in Brian's throat. Macklin's story suddenly took on a whole new meaning.

"I-I must have misunderstood," said Brian hurriedly. "You know how it is – the parties, the smoke, a few drinks. I obviously misheard."

"Forget it," said Laura. "Gene turned a little strange as he grew older. He started imagining all sorts of things. Best to ignore whatever he told you. Let's talk about this new novel of yours instead."

Talk they did, reaching a deal for her to act as his agent starting that afternoon, confirmed by fax that evening. A month later Novel Library paid $75,000 for *We Are the Dark* in a heated auction with three other companies. An option for movie rights came soon after, with a $50,000 guarantee and escalator clauses raising the price into six figures if the picture actually went into production.

Suddenly, Brian was very hot. Glowing reviews of his first two novels appeared in *Science Fiction Times* and *SF News*, where he was proclaimed to be a 'bright new star in the horror field'. There was no mention why neither book had been reviewed when originally published.

Small press magazines which had managed to ignore his work until his big sale clamored for interviews. They also wanted short stories from him, or excerpts from his new novel. Several proposed publishing special Brian Cassidy issues. Numerous conventions, large and small, invited him to attend, some even offering to pay his way. By and large, he ignored all of the attention and kept busy writing.

He met Laura in person for the first time in late June at the Horror Writers of America Banquet in New York City. As usual, Brian had no desire to attend the gathering but Laura insisted, hinting mysteriously at big news she wanted to reveal to him in person. With the money he had earned in the past few months gathering interest in his bank account, Brian found that he had no excuse for not going.

A short, petite woman with blonde hair and blue eyes, Laura was everything that he expected from an agent and more. She burned with nervous energy. Pushy and sarcastic, she reminded Brian of a typical brash stage mother, out to get the most for her child. Five minutes after meeting her, he felt confident that any deals Laura negotiated for him would be the best ones possible.

She insisted that they have lunch Saturday at the Carnegie Deli, located only a few blocks from the convention hotel. Over corned beef sandwiches so huge they had to be held with both hands, she revealed his latest triumph.

"Paramount is definite on *We Are the Dark*. Coppola's set as director, and there's rumors that Michael Douglas wants to play Landros.

Slowly, Brian lowered his sandwich to the plate. "What's this mean to us?" he asked, his voce trembling.

"Money," replied Laura, grinning. "Big money. But, that's not all."

"There's more?"

"Remember when I called you after the ABA and told you that there was lots of foreign interest in the novel. I thought that would be the case. That's why I refused to give Novel Library worldwide rights, even though they offered more for them. Well, we've just gotten offers from England, Germany and Japan. Together, they should equal or top the money you got for the U.S. sale."

Brian stared at his sandwich suspiciously. "Can I eat now? Or is there more?"

"The Book-of-the-Month Club wants *Dark* for its November release. The publisher signs the papers next week. And, tomorrow night, we're having dinner with Ross Cavanaugh."

"The President of Novel Library," said Brian shocked. He wondered if all of this was a dream.

"You bet. I sent him your proposal for *Forever the Night* last week and told him he had two weeks before I showed it to anyone else. I think he wants to make an offer. I know he does. A substantial offer."

"But *We Are the Dark* hasn't even appeared," said Brian, puzzled. "It's not due out for months. Why would they buy another book from me before the first hits the shelves?"

"Advance orders have been incredible," said Laura. "A friend of mine works at Novel Library and she tells me the numbers from the sales reps have been astonishing. Everyone there expects the book to debut on the *New York Times* Best Seller list." Laura paused dramatically. "High on the list."

Still in a daze, Brian parted with Laura in the hotel lobby. She had a meeting with another client at the bar in a few minutes, and he wanted to return to his room to rest and recuperate. So much good news at one time had him reeling.

It wasn't until after he stepped into the elevator going up

ROBERT E. WEINBERG

that he realized he wasn't alone. Standing in one corner of the car was Amos Sawell. Cuddled close to him, one of his big arms around her shoulders, was Talia Van. She smiled slightly and dipped her head as if in greeting. Sawell, reeking of liquor, scowled but said nothing.

They always dress in black, thought Brian, as he tried to keep his eyes to himself. Talia wore a sleek, knit catsuit that emphasized her sleek curves and lean, long legs. She clung so tightly to Sawell that she seemed almost a part of him. Like a leech sucking out his life's blood.

Brian's room was on the ninth floor. The only other button pushed was for the twenty-fifth. Stepping out of the car, Brian glanced back at Talia. Already, Sawell was clumsily pawing at her body. She hardly seemed to notice. Her eyes were fixed on Brian. Licking her lips slowly, sensuously, she winked. Then, the door of the elevator closed and Brian was alone and very, very scared.

5.

There was a cocktail party that evening, at the penthouse on the fortieth floor of the hotel. Laura had warned Brian she wouldn't be there until late, due to a meeting with an important editor, but he didn't mind. Instead, he went hunting for Jack Landers.

It didn't take him long to find the Texan. As usual, the writer was surrounded by a gaggle of followers, all laughing loudly at his outrageous anecdotes about his days working on a farm before he became successful as a writer. Nervously, Brian nursed a coke until Landers spotted him.

"Brian, buddy," said the Texan. "Good to see you."

Then, as if sensing something wrong, Landers turned to the crowd. "Scuse me folks. But me and my friend Brian got some catching up to do. Been a long time since we got to socialize. Talk to you-all later."

Landers peered at Brian through narrowed eyes. "You look like somebody hit you in the head with a two-by-four, boy. Something's troublin' you. Want to talk about it?"

"Maybe," said Brian. "Depending on whether or not you'll

170

think I'm crazy."

"Never thought nobody was nuts," said Landers. "A bit touched in the head, maybe, but never crazy. I've seen too much in this world to disbelieve anything I hear. You want we should move to a less crowded spot?"

Off in a corner of the room, Brian related his tale to Landers. He started with his meeting with Gene Macklin and their encounter with Talia Van in the elevator. In exacting detail he told of Macklin's strange story of party people and Laura Armstrong's lack of knowledge about any such work. He concluded with his most recent sighting of Talia, in the elevator with Amos Sawell.

Landers didn't say a word until Brian was finished. Frowning, the Texan shook his head. "I don't know what to make of it, Brian. I'm not denying there's author groupies. It ain't like rock-and-roll, but there's a bunch of women anxious to sleep with an honest-to-God writer. This Talia chick, she sounds like one of them. But, a succubus? I'm not so sure."

Jack shrugged his shoulders. "It's common knowledge that Amos Sawell's lost what little spark he ever had as a writer. But, is that due to some sort of elevator girls draining him dry or him just attending too many of these conventions and not spending enough time concentrating on the business of writing? What I'm saying is that I'm not sure there's a supernatural explanation behind it all. Lots of writers burn out. Playing fast and loose with some women might be responsible, but that doesn't make them ladies monsters. Even if they do wear black."

"Then you think I'm imagining all this?" asked Brian, recognizing the wisdom in his friend's words.

"Ain't saying that either," replied Landers. He patted the strange little idol holding his string tie together. "Like I told you, my wife makes me wear this goofy charm every convention I attend. She checks up on me too, every time we talk on the phone, making sure I got it on. Won't tell me the reason why, but I ain't ever been approached by anyone like the type of woman you've described. Maybe the wife knows something us men don't. My advice is to stay away from this Talia babe, no matter what she's wearing. Girl sounds like trouble, Brian – big trouble."

"I agree," said Brian. He looked down at is watch. "You going to be here for a while? Laura brought me over a bunch of bound galleys of *We Are the Dark*. I left them down in my room. I want to give you one."

Landers grinned. "Why, thank you kindly, sir. I'd surely like to see one of them. Word is out that it's going to be a blockbuster."

"Be back in five," said Brian, his spirits rising.

Lander's advice made perfect sense. He had been getting upset over nothing. Vampires only existed in horror novels, not in real life. Smiling, he stepped into the elevator going down. And found himself alone in the car with Talia Van.

The door slid closed before he could react. Automatically, without thinking, he pressed the button for the ninth floor.

"Brian," she said softly, her voice like the purr of a cat. "I was hoping to run into you tonight. I've been hearing wonderful things about your work. You sound so... creative."

"Uh, thanks," said Brian. Despite himself, he found he couldn't help staring at the young woman. She wore a short black leather dress that left her shoulders bare and barely came down to her thighs. Centered between her breasts, a silver zipper with a large pull tab descended the entire length of the outfit. As before, she wore black stockings and spike heels.

"Like it?" she asked. "I wore it special for you."

"It's very attractive," said Jack, looking at the floor indicator. The elevator hardly seemed to be moving.

"I find you *very* attractive," said Talia, and with a rustle of leather, was beside him. Before he knew what was happening, her arms were around his neck. Her body pressed tight against him. Her skin sizzled. It felt like she was on fire. It took only the slightest amount of pressure to bring their lips together.

What resistance he had melted with that embrace. The kiss burnt Brian to the depths of his being. He had never experienced passion like that before, and knew that he would never experience its like again unless it was with Talia. Hungrily, he kissed her passionately, wildly, no longer worrying about the slowness of the elevator or their eventual destination.

Lust overwhelmed him. Reaching down, he grabbed her by the buttocks, pulling her body ever closer, wielding them together. Shamelessly, she reached down and grabbed his erection through the cloth of his pants. "I want you," she growled. "I want to feel you inside me."

A small part of his mind, a very small insignificant part, was screaming for him to stop, to realize what was happening. But, he ignored it. All he knew was that he had to possess this woman, he had to make love to her as soon as possible.

By the time the elevator reached the ninth floor, Brian was ready to explode. It took all that remained of his self-control not to rip Talia's clothes right off in the hallway and take her right there on the floor. Her breath, coming in short, intense gasps indicated she wouldn't object. Hurriedly, they half walked, half ran down the hallway to his room.

He hardly noticed Sarah Milhouse coming from the other direction. Nor did he see the strange expression that passed across her face as he and Talia swept by. His entire existence, his entire being, focused on one thought. He had to fuck Talia Van. Immediately.

Hands trembling with emotion, he unlocked the door to his room. Talia entered first, Brian following. It never even occurred to him to lock the door. Nothing mattered other than the woman he was with.

"Take off your clothes," she commanded, her voice heavy with passion. She pointed to the king-sized bed. "I want you there – naked – now!"

Brian kicked off his shoes, then ripped off his clothes. In seconds he was lying on the sheets, flat on his back, his erect penis throbbing so hard that it hurt.

Eyes glowing with desire, Talia tugged at the clasp to her zipper. Slowly, she pulled it down, revealing her nakedness beneath.

She wore no bra or underwear. Her white skin glistened in the dim light of the room. Brian gasped in excitement. Talia was the most exciting woman he had ever seen. He couldn't define what made her so desirable. All he knew what that he wanted this woman like no other in his life.

Cat-like, she stalked over to the bed. "I knew you were next," she said mysteriously, "ever since that night in Seattle. I sensed it then. The talent was there, waiting to be released.

That's when I put my mark on you, warned the others to keep away. You were mine, all mine."

"Others," said Brian, his hands reaching for her, hardly listening to what she was saying. "What others?"

"Leah, Katie, Janise, and the rest," answered Talia. "The rest of my kind. My sisters."

"Your sisters?" repeated Brian, trying to shake the cobwebs from his mind. He felt strange, so very strange.

"Hush," said Talia, crawling onto the bed, next to him. She pressed her lips, her burning lips on his. "Forget them. Forget everything, except your desires."

As she sunk into his embrace, he felt her body covering his. Her breasts, the nipples hard and excited, pressed against his chest. Her thighs encircled his waist, her dampness grazing the tip of his erection. Gathering his strength, he raised his hips, trying to thrust into her. Chuckling, she arched her back, pulling away.

"No, not yet," she said, lifting her mouth from his. Her dark eyes glowed with an inner light. "Let me do all the work. I want to fuck you."

Brian's body tensed as slowly, teasingly, Talia started to lower herself onto him. He gasped with pleasure as he felt her warmth begin to engulf him, drowning him in ecstasy.

Then, without warning, she screamed! Shrieking in pain, she leapt off of him, her face contorted in rage. "Bitch!" she howled, poised at the edge of the bed, her hands extended claw-like in front of her. "I'll rip you to shreds!"

As if waking from a dream, Brian groggily looked first at Talia and then the woman she confronted at the other side of the bed. It was Laura Armstrong. In one hand, his agent held a small but ornately engraved crucifix.

"Try it, and I'll brand you worse than that," said Laura harshly, waving the cross in the general direction of Talia's buttocks. Astonished, Brian saw there was a red mark, corresponding in size and shape to the crucifix, on Talia's hip. "I believe in protecting my clients. Now get the hell out of here before I really get mad."

Snarling, Talia grabbed up her clothes and shoes and headed for the door. She didn't even bother getting dressed. "I won't forget this," she vowed angrily.

"I'm shaking," said Laura sarcastically.

Talia exited, slamming the door behind her. Laura turned to Brian, who hastily covered himself with a sheet.

"Here," she said, throwing him his clothes. "Get dressed. You can thank your lucky stars I ran into Sarah Milhouse in the elevator going up to the penthouse. She said just enough to get me worried."

Laura grinned. "Leaving your door unlocked helped too. Though I doubt if you were in any condition to notice."

Face red, Brian hastily donned his clothing. "You said Macklin never wrote that book."

"He didn't," said Laura, nodding approvingly as Brian stood up. She brushed off his shirt and straightened his collar. "Good. You look reasonably respectable. There's several important people upstairs I want you to meet. Come on. They're not the type who like to be kept waiting."

"But," said Brian.

""Macklin never wrote a word," said Laura, half escorting, half dragging him into the hallway. "But you're not the only one he told of his suspicions. That's why I always carry this crucifix with me when I attend conventions." She grinned. "It comes in handy from time to time."

Brian shook his head in disbelief. "Then they actually exist, these party people, going to conventions, preying on authors, draining them of their creativity."

"Elevator girls, I call them," said Laura impatiently. "Because they spend their time in elevator cars waiting for their victims."

"But shouldn't we be doing something?" said Brian, angrily. "Like warning the other attendees."

Sighing, Laura grabbed Brian by the shoulders. "Two points, Brian. Two extremely important points. Listen carefully and don't forget them."

"First, consider the state of most male writers attending this conference. If you could convince them that there are incredibly beautiful female vampires roaming the hotel, willing to fuck them in exchange for some of their creativity, you'd never be able to get on an elevator again due to the overcrowding. Hell, assuming there are elevator boys as well as girls, you could add most of the women writers to the list.

"Second and more important, this is the 21st century. No one believes in vampires any more. They'd all think you're nuts or looking for publicity. Publishers don't like dealing with crazy people, even incredibly talented ones like you. Go upstairs and tell everyone what happened and you can kiss that movie deal goodbye. Not to mention the Book-of-the-Month Club. And the best seller list."

Brian shook his head. "Then, you're saying I should just forget the whole thing. Treat the entire incident like it never happened."

"Exactly," said Laura, smiling and taking him by the arm. "Just make sure from now on you wear a cross whenever you go to a convention. Now, let's move."

"Laura," he said as they waited for the elevator to the penthouse. "Assume for an instant that I wasn't your client. And somehow you discovered Talia had taken me back to my room to seduce the creativity out of me. Would you have bothered saving me? Truthfully."

She hesitated only an instant before answering. But it was enough for Brian.

"Of course I would," she lied. "You know that."

"Of course," Brian lied back.

As they rode up to the penthouse, he remembered what Jack Landers had said about agents. The Texan had been absolutely correct. Elevator girls were by no means the only vampires attending the convention. ❧

The One Answer That Really Matters

1.

The room was bleak and colorless. The walls were painted a neutral shade of gray and there were no windows. The only furniture was a rectangular table, made of metal, its four legs welded to the steel floor, and two chairs. Taine sat down in one of the chairs. And waited, in silence, for the man who had summoned him to this place, to come and sit in the other.

Behind Taine, standing at attention, his back almost touching the wall, was a prison guard. The man, six foot four inches tall, had a face made of old leather and hands to match. In his holster he carried a Colt .45 revolver. Before they entered the interrogation room, the unnamed lawman had made it very clear to Taine that he knew how to use his weapon and that he'd be glad to save the state the cost of the execution two nights later.

Taine had no argument with that opinion. While he hadn't paid much attention to the sensationalized trial, it seemed like an open and shut case of homicide twenty-seven times over. MacDonald had been tried and convicted by a jury of his peers. The sentence had been death. The killer's attorneys had exhausted every possible appeal. It hadn't helped much that MacDonald had whipped up public sentiment by proudly bragging about the murders on several local late-night radio talk shows and one memorable morning call-in gab-fest. MacDonald had never shown a hint of remorse for his killings. Not the least bit.

The worst mass murderer in Illinois history entered through the door across the room from Taine. Anson MacDonald didn't look very dangerous. Around thirty years old, he stood five ten, weighed a little more than a hundred and fifty stripped, and had a receding hairline. His fingers were long and delicate. Clad in a bright orange prison uniform, he looked extremely ordinary for a man who had killed twenty-seven people. Then again, he had poisoned all his victims, not strangled them. Strength had played no part in his crimes.

As befitting his status as Chicago's number one mass murderer, MacDonald wore heavy shackles on his wrists and ankles. He sat down in the metal chair facing Taine. With an effort, he put his hands up on the table separating them.

"Thank you for coming," said MacDonald. He had a soft, pleasant voice. Not the voice of a mass murderer, whatever that might be.

"You made an offer I couldn't resist," said Taine.

"Others turned me down," replied MacDonald.

"My wife died six months ago of cancer," said Taine. My son's attending college in California, where his grandparents are spoiling him rotten. I got bored sitting at home watching reruns of *Law and Order*."

"Still, you didn't need the money."

Taine nodded. "My wife left me a substantial fortune. I donate my fees to charity. Your money will fund good works."

"How nice," said MacDonald.

Taine glanced down at his wristwatch. "You better start telling me what you want me to do, Mr. MacDonald. We've only got a half hour. Time will be gone before you know it."

"My time will be gone in short order," said MacDonald with a short, sharp laugh. "I'll be honest with you, Taine. You're not the first investigator I've hired. You're the fifth. None of the others were successful. I'm hoping you'll succeed where they failed. The others were big agencies. You're just one man. The newspapers call you the Occult Detective. Maybe that's what I need – a detective with 'supernatural connections.'"

Taine shrugged. "I can't perform miracles. No matter how much you pay me."

"Like prove me innocent?" said MacDonald, chuckling. "Not to worry. I'm guilty, guilty as sin. I'm ready to pay for my crimes. All I want you to do is to find the answer to a single question. It's the question that's haunted me all my life. I thought I would find the solution by killing all those people.

But I didn't."

MacDonald gazed piercingly across the table. "I poisoned twenty-seven of my best friends and closest relatives in the whole world believing their deaths would provide me with the right answer. But I was wrong and now I'm scheduled to die. I have exactly two days to live. Forty-eight hours, give or take a few, from now. Not a second more. It's a mystery I hope you, Sidney Taine, can answer. I'm willing to gamble a million dollars that you can."

"*A million dollars?*" repeated Taine. "You'll pay that for the answer to one question? I don't get it."

"I was born incredibly rich, Taine," said MacDonald. "Old money, the court can't touch it. All of my close relatives are dead – I murdered them. After my execution, my estate is going to be fought over by distant cousins for the next hundred years. Answer my question and I'll donate a million dollars to your favorite cause. The money will be paid the minute you find the solution. I guarantee it."

"What if I can't answer the question?" asked Taine. "Some riddles don't have an answer."

"I might be rich but I'm not stupid. This question has an answer. I'm sure of it. The money depends on you finding that answer and telling it to me. If I'm satisfied it's correct, the charity gets the money. There's no payment for just trying. I want results."

"What if I find the right answer but you don't like it?" asked Taine. "Or more to the point, what if you try to tell me the answer is wrong?"

"I have no reason to lie," said MacDonald, "but I can understand your concern. A bad reputation is hard to shake. I'm not known as being the most trustful person in the world, or the most truthful. How about we let my lawyer decide? She's honest and she has no reason to lie. She'll be the judge as to whether the answer is correct or not."

"Fair enough," said Taine. "Tell me the damn question already."

"First, I need to tell you a brief story," said MacDonald. "No more interruptions. There's not enough time. Any other details you can ask my lawyer, Amanda Blaylock. She's been working exclusively for me the past year and knows everything about me worth knowing. The woman's sharp, real sharp. Now, let me talk, so you'll understand exactly what I want answered."

MacDonald sucked in a huge breath of air then released it and started talking. He seemed totally unconcerned of the three guards watching him intently. He was focused entirely on telling his story.

"I'm thirty-four years old," he began. "I was born into money. My grandfather made his millions during the first half of the century in oil. Then my father came along and expanded the empire into everything from fast food to computers. By the time I came into the world, there was nowhere left to expand. Along with my older brother and younger sister, I was one of the richest children in creation. According to *Forbes*, we're the second richest family in the world, right behind some Saudi oil prince.

"Oddly enough, my father was a science fiction and fantasy fan. The stories provided him with much of his inspiration. Growing up, I fell into the same groove. I read extensively in his collection, both in books and paperbacks, as well as the huge files of magazines never reprinted in book form.

"I'm first to admit that I'm a geek. Plus I possess a near perfect memory. My parents never objected to my mania. They were glad I loved to read. It didn't matter much to them what I was reading, as long as I was reading. That's more than could be said for my brother, who was always getting in trouble gambling, racing fast cars and playing with fast women. And then there was my sister, who was always getting into trouble without resorting to gambling, cars or women. She was heavily into drugs.

"My father and mother died when I was fourteen. They were killed in a casino fire. My older brother died in a drag racing accident a year later. My sister overdosed on drugs when she heard the news. It took her two months to die, a very painful end. Their deaths left me, at sixteen, the fourth richest person in the world. I was the most eligible teen in America according to one heartthrob magazine. A few years later, I was promoted to most eligible bachelor in the country. A meaningless title, as I didn't believe in long-term relationships. To me, life had no meaning without the truth.

"The truth," said MacDonald, pausing for effect. "Reveal to me the truth about our existence, Taine, and I'll give you that million dollars. Tell me the truth and I'll die happy."

"I don't have a clue what you're talking about," said Taine. For the first time since entering the interrogation chamber, he felt uneasy. What exactly did the mad billionaire want to know?

"The world isn't right," said MacDonald, his voice rising slightly in excitement. "Our world feels wrong. Something isn't real about the universe around us. All my life I've felt it. Life seems false, vaguely artificial. It's like we're all stumbling around in some sort of play, only we don't have a script. Things happen – good things, bad things, but none of them make any sense. Actions have no meaning beyond the very personal."

Taine shook his head. "No. Sorry. You're just projecting your own social disorders onto the universe. My wife died from cancer six months ago. I can assure you I felt her pain. I suffered with her, and when she was gone, I grieved long and hard. Her death hurt me worse than a bullet. I grieve for her every day."

"That's part of the problem," said MacDonald. "Pain, hurt, suffering; if you strip away the noise, the scenery and props, could those feelings be the *real* reason we're here? Are they what life's all about? Could the only meaning of life be the continued agony of existence? Is the tie-that-binds just the horror that lurks just around the corner?"

"What are you saying?" asked Taine.

"Are we dead?" asked Anson MacDonald. "Is this world just a façade? Are we really in Hell?"

"That's crazy," said Taine.

"Am I?" said MacDonald. "Years ago, I read a fantasy novel that asked that question. The author postulated that Earth was really Hell and everyone born on it was a sinner. The greater your crimes, the longer you lived. Of course, no one realized the truth except for one or two sinners, the very worst of the worst, and everyone else thought they were insane. It was a crazy idea, but it made perfect sense. It started me thinking, wondering if it might be true."

"Using the same logic, you have to consider love, happiness, and good cheer," said Taine. "Which means this could be Heaven."

"I read another story," said MacDonald, nodding his head in agreement. "An old man died and went to Heaven. It turned out to be just like the street he had lived on all his life. Nice, safe, comfortable. But he didn't understand; he couldn't adapt to the surroundings. He felt cheated. It wasn't the huge white marble palaces he thought would be everywhere in the afterlife."

"So we could be in Heaven – or Hell – and not realize it," said Taine.

"Two minutes," said the guard behind Taine. He sounded bored.

"Exactly," said MacDonald. "We could be in either place, with no sure method of learning the truth. The concept gnawed at me, Taine. It whirled and whirled around in my brain, driving me crazy until I had to find the answer. I had to! So I invited all my friends and living relatives, my closest and dearest companions, to a huge dinner party and poisoned them. I assumed that doing so would make it absolutely clear to me whether I was living in Heaven or in Hell. But, lo and behold, I was wrong. I felt nothing. Some sorrow, some regret, but no great revelation." MacDonald clutched his hands into fists, squeezed his fingers until they were blood red. "I found *no answer*."

"One minute," said one of the two guards behind the chained man. "Finish up, Mr. MacDonald. You've only got sixty seconds left."

"I want you to discover the answer, Taine," said MacDonald, his pale blue eyes shining with a glint of madness. His voice grew louder and louder. "Our existence is artificial, it's not real. We're not alive, none of us are. We're dead and we've gone somewhere. It's Heaven or Hell, Taine. One place or the other. You tell me which one in the next two days and I'll donate a million dollars to your favorite charity." By now, the killer was shouting at the top of his lungs. "*I must know the truth!*"

"Time to go," said the other one of MacDonald's guards, tapping the hysterical prisoner on the shoulder. At the touch, MacDonald turned and it was as if a switch was thrown. All of the passion drained out of him, and the quiet, subdued prisoner was back.

The murderer rose to his feet. "Heaven or Hell, Taine?" he said in a rush, his voice soft and very desperate. "I must know. Find me some *proof*."

2.

Taine arrived at his office at 10 a.m. the next morning. His ever-efficient secretary, Mrs. McConnell, was already there, sorting files and preparing papers for the accountant. Fifteen years away from the job, yet she had agreed to return to work the moment he had called her. It was as if his retirement had never taken place. She looked up when he entered.

"Busy on a new case?" she asked.

"How did you know?" he replied. "Psychic powers? We should be getting a check this morning. A nice, fat one."

"You always come into the office smiling whenever you've signed a new client," said Mrs. McConnell. "Today, you're grinning like a Cheshire cat. It isn't hard to deduce the obvious."

"You'd make a fine detective," said Taine. He opened the door to the inner room that served as his office. "A woman, a lawyer named Amanda Blaylock is due in a few minutes. I'll see her as soon as she arrives."

"Amanda Blaylock," Mrs. McConnell rolled the name on her tongue. "Her name sounds familiar. Didn't you once tell me that you attended law school with an Amanda Blaylock? That she was determined to be a full partner in a major law firm before she was thirty?"

"Right you are," said Taine. He frowned. "We even dated for a semester. I was young and foolish in those days. She lived in Los Angeles. It's hard to imagine she's the same person."

It was. As soon as Mrs. McConnell ushered the woman into Taine's office, he recognized her. Twenty years had not changed Amanda much. She was still incredibly beautiful. She was tall, with long blonde hair, sparkling green eyes, a nicely curved figure, and the bronzed skin of a surfer goddess. Nor had the predatory, almost wolfish look of her face changed. If anything, it had grown more pronounced.

"Sid Taine," she said, reaching out to shake his hand with ice-cold fingers. "How bizarre. After not seeing each other since graduation twenty years ago, we finally run into each other courtesy of a mass murderer. Fate works in mysterious ways."

"Have a seat, Amanda," said Taine. "I must admit I never expected to see you in Chicago. The winters are too cold. I believe you have a check for me?"

"I gave it to your secretary," said Amanda. "Courtesy of my client, Anson MacDonald, confessed killer and pulp fiction philosopher. When he mentioned your name, I wasn't sure it was you. Chicago's a long way from Los Angeles. I moved here late last fall to lend a hand with Anson's defense. The firm thought I might be able to somehow pull a rabbit out of a hat. No such luck. Since then, I've been handling all of his appeals and side jobs. Like hiring detectives to chase down the answer to this crazy question he's obsessed about."

"He paid each of them thirty thousand dollars?" asked Taine.

"You got it," answered Amanda. "The one thing you can count on is for Anson MacDonald to pay his bills. He gave them each a thousand dollars a minute to listen to his story. None of them, however, came up with a satisfactory answer to his question. Some of their ideas were fascinating. Several of them were also quite obscene. I think they were making a play for me. It didn't work."

"You didn't tell MacDonald we dated for a semester in college?" said Taine.

"I didn't think it was necessary," said Amanda. "Besides, he was determined to hire you. If I've learned one thing working for Anson, it's that what he wants, he usually gets. Besides, you and I were never a real item."

"We did make an odd couple," said Taine, chuckling.

"An odd couple indeed," said Amanda. There was a strange, almost wistful sound to her voice. Taine would almost classify it as regret if he didn't know Amanda so well. She never regretted anything. Introspection was not one of her faults.

"I have a check for a million dollars in my briefcase," said

Amanda. "However, it requires my signature before you can cash it. You'll get it if you answer Anson's question to my satisfaction, in the required time allowed. Unfortunately, that means you need to act fast. The deadline is tomorrow at 5 p.m. Anson walks the last mile then. If he doesn't hear the answer, the deal's off. Agreed?"

"Agreed," said Taine. "With you as the judge?"

"I'm honest," said Amanda, with a laugh, "which, these days, is a virtue." Then, for a moment, the hard shell was gone and she was a real person. "I read about your wife in our background check. I'm sorry, Sid. I'm truly sorry."

"Thank you," he said.

There was an awkward silence during which Taine found himself at a loss for words. Then Amanda spoke.

"I'd be interested in learning how you plan to find an answer to Anson's question. I must admit that I remain a skeptic when it comes to the supernatural. If it's not too much trouble, I'd like to go along with you on your investigation?"

"Why not?" said Taine. "It'll be less boring with two of us. And maybe I'll make you a believer."

Amanda smiled. "I doubt that very much. One thing you should remember about me from our college days, Mr. Sidney Taine, is that I'm a hardheaded realist. For the record, to me, the occult is merely another word for fraud. Convincing me that we are actually in Heaven, or Hell, is not going to happen. I'm going to want proof. And that's just not possible."

"Just for the record," said Taine, with a wry smile, "I intend to answer your client's question. He might not like my explanation, but I'll answer him before he dies."

Amanda shook her head. "You haven't changed a bit since college, have you, Sid? I'm not sure who's crazier. Anson Mac-Donald or you…"

"One thing you should know about me, Amanda," said Taine. "I don't take cases I can't solve. Never."

3.

Taine told her to be ready at 9:00 p.m. He told her to wear her most striking, sexy outfit. He didn't say where they were going, but he assured her their destination tied in with his investigation for Anson MacDonald. He said that they would spend the night determining if they were in Heaven or Hell. He seemed quite confident that they would find an answer.

Amanda had to admit that the thought of spending the entire evening with Sid Taine excited her. She couldn't explain exactly why but the detective set the blood boiling in her veins. Taine had always appealed to her. He was one of the few men she didn't intimidate. One of the greatest challenges attending law school had been playing the frigid virgin while dating Taine. Maintaining that guise had kept her sharp, on her toes. It had taken all of her concentration and determination not to rip off the big man's clothes and make passionate love to him until they both were physically and emotionally exhausted. Taine had always been too much the proper gentleman to try anything, though Amanda felt certain he harbored much the same desire for her as she for him. They had both been too focused on their grades to allow themselves to be distracted by passion. It was a fault she had corrected after college. Three husbands later, she was still correcting it.

The detective still looked good – damned good – after twenty years. At six foot two, two hundred and twenty pounds, he was trim and in tip-top shape. Not flabby like husband number three. Plus Taine's features, always deep set and serious, had only improved with age. His face, with high cheekbones, deep set eyes, and wide brow could have been cut from stone. And his dark eyes were still deep with mystery. Those eyes were like twin pools of darkness she could dive into and swim around forever.

That he had been married and lost his wife to cancer didn't worry her much. Time healed all wounds. Loved ones died all the time. During the hour she had spent in Taine's office, she had sensed he was ready to move on with his life. Why not, she reasoned as she dried herself off with a fluffy white Turkish bath towel, with her?

Amanda smiled at the thought. At forty, she still looked spectacular, and unlike many of her contemporaries, was untouched by a surgeon's knife. She was all natural and intended to remain that way. An active lifestyle, good eating habits, and an excellent gene line all combined to give her the body of a

THE ONE ANSWER THAT REALLY MATTERS

twenty-year-old with the mind and outlook of a woman of forty. She had made her share of mistakes in life; picking husbands was not one of her strong points. But, what she lacked in marital skills she made up with in brains and business acumen.

While she had to remain strictly neutral regarding the answer to Anson MacDonald's question, she was first to admit that she hoped Sidney Taine had some miracle up his sleeve.

Jasmine-scented body powder, a touch of perfume behind each ear and between her breasts, black silk undergarments provided the proper foundation for a jet black, long sleeve mini-dress with slightly daring cleavage. Next came a pair of thigh-high black nylons, black leather boots, a black opal brooch around her neck, and matching black opal earrings. She debated a hat then decided against it. Surveying herself in the mirror, she decided that if looks could kill she would easily match Anson MacDonald's victim count. The thought amused her as she hurried into the living room to buzz Taine in through security.

Five minutes later, he was in her apartment, sipping a glass of white wine and staring out at the city from the giant picture window that made up one entire wall of her living room. Living on the twentieth floor had its benefits, and though it cost a lot more than a condo on a lower level, Amanda felt it was worth the difference in price.

"It's quite beautiful," said Taine, walking right up to the glass and staring out into the city. Most people found the edge of the window intimidating and had a hard time standing so close to the rim of the room. Not the case with Sidney Taine. He was not most people. "I'm impressed. My office overlooks the lake, but the view is nothing like this."

"Life is filled with unexpected surprises," said Amanda. She held up the wine bottle. "Ready for a refill?"

"No, thanks," said Taine, putting his glass down on the coffee table. "We better get going."

"Where?" asked Amanda. "Clubs? Nightspots?"

"Certainly," said Taine. Reaching out, he placed one massive hand on each of her shoulders. His fingers held her gently but firmly as he looked into her eyes. His face grew serious, intense.

"Now, listen to me," said Taine. "We're investigating Heaven and Hell. Those are extremely powerful words to some people. Don't get into arguments with anyone. Speak in vague terms, and never mention your name, where you live, and most of all, what you do for a living. These people do not like lawyers, and some of them are very, very nasty individuals. Remember, Heaven or H-E-L-L. Do you understand?"

"Yes, sir," said Amanda. Though she suspected Taine was exaggerating the danger, she also knew there was more than a little truth in what he was saying. "I might be cynical, but I'm not stupid."

During her early days as a lawyer, she had litigated a number of drug cases involving Hollywood's rich and famous. She had learned quickly enough that beneath all the glitz and glamour, there was a core of dirt and mean in just about everything.

Taine released his grip on her shoulders. Amanda couldn't help but notice that the detective carried an automatic in a shoulder holster nestled beneath the left sleeve of his perfectly tailored suit jacket. More than anything he said, the sight of the gun convinced her that they might be in real danger tonight. The Sid Taine she remembered from college abhorred violent behavior. If he was carrying a gun, they were definitely going into peril.

"Ready?" asked Taine, standing at the door.

"Ready," answered Amanda.

"One more thing, Mandy," said Taine, his voice softening, as he used a nickname she had abandoned many years ago.

"Yes, ST," she replied, using her own pet name for Taine from their college days.

"You look quite beautiful tonight," said Taine. "Absolutely stunning. You haven't lost a step since college."

"Thank you," she said. Standing on her toes, she leaned against the detective's chest and gently kissed him on the cheek. "You look pretty good yourself."

With that, they were gone, out into the night, searching for Heaven or Hell.

4.

Their first stop caught her completely by surprise. No question, Taine was determined to find an answer to Anson's question. Wherever that search might take them.

"Off with your necklace and earrings," said the detective steering his car onto Michigan Avenue. "Put them in your purse and hide the bag under the seat. Reach in the back; I borrowed a shawl from Mrs. McConnell. Toss it over your head and shoulders. It should conceal your looks. And remember closely my warnings a few minutes ago. Just watch and listen."

Amanda did exactly what Taine told her to do. The detective's tone breached no back talk. That he was willing to share some of the darker side of his career with her she took as a tremendous compliment. All she hoped was that whatever they were going to do wouldn't wind up with them in jail; or worse, dead.

"Twenty-Seventh Street off Michigan Avenue," said Taine ten minutes later. He was driving the car at a crawl, in the lane closest to the sidewalks. Amanda huddled down in her seat, trying to be inconspicuous. A half-dozen, heavily painted black women were shouting gutter phrases at the detective, quoting rates and promising pleasures beyond imagining. Finally, reaching the end of the block, he gestured to one of the women with a huge bosom and matching rump, along with gobs of black hair streaked with blonde tints. As the hooker walked closer, Amanda was horrified to see the woman was casually scratching herself all over. No doubt she had fleas.

"Hey good lookin'," said the hooker. "Whacha got cookin? You anxious for a trip around the world? I got yer ticket."

"How much?" asked Taine.

"For you," said the woman, "fifty bucks. For you and your friend, a C-note. Nothing too kinky or that leaves marks. I gotta look my best for my many satisfied return clients."

Reaching into his suit coat, Taine pulled out the roll of hundreds. The hooker's eyes widened and then narrowed. "I'll pay you two hundred if you give me an honest answer to one question," said Taine. "But I want the truth so help you God and the Holy Virgin Mary."

"So help me God and the Holy Virgin," said the prostitute. "For two C's I'll tell you the story of my life."

"That won't be necessary," said Taine. "My question is much less complicated. But if you lie to me, I'll know. I've got the power, the hoodoo power. I can see right through you."

"You've got the power," repeated the hooker. "I can feel it. Ask away. I'll answer you with the truth. I swear it."

Taine asked. Were they living in Heaven or Hell? The hooker thought for a few moments before answering. She offered no explanation for her reply nor did the detective ask for one.

Thirty minutes and five whores later, the answer remained the same. Amanda was surprised. She had assumed that all the women would select Hell. None of them had. Heaven was the unanimous choice.

"They had to be lying," she said to Taine. "None of them looked like they were spending their time in Heaven."

"Well, so much for the power of hoodoo," said Taine, with a laugh. "They said what they assumed their pimps would want them to say. No surprise. Truth is elusive, except when you're dealing with desperation. These women are lost souls, but they're still not without hope. For that, we need to make another stop."

"Not the street again, I hope," said Amanda.

"Worse," said Taine. "Under a bridge."

The detective drove his car down Michigan Ave. then headed east to the Fifty-Ninth Street overpass. In the darkness and in this neighborhood there was no traffic. Taine again slowed the car to barely walking speed. Beneath the bridge, caught in the headlights, were more than a dozen bums. Homeless men, they were dressed in rags, unshaven and dirty, and sat on the ground passing around a bottle of cheap whiskey. Amanda had seen men like this, begging on the street, standing alone in the rain, hiding beneath underpasses for shelter at night. Still, she had never seen them from so close.

Taine put the car in park and shut off the motor. "You'll have to trust me," he said. "Lock the doors after I leave. These men aren't criminals but sometimes they get desperate."

"I really don't think it's necessary to ask them, ST," said

Amanda. "I'd be willing to assume we know what they'll say."

"No assumptions," said Taine. "Lock the doors. I'll be back in five minutes, ten at the most. Don't be frightened. You'll be fine."

"Easy for you to say," replied Amanda.

Taine was out the door before she could argue further. Not willing to play the coward, she counted to ten before she locked the car doors.

The detective returned after eight minutes. His features were white, his eyes blazing with anger. "It's hard to believe that veterans in America, the richest country in the world, are living under bridges. Fourteen men, living in Hell."

She could have said, "I told you so," but knew better.

5.

Fifteen minutes driving north on Lake Shore Drive with the windows open cooled Taine off, physically and emotionally. Amanda breathed a sigh of relief when the big detective told her she could remove the shawl she was wearing and put back on her earrings and jewelry. Their new destination was *The Happening*, a well known nightspot located at the edge of the Loop, overlooking the Chicago River. As benefited the expensive location, there was a $100 cover charge and the people lined up waiting to get in were dressed to the Nines.

Amanda had visited *The Happening* a few times with Husband Number One who liked being seen where the "In Crowd" hung out. The liquor was top-notch and the music laid back and not constantly blaring at bone-shattering decibels like many other clubs. It was a place notorious for politicians and publicity-hungry Hollywood stars. Having worked in the Hollywood office of Elgin, Baylor, and West for years, Amanda knew many of the top celebrities in L.A. and usually handled their legal affairs for them when they came to Chicago. Husband Number One enjoyed living in his wife's shadow. A body-builder and physical trainer, he was every woman's dream lover. Gavin was incredible in the sack and he was handsome eye-candy on her arm when she went out, but he lacked one thing necessary to make him a dream husband: brains. Her first leap into marriage had lasted one month, having run out of things to talk about after two days and three hours.

Amanda had no worries about running into Husband Number One at *The Happening*. After their divorce, he had settled down as the trainer and live-in boyfriend for an Olympic gymnast. Evidently, the young woman didn't require her lover to think, merely perform. They were definitely not a couple that showed up at clubs. One photo taken at *The Happening* would ruin any possible future endorsement deals.

Taine, spending some of Anson MacDonald's money earned the day before, slipped the gatekeeper a hundred to let them pass into the club without the customary hour wait. Several people who had been standing in line patiently complained bitterly as they watched Amanda and Taine walk into the bistro's entrance. With just the hint of a smile, Taine held up his right hand, making a peace sign. Between the V formed by his index and pointer finger he held a wad of hundred dollar bills.

Amanda laughed. Obviously she wasn't the only one who had changed since college. Twenty years ago, Sid Taine had been so straight-laced, so honest, so contemptuous of people who used their money or their influence to get ahead. Of course, he had also derided violence as the admission of the absolute failure of diplomacy. The big detective glanced down at her and there was a glint of amusement in his eyes. Without doubt, he realized what she was laughing about.

"So," he said, "you get older and wiser. You learn that the idealism of youth is no match for the treachery of old age."

"You, sir," said Amanda, "are not old. And compared to the people I work with every day, are definitely not treacherous."

Inside the club, they decided to split up with an agreement to rendezvous at the bar in an hour. Each was to get opinions on Heaven or Hell from people they knew in the bistro. Considering the circles they ran in, Amanda felt confident that the possible overlapping of opinions would be negligible and that she would easily double Taine's totals.

"Loser pays for drinks," she said, feeling quite confident Taine would be unable to resist the challenge. "And I only drink the best."

"I'll take that bet," said Taine.

At that, they parted, Amanda heading for a nearby booth where she spotted a junior partner of the firm. With the young lawyer's help and her own contacts, Amanda felt certain she should easily be able to question fifty people within the hour. The taste of victory was sweet, especially when someone else picked up the tab.

An hour and forty-seven responses later, Amanda headed to the bar. Though it was approaching midnight and the place was jumping, finding Taine wasn't difficult. He was the man with the biggest shoulders in the room, standing with his back to the crowd, sipping a tall drink and talking to one of the bartenders. Feeling bold, the result of several stronger drinks foisted on her by friends during the course of her wanderings, she edged up close to him and reaching up, ran the tips of the fingers of one hand across the back of his neck.

Unlike the movies or TV shows, Taine neither turned in a rush nor shivered in pleasure. Nor did he choke or gulp down his drink.

"Ready to pay up?" he asked, his tone casual.

"How did you know it was me and not some cheap bimbo looking to make time with the handsomest man in the room?" asked Amanda. "Sixth sense refined by years of detecting?"

"Two eyes," said Taine, gesturing with his head at the large mirrors positioned above the bar, reflecting much of the night-spot's floor and inhabitants. "Good vision."

"I'll have whatever Mr. Taine is drinking," Amanda told the young man waiting bar. "Make it a double and put it on his tab."

"Yes, ma'am," said the bartender. "One double ginger-ale coming up. Would you like a cherry in it?"

"Ha, ha, very funny," said Amanda. She grinned, looking Taine straight in the eyes. "Sticking to the cheap stuff, knowing I'd be ordering the expensive booze?"

He sighed dramatically. Amanda couldn't resist giggling. "I got forty-seven," she said, triumphantly. "Fourteen in Hell, thirty-three in Heaven. Match those numbers, big boy?"

"Fifty-seven voted for Hell," said Taine. "Forty-four choose Heaven."

Amanda choked on her ginger-ale. "A hundred and one replies? That's impossible."

"I never lie," said Taine. "At least, not often. Never to a beautiful woman."

"How did you do it?" asked Amanda. "This bar is filled with my crowd, the movers and shakers of Chicago."

Taine waved one hand at the bartender. "*This* is my crowd; the workers and the washers of Chicago. I helped some good people looking for honest work in the kitchen here. Plus, I trained the security crews at most of the bars and lounges in the city. You'd be surprised how many people it takes to run a place like this on a busy night."

"No, I wouldn't," said Amanda, secretly pleased that Taine had once again referred to her as a beautiful woman. "What do you really want to drink? I always pay my debts."

"The ginger-ale went down smooth," said Taine. "Besides, we still have another club to visit tonight. Let's move."

Amanda wasn't sure she could handle much more alcohol, but she was determined not to say a word to Taine. Though she wondered what other bar he wanted to visit?

6.

Their last stop of the evening was at *Cemetery*, a trendy hip-hop dance club in the northwest corner of the city. Amanda had never been there but knew the place by reputation. All the political big-shots in the city went to *Cemetery*. A reputed mob hangout, it was where the big spenders could rub elbows with the city's most dangerous hoodlums. And if the gossip columns were to be believed, make deals benefiting them both. There was a line of twenty or so people waiting to be let in, but Taine steered Amanda right up to the bouncer who was handling admission. The man was huge, several inches taller than the big detective and at least a hundred pounds heavier, with all the extra weight distributed around his waist. He wore a bright yellow muscle-shirt that left his arms, the size of deli salamis, bare. His blotchy skin was off-gray in color and he was totally hairless, bald and without eyebrows.

"Good to see you tonight, Mr. Taine," said the doorkeeper, waving them down the path to the front door of the club.

"That man was immense," Amanda said to Taine as they reached the front door. "He must have weighed four hundred pounds."

"Probably more," said Taine. "Wait till you see his brother, Big Sal. Then you'll know why they call the bouncer, Little Willy."

In contrast to the bouncer, a pencil thin black man wearing a tuxedo pulled open the club's front door. Taine tipped him twenty dollars as he and Amanda entered *Cemetery*. A step inside and they were slammed by a wall of noise, combining equal parts blaring music and hundreds of people engaged in loud conversations. A circle of a dozen green fluorescent lights sunk in the high ceiling reflected off the patrons' skin, giving everyone a pale, undead hue. Their spooky appearance gave the dance club its name.

The nightspot consisted of a gigantic ballroom; with a line of booths against the walls, a huge dance floor, and a bandstand at the rear. The room was packed with people, most standing in small groups talking or swaying to the loud music. There were a half-dozen exits at the rear of the club, their signs glaring bright orange in the near darkness. A stampede at a packed nightclub years before had killed nearly two dozen people. Exits ever since then were plentiful and clearly marked.

Taine looked out of place with his dark suit, white shirt and conservative tie. Most of the men were wearing jeans and sport shirts. Some were dressed in muscle-tees. More than a few wore suspenders. Amanda fit right in, though her short-short dress was one of the longest in the club. Micro, not mini, was the style and more than a few skirts or dresses barely covered their owners' bottoms. There was a lot of skin on display and a number of women – both young and middle-aged – didn't seem to consider underwear a necessity. Amanda, who considered herself not easily shocked, was suitably surprised by what people were wearing – or not wearing – in the nightspot.

"I feel a hundred years old," she said to Taine, half-shouting to be heard over the constant din. "What happened to good taste?"

"It dies a little bit more every day," said Taine. "Kicked in the teeth lately by Paris Hilton and the Kardashian sisters."

ROBERT E. WEINBERG

Taine steered her past a large group of old men bumping
their thighs against the bottoms of a gaggle of young bleached-
blondes wearing too much makeup and very little else. The old
crows were grinning broadly, as were the bottled-blondes – but
for very different reasons, Amanda suspected.

"Heaven or Hell?" asked Taine.

The question hit her in the face. The sight of the horny old
fools and the cheap tramps grinding up against them suddenly
didn't seem so funny. Lust sometimes had its charms, but this
wasn't one of them.

As they followed some invisible yellow brick road that only
Taine could sense, wending their way through the crowds at
the nightspot, Amanda was astonished at some of the people
she saw. More to the point, the people she saw together. Big-
name lawyers sat at booths tossing down drinks with circuit
court judges, often times with a well-known criminal or two
joined in the mix. Several of the mayor's inner circle were ac-
tively making time with women half their age and definitely
not their wives. An amazingly popular celebrity chef, in town
for a dining convention, was busily drinking down his supper.
There were no drugs openly on display, but a number of people
looked like they were buzzing on coke or crack. Amanda suspected most of the action and dealing took place in the men's
and ladies' rooms.

Finally, Taine came to an abrupt stop in front of a wide
booth located on the far side of the nightspot. A half-dozen
very attractive women, looking to be in their early twenties,
were crowded around a behemoth of a man who sat behind an
immense table filled with food. Off a few feet to the side, trying
to look invisible, were a pair of guards, each man armed with
an Uzi.

The giant figure, who had to be six hundred pounds or
more, had features that bore a close resemblance to Little Willy at the front door. This was his brother, Big Sal. Amanda had
never seen such a huge person before. Sal's head was nearly
double that of a normal man's skull, and his eyes were the size
of light bulbs. His fingers were as big as hot dogs, and he must
have had a sixty inch waist. Big Sal was really *big*.

Amanda recognized the man immediately, though she had

never met him in person. Every lawyer in the city knew Big Sal Vecchio. Reputed gang lord and mafia Capo, he ran the rackets on Chicago's north side. Arrested more than twenty times, he had never spent a day in jail. Big Sal was as smart and ruthless as he was fat.

7.

The table in front of the gangster was filled with plates of spaghetti, ravioli, manicotti, lasagna, shakers of several kinds of cheese, and several large loaves of garlic bread. Sal was raising a quart-sized tankard of beer to his lips when he first spotted Taine. Instantly, he slammed the metal cup down on the table, sloshing beer everywhere. "Hey, Taine! My favorite magic man. Welcome!"

The detective smiled and raised a hand in greeting. There was no way he could reach Sal with the crowd of women who surrounded the giant. "Big Sal," said the detective, "I swear you get more handsome every time I see you."

"Yeah, yeah," said Sal nodding his gigantic head. "Eating makes me look good. Why you here, Taine? My boys ain't killed nobody in months. We've been good citizens."

"I know, Sal," said Taine. "All I want is to ask you a question."

"A question?" repeated Sal. He frowned, creasing his huge brow with deep wrinkles. "You know the rules. No talking about business at the table. For you, Taine, I'd make an exception, but I wouldn't like it."

"No, no," said Taine. He kept Amanda behind him, as if afraid once Big Sal saw a lawyer, he would clam up and not say another word. Stranger things had happened. Tonight, she was primarily keeping her head low and her ears open. "I'm doing a little survey. Just asking one question. But I need an honest answer. No BS."

"Working for that Anson MacDonald?" said Sal as he gobbled down a half-dozen ravioli. He laughed, obviously amused by the surprised expression on Taine's face. "You can't keep things hidden from a Boss, Taine. You neither, Miss Blaylock. No reason for you to hide behind my friend Sidney. I don't bite. Not even lawyers."

"I didn't think you did," said Amanda, flashing what she hoped was her most winning smile. "I just didn't want to be a distraction when you answered Mr. MacDonald's question."

"Heaven or Hell?" said Big Sal. "That' a question for a Bishop, maybe even a Pope. Not the sort of question you ask a mob boss. But, Taine's a special friend and I owe him a lot. Ask him someday, Miss Blaylock, to tell you the story about how my grandson was kidnapped a few years ago and how Taine saved Luciano from being made into stew by some big-city cannibals. I owe Sidney a blood debt and that's not a debt that can be repaid easily. Nothing I wouldn't do for my friend, Taine. Nothing."

"Good," said Taine. "Then answer the question."

"Heaven or Hell?" repeated Big Sal. "I've been pondering the choice all day, Taine. When I was in good shape, twenty, thirty years ago, I woulda told you Heaven, that's for sure. These days, I'm not so positive. The world looks a lot different when you're trapped inside your own body."

Big Sal waved a huge arm, fingers spread wide, around in the air. "Sure I got my club; and my women; and my food; and Little Willy, simple-minded as he might be; and my grandchildren, the light of my life. I got plenty, Miss Blaylock. More than most people, that's for sure. But Heaven or Hell? The choice isn't as easy as it sounds. I'll vote for Heaven, but to be honest, I have my doubts. I have big doubts."

"Thanks, Big Sal," said Taine. "We have to run."

Then, they were back in the crowd, heading for the front door.

"Interesting answer," said Amanda, "but definitely not conclusive. Wait a sec'."

Amanda tapped the shoulder of one of the peroxide blondes dancing with the old geezers. The young woman's features twisted with annoyance as she turned to face Amanda but settled into a thin-lipped smile when she saw the hundred dollar bill Amanda was holding between two fingers. Amanda leaned forward and whispered in the girl's ear. Just a few sentences.

"Hell," said the blonde without hesitation. She glanced over at her dance partner who was staring at the girl with ill-concealed impatience. "Definitely Hell."

"Point taken," said Taine. "It seems that age and circumstances are major factors in forming opinions. No surprise there. The poor think we're living in Hell. The rich believe it's Heaven. They both think the world is merely a question of circumstance."

"Speaking of circumstances," said Amanda. "Big Sal's grandson Luciano's encounter with big-city cannibals. That's one story I want to hear. I thought you retired when you got married?"

"I did," answered Taine. "From being an investigator, not from living. I closed my detective agency and spent all my time with my wife, Janet, and her son, Tim, who I adopted. Janet and I ran her father's business, a multi-national corporation she inherited when he died. During the summer when Tim was off from school, we traveled, here and abroad. When necessary, I helped friends in trouble, using skills I developed while working as a detective. Big Sal's problem was one of those cases."

Taine paused, then continued, his voice barely above a whisper. "Around two years ago, Janet started feeling sick and suffering from back pains. No one suspected pancreatic cancer as it was more common in men; in people in their sixties and seventies; and among smokers. By the time her doctors finally diagnosed pancreatic ductal adenocarcinoma; the most fatal form of pancreatic cancer, tumors had formed throughout most of her body. The disease was already in an advanced state and was inoperable. She tried every form of recognized treatment and several experimental cures. Nothing worked. It was a terrible, terrible time. Not even the supernatural can heal cancer. The most I could do was lessen her pain. She died six months ago, on Christmas Day. It was the worst day of my life."

Amanda sighed. No reason to ask Taine whether he thought they lived in Heaven or Hell. She already knew his answer.

8.

They visited two more clubs, with much the same results, before they finally decided to call it a night. They agreed to meet at Taine's office the next day at noon. It was five hours before Anson MacDonald was scheduled to die. Amanda had no idea what Taine was going to say to MacDonald, but she hoped the detective had some trick up his sleeve. Otherwise, the million dollars would go unclaimed. And that would be one more crime which her client could add to his list.

She said as much to Taine shortly after he ushered her into his private office and invited her opinions of their survey the night before. Sitting in the middle seat of three red leather chairs that encircled the detective's desk, she laid out her feelings in no uncertain terms.

"Interesting opinions," Amanda concluded, after speaking passionately for approximately ten minutes, "but no one convinced me that we live either in Heaven or in Hell. MacDonald can believe anything he wants but he killed those people for no reason."

"Somehow I expected you to say that," said Taine. Getting up from his chair behind his desk, he walked to the door of his office and locked it. Amanda felt a sudden twinge of concern.

"Magic requires privacy," said Taine. "Best that we not be disturbed for the next few minutes."

"Magic?" asked Amanda, wondering what Taine had in mind. She trusted the big detective. Or at least she thought she did. Until now.

"You've expressed strong doubts in the supernatural," said Taine. "I can't say I blame you. Our world is filled with frauds and deceptions. There are too many crooks and cheap hustlers who know nothing of the deep mysteries that surround us. Hold my hands and I'll show you why I'm known as the 'Occult Detective.'"

Taine sat down on the red leather chair to her right. He stretched both hands to her, palms up. Not knowing what to expect, Amanda placed her hands palms down on his. The detective smiled.

"God created the universe by inscribing his perfect name on the void," said Taine. "He extended his identity to all things. Thus, knowing the true names of things and how those names are pronounced gives a magician power over them. It enabled him to see things not visible by ordinary people. Like Heaven."

Taine spoke a word. The syllables slid through Amanda's mind, refusing to stick. Yet the word was complete.

Her mind was suddenly *elsewhere*, floating along on a cool, comfortable breeze, in a place of many bright lights. She felt calm, relaxed, at peace with the world, knowing without question the world was at peace with her. The air was filled with soft music that spoke directly to her inner soul, embracing her with love. She felt content.

And then it was over.

The sensations ceased, the music stopped, and she was back in Taine's office, sitting on the red leather chair, facing him.

"What happened?" she asked when she was once again able to frame a coherent sentence. "Was that some form of hypnosis?"

"As best as it can be understood by a human mind," said Taine, "that was Heaven."

"You—?" said Amanda.

"I am one of the last true magicians," said Taine. "I know the name for Heaven. As well as the name for ----------."

Pain. She was experiencing absolutely incredible pain. Amanda's entire body shrieked in sudden, intense, overwhelming pain. Her bones felt as if they were being smashed by steel hammers, being shattered into thousands of shards, each ripping into her flesh from the inside out. Her eyes were wide open but there was nothing to see other than flames. She sensed rather than saw other people nearby engulfed in the same fire. She could hear them screaming, screaming in dreadful agony. Her own mouth was open and she screamed.

Her cry of pain echoed against the walls of Taine's office. The agony vanished in an instant but it took Amanda several minutes to regain her composure. There was no doubt in her mind, none. This was not trickery, not hypnosis, not some sort of fraud. This was truth. Heaven and Hell revealed. Finally, she could speak.

"Heaven is serenity and Hell is unending, unwavering pain," she said, her voice trembling. "Not exactly what I imagined but beautiful and horrible nonetheless."

"Everyone sees them differently," said Taine. "Your vision of Hell is much different than mine; your vision of Heaven too."

"Then Anson MacDonald was wrong and his obsession was wrong and we aren't dead and this isn't Hell," said Amanda. "And last night was a waste of time."

"Don't jump to conclusions," said Taine. "Last night wasn't only about Heaven and Hell."

"You knew all along that Anson was wrong," said Amanda. "I thought he was playing you for a fool. But, in reality, you were playing him. Why?"

"I'll tell you when I tell him," said Taine. He glanced down at his watch. "If we hurry, we should be able to make it to his cell just in time."

They hurried. It helped that Amanda was MacDonald's lawyer and that her law firm was the biggest and best connected in Chicago. Taine had connections as well, including an in with the governor. The big detective had influential friends. Together, they got five minutes alone with the prisoner. But, after that, he would walk the final steps to his execution.

"So," said MacDonald leaning casually against the bars of his cell. "Do you have the answer? Is this Heaven or Hell? And, most important, do you have proof?"

"It's neither," said Taine. "There's a third choice, a much more likely scenario. I spent the previous evening pointing out to your lawyer how much more likely it is than Heaven or Hell. The third choice doesn't much matter if we're living or we're dead. God sees us in either case and watches what we are doing either way."

"A third choice," repeated MacDonald. The first traces of fear were visible in his eyes, the way he stared at Taine. All of the color drained out of the killer's cheeks. "Then I killed all those people for no reason. The murders had no meaning."

"They had meaning," said Taine. "The land cries out for justice. Whether we are living or dead, it doesn't matter. This is the place where we are judged. Heaven or Hell comes afterward."

It was time for MacDonald to be marched down the last mile, the steps to his execution. Going to meet his maker. Time only for a few last words.

"This isn't Heaven or Hell," said Sidney Taine, in a voice that could not be denied. "It's *purgatory*." ⟍

Maze

The heavy steel door had been ripped off its hinges. Beyond the wreckage, the corridor was pitch black. A bright beam swept across a floor littered with exploded light bulbs. The white cement was stained crimson. Blood covered the walls and ceiling as well. But there were no bodies. There never were any bodies – or remains of the victims. Daemons fed on human flesh.

"Spread out," he declared, his voice thick with anger and frustration. "You know the routine. Search the entire installation. See if anyone's alive. Twenty minutes then rendezvous back here. I told the men outside we'd return to the tanks in a half-hour. They won't wait if we're late and walin' back to the Zone ain't an option. Be careful. The Daemons are probably gone, but you never can tell. This place could be a trap. Stay alert."

No need to warn his men. A dozen veteran soldiers, they were survivors of the worst the wasteland had to offer. Clothed in Deathware and armed with massive Last Rights assault rifles, they understood the slightest mistake or miscalculation meant death. Or worse.

Pairing off, five teams scurried down the concrete and steel corridors that crisscrossed the subterranean research station. The remaining two men, Cleveland and Moss, stayed with Allison as bodyguards. Moving slowly, the three soldiers started down the main tunnel leading to the station's command center. The ghosts of the station's vanished personnel marched with them. This base wasn't the first one Allison had found gutted in his years in the Wasteland. But it never got any easier.

Yesterday, forty men and women had worked here, at the edge of forever, searching for answers in the unending war against the forces of Hell itself; forty living, breathing, eating, sleeping, loving, talking, human beings, knowing the risk they were taking but refusing to surrender to the darkness. Hoping that in some small measure they would contribute to mankind's ultimate victory over the forces of night. Now, they were all dead. And the war between humanity and daemon continued as if they never had existed.

Allison had arrived with his crew at base 412 in the Wasteland in two Roll-Cage tanks a little more than an hour ago. They'd come from the Zone in response to an urgent message received at Volksag Corporation headquarters thirty hours earlier. The communication, sent by Dr. Sinclair, chief scientist of the research facility, had been short and to the point. *Found sleeper. May have necessary answers.* Require immediate assistance. No one at Volksag was sure exactly what the words meant, but Sinclair was not given to exaggeration. Allison and his squad, armed and ready for battle, had been dispatched immediately. And still arrived too late.

Necessary answers. The words echoed through Allison's mind as he hiked down the tunnel leading to Sinclair's laboratory. A big, powerfully built man, standing well over six feet tall, with shaven head and a dark black fringed beard, the expedition leader was as tough as he looked. Still, Allison had been sent on this mission for his brains not brawn. He had a sharp mind and steel trap cleverness. Sinclair's message hinted at a major discovery. Whatever answers the scientist had discovered, Allison meant to find them, no matter the cost.

The research director's main laboratory was a mess. The equipment and files had been smashed flat and burned black. Nothing remained but jagged slabs of fused steel and molten glass. A solitary crimson handprint on one wall was the only sign that anyone had been in the office when the Daemons had arrived

"Captain," came an unexpected voice in Allison's transcom as he watched his two assistants sort through the wreckage, hunting for anything of value. "McCay here. Down on level three. Better come quick. I think we found something."

"On my way," answered Allison, beckoning for his men to follow. The stalking Daemons had been on a search and destroy mission. Hard to believe the ravagers would miss anything important. Hell's minions were extremely thorough. Still, they weren't smart. At least, not the ones who handled massacres in the Wastelands. It wasn't much of a hope, but it was the only one Allison had.

Level Three was located a hundred feet below ground. It was where the electrical generators and air filtration plant that kept the underground center livable were located. Except for the scattered red blots that marked where a technician had perished, this quadrant appeared undisturbed. Daemons found huge machinery disturbing and stayed as far away from it as possible. Only the temptation of living flesh could lure them down to this level, and not for any longer than necessary.

"There," said McCay, an unshaven mammoth of a man. His right hand pointed at a column of massive steel storage drums wedged up against the rear wall. "Take a look at the one on the end." McCay nodded at his companion, "Creed noticed the scratches on the floor. That container is different than the rest. Similar but not the same.

"Damned if it ain't," said Allison, staring at the metal tank. Twelve feet high and six feet thick, it was scarred and pitted with age. Odd markings for a storage unit kept in the basement of a research center. Unless the drum wasn't originally from inside. Possibly, it had been found in the Wasteland and brought into the complex for study. And when the Daemons attacked, desperately hidden in plain sight.

"Turn the thing on its side," commanded Allison waving a hand at one of the storage cranes hunched up against the wall. "And, Cleveland, signal the Roll-Cages we might be a little late. We're not leaving until I find out what makes this drum special. Hard to imagine the Daemons would attack a station because of a storage tank.

Not so hard to imagine when they got the drum on its side and saw the thick glass insert covering the side of the unit that had been turned to the wall. And the sleeping man who floated within the tank on a sea of sparkling green foam.

It took Allison ten minutes to find the recessed metal clips that popped open the top of the tank. The green liquid was so cold it burned Allison's fingers even through his gloves. Strangely, the figure resting in it seemed unaffected by the temperature. The man's eyes were closed but his breathing was deep and normal. He appeared to be sleeping, though all their shaking couldn't wake him.

"Can't waste any more time here," declared Allison after a few minutes. "We gotta get moving. I suspect we found what those Daemons were hunting. Seems likely they might decide to take another look. Best we be long gone when they return."

McCay and his partner, Creed, went first, their assault rifles level and ready. Grim-faced, they searched every shadow. Behind them came Cleveland and Moss, the stranger half-carried, half-dragged between them. The limp figure was heavier than he looked. Last marched Allison, busily directing the rest of his forces out of the base. A sense of urgency gripped him by the throat. It was a feeling that wouldn't be gone until they returned their prize to the Zone. Again, his mind returned to Dr. Sinclair's message. Found sleeper. May have necessary answers. Obviously, the words referred to their discovery. A sleeper. What did the words mean? And more important, what were the questions to which the man might know the answers?

The Daemons attacked just as Allison and his men emerged from the underground tunnels. They burst out of the horizon, moving with unnatural speed, screaming with inhuman savagery. Five of them, each twenty feet high, with four arms ending in huge pincer-like claws. Obscene parodies of humans, with mottled red-grey skin, they hurtled themselves forward at the men in the corridor mouth, totally ignoring the automatic cannon fire coming from the troops stationed by the Roll-Cage tanks.

"Aim for their legs!" Allison roared into his transcom, the massive Last Rites assault rifle jerking in his arms. "Cut them down to size!"

There was no time for orders, just survival. Of the five that attacked, three fell victim to the assault cannon before they reached the mouth of the tunnel. But two did not. A hand the size of a shovel swept past Allison's face. Monstrous claws snapped.

Cleveland screeched in agony, blood spurting like a fountain from a massive gash in his side. Allison swung his rifle upward, the gun belching explosive shells. Twenty feet above him, a Daemon's face exploded in a rain of blood and gore.

"Down!" yelled Moss from behind him. Allison dropped. Heat rippled across his back, but his body armor kept him safe from the liquid fire that slammed into the remaining abomination. The creature shrieked once as its massive frame melted into a raging napalm inferno. Whatever hell they came from, Daemons were not immune to fire. They burned with a satisfying finality.

The entire fight had taken less than twenty seconds. Cleveland and Creed were dead, as were the five Daemons. A fair trade on this harsh world. Not one that Allison liked making. Good fighting men were precious. They were not easily replaced.

"Daemons," said a voice from Allison's right. It was the stranger from the tank. He stood unsupported, bright blue eyes wide open. His voice betrayed neither surprise nor fear. "Dr. Sinclair spoke of them. Creatures from the circles of Hell. I had no idea they were so large."

"These punks are nothing compared to their big brothers," said Allison, grabbing the stranger by an arm. The man didn't resist. "Those mothers can block out the sky. They'll stomp us like bugs."

"That sounds unpleasant," said the stranger. He turned, looked at the tunnel leading underground. "Dr. Sinclair? The others in the station?"

"They didn't make it," said Allison. "You're the only one left."

"I suspected no less," said the stranger, "when the attack began and Sinclair insisted that I return to the capsule. He was a brave man."

"Yeah," said Allison. "Same's true for anyone who works in the Wasteland. Ain't a job for somebody looking to live forever. Now, enough chattering and let's move. Or we're bugs."

Thirty minutes later, inside one of the Roll-Cage tanks heading straight for the Zone, Allison felt slightly more secure. Nothing less than a full Daemonic incursion could stop them now. And whatever danger the stranger represented, Allison doubted that any imaginable threat could forge the eternally feuding realms of Sheol into some sort of alliance. They were safe. At least from the evils without.

"Who are you?" Allison asked the stranger. The man, well formed and slender, looked quite ordinary. He appeared perhaps thirty years old. His only garment was a silvery metal membrane that covered him from neck to toes like a second skin. "And what makes you so important?"

"My name is Maze," said the man. "As to my importance, I'm not sure what you mean. You and your men come from the fortress called the Zone? Earth's last refuge?"

Allison nodded. "Its been called that. I'm Allison. Work for Volksag Corporation, just like everyone at base 412. Sinclair sent my boss a message requesting help. Said he found a sleeper. That you?"

"A sleeper?" replied Maze, smiling. There was something odd about the man though Allison couldn't say what. Maze seemed too relaxed, too calm. Unconcerned about the Daemons or the carnage they had caused. Almost as if he was playing some sort of game. The stranger definitely did not believe in talking about himself. "An interesting expression even if not quite accurate. This Zone? Dr. Sinclair said it's nearly three miles high and over forty miles in diameter. Built of reinforced steel and concrete, with hundreds of sectors and levels. Except for a small sprinkling of scientists and Wasteland Mercenaries like himself, all of humanity resides within its walls. Correct?"

"Yeah, pretty much so," said Allison. He wasn't sure he should be answering Maze's questions, but could think of no reason not to. "Home sweet home."

"Sixty million people?" asked Maze. "All jammed into one monolithic structure?"

"Give or take a few hundred thousand," replied Allison. "What makes you so curious?"

"Nothing like it in my time," said Maze. "It sounds fascinating. A place with opportunity for someone like me."

"Your time?" repeated Allison, picking up on that phrase.

"Before the Daemons," said Maze, with the flicker of a smile. "Before the gates of Sheol opened and Hell's legions poured out across the world. I entered the cryogenic shell in 2025. As best as Dr. Sinclair could determine, approximately two hundred and seventy-five years ago."

"I don't understand," said Allison. "It doesn't make much sense."

"I know," said Maze. He laughed as if amused by Allison's suspicions. "But you will. Once we reach the Zone, you'll know my entire story. I promise you that."

Staring at Maze, bright blue eyes shining, Allison shivered with sudden worry. He was merely following orders, being a good soldier. Working for the Corporation, doing his part for the Zone. Sinclair's message had said Maze might have the necessary answers. But at what price?

It was a question Allison suspected was going to be asked many times during the next few days. Many, many times .... ◣

NATE KENYON grew up in a small town in Maine. His debut novel, *Bloodstone*, was a Bram Stoker Award Finalist and P&E Horror Novel of the Year award winner. *The Reach* was also a Stoker Award Finalist, received a starred *Publishers Weekly* review, and is in development as a major feature film. His third novel, *The Bone Factory*, was called "masterful" by *Booklist*. His fourth novel, *Sparrow Rock*, will be released in limited edition by Bad Moon Books and in paperback by Leisure Books in May 2010, and his novel *StarCraft Ghost: Spectres*, based on the bestselling videogame franchise by Blizzard Entertainment, will be released by Pocket Books around the end of the year.

Kenyon's sci-fi novella *Prime* was released from Apex in July 2009. He has had stories published in a number of magazines and anthologies including *Terminal Frights*, *Shroud Magazine*, *Northern Haunts*, *Monstrous*, and *Legends of the Mountain State 2*. He lives in New England with his children and their ferocious dog, Bailey, where he is at work on his next novel.

Visit Nate online at www.natekenyon.com.

Nate Kenyon

Breeding
the Demons

Fowler's pink, chubby face glistened, and he held the hungry-dog look of a man waiting out his obsession.

"Been here long?" Ian said.

Fowler grunted and motioned for the photographs, his eyes glazed and mouth stained red from drink. He smelled of sweat and cheap cologne. Three Bloody Marys lay drained upon the nightclub table, and Fowler had loosened his tie.

Ian slipped into the booth and put his leather portfolio on the table, enjoying making the man wait a little. But Fowler would not be denied. He grabbed the portfolio and rifled through its contents, and his breathing quickened as his eyes devoured the pictures within.

Finally he sighed and straightened his head. He removed the photos and slipped them into a plain manila envelope, which he stuck inside his jacket. "You are a fucking genius," he said.

"I had to give bribes. It's expensive —"

"Your business." Fowler waved a sausage-fingered, jeweled hand. "Keep it to yourself."

Ian shrugged. He had expected this. Fowler didn't want to know how he did it, any more than the purchasers of a pornographic magazine wanted a detailed description of how the models were selected and positioned, lighted and airbrushed.

"When can I have the next set?"

"I need some time. And I can't keep paying everyone off and expect to get away with it."

"Well, come up with something else then." Fowler looked irritated that he had to offer advice. "I don't have to tell you what happens if you just stop. I'm barely keeping them satisfied as it is."

"I'll get it done as soon as I can."

"Have a new batch by the end of the week."

"The end of the *week*? How the hell am I supposed to-"

The envelope appeared as if from nowhere. It looked thick tonight; a good ten grand, if his eyes served him right. More than enough to put him back to work. At least for now.

"All right," Ian said. "End of the week."

~φ~

Fowler hadn't always been that way. Ian remembered a slimmer version, eager for nothing more than his next square meal. But he catered to a very eccentric group of customers, and their money was a powerful drug. And they were insatiable. If the eyes were windows to the soul, then Fowler had been blinded long ago. It would not be long before he crossed over completely and became like those he chose to serve.

Back at his studio apartment, Ian searched for his muse among the shadows that lined his walls. He had cleared most of the central space for his work. He had kept only a bed and two ragged chairs in one corner, and installed a slightly con-cave sheet-metal stage with a drain in the middle of the room. The floor he kept bare and polished in case of spatters. The large, two-story high warehouse windows let in plenty of light when he wanted it. But for the most part he kept the monstrous blinds drawn, preferring to work by candlelight, or the dark.

One of his two walk-in freezers still held a few loose ends, but nothing spoke to him as he stood within the drifting mist. It wouldn't do to throw something together with spare parts. He had something in mind, but he needed to gather the right materials.

He stopped first at Anna's place. She lived in a brownstone overlooking the river, and the stench of industrial waste wafted up through closed windows and doors and into kitchens and bedrooms and clung to the clothes hanging in closets. But to-night the air was clear, and Anna answered his knock in nothing but a nightshirt and the black silk underwear he'd bought her for her birthday three weeks before.

"Want a drink?" she asked him as he followed her smooth, bare legs into the kitchen. "I was just going to make up something fun."

"I'll take anything wet."

She took ice from the freezer, threw tequila and a sweet mix into a shaker and poured liquid over misted glass. He heard a soft pop as an ice cube cracked, and took a sip through slightly tender lips.

"Business?"

"You don't want to know."

She shrugged. "You're busy. My sister's in town next week. Will you be too busy for that?" She leaned back against the counter. A slight arch in her spine outlined her nipples against the fabric of her shirt. He took a long, slow look, from blood-painted toes and shapely calves past round hips and tapered waist, up to a face that held a full Spanish mouth and almond-coffee eyes.

"God, you're something. How did I get so lucky?"

"I'm not all that much. And don't try to change the subject."

"You're the most beautiful woman I've ever seen. I'm a frog and you're a princess." He took another mouthful and held it, set the glass on the counter and pulled her shirt up to her shoulders. She shivered as he held an ice cube in his cheek and bent his head to trace a breast with his tongue, blowing frigid air gently across puckered flesh.

Later they lay in darkness across tangled sheets. Ian's sweat trickled down into the hollow of his throat. The air smelled of sex. His lungs burned with every breath.

Anna twisted a strand of hair in long, slender fingers. "I saw ants in the kitchen today," she said. "They were marching in a line from somewhere under the fridge, up and over the counter, and carrying some dried rice from a bowl I'd left out last night. Two of them started fighting so I squished the bigger one with my thumb. And you know what the other one did? He grabbed the dead one by the head and dragged it back down to the floor and out of sight."

"That's gross."

"I know." She sighed. "I kept wondering what he was going to do with the body. Do they eat each other or something?"

"Knock it off, will you?"

"What are we doing, Ian? We've been seeing each other for three months now. I really like you. But you shut me out. I bring up something like my sister coming for a visit and you just fuck me to shut me up."

"It isn't like that at all."

"You have secrets. Where were you tonight? I called your place, the place I've never even *seen*. I don't want to stalk you. But you're playing this mystery man thing too far. Maybe I'll lose interest." She slid a sweat-slick leg out from under his, and wriggled up on one elbow to stare at him.

"It was nothing. I sold some more pictures, that's all."

"Really?" She hunched a little closer. "That's great. Can I see them?"

"Nothing to see. They're just environmental shots, boring stuff." He stood in the dark and put on his shirt and pants. *You wouldn't understand.* What an understatement. "Why don't you make a lunch date with your sister and let me know the time? Call me tomorrow."

~φ~

Hours later he drove back across town, dirt clinging to his clothes and his new materials safely packed away in the rear of his van. He wondered how he slipped so easily between two worlds. A starving artist made an offer he couldn't refuse? But it had been more than that. Years ago he had held several shows in little galleries in New York, mostly mixed-media exhibitions staged by old college friends, Warhol-style trash reshaped and resold, recycled. He had never had Warhol's vision and the public knew it. His true tendencies were darker and more disturbing.

Time after time they turned him away with little or no money in his pocket, and after a while even those few friends who remained stopped lending him space. For several months he wandered, mired in depression and faced with the failure of his life's dream. He never doubted he had talent (or not for long, anyway), but it remained frustratingly coy. It spent less and less of its time with him, and he began to wonder if the struggle was worth it.

He took up work in a meat market, carving up legs of beef and lamb. There he met Fowler. Fowler introduced him to another world that existed between the seams of light and behind every dark alley and shadow. Fowler's clients were the eyes staring at you from the depths of your closet. They were the chill winds lurking at automobile accidents and behind the gaze of serial killers and madmen. Ian didn't think Fowler had understood what he was getting into at the time, any more than Ian had understood himself. But soon it was too late.

He took the old freight elevator from the back lot and lugged his stinking, soggy cargo through quiet corridors. He had to make several trips. It was late and the building was all but deserted anyway; he had seen to that soon after he had moved in, renting the space around him whenever something opened up.

Once inside he lit several thick candles and began to pace the floor, seeking that elusive well of creativity. This would be his masterpiece. It would have to be entirely new. And it had to be raw. He would create something born from the butcher's block, an assembly of everything foul and bloody the mind could imagine. They would be astonished, amazed, excited to a frenzy of lust. And they would pay with the almighty dollar.

Ian slipped his tools from their place on the wall. This section of the huge room resembled a medieval torture chamber, a look he had purposely cultivated for mood. Unfinished brick ran dark with water stains, edges of bone-scraping steel winked and smiled from hooks. Stravinski's Mavra playing softly in the background, he crouched on the giant metal basin and separated the limbs of the two corpses, a child and its mother, with blade and saw. He paid careful attention to the areas less preserved from lying in particular positions. Slime and clotted blood quickly covered his hands. He did not wear his gloves, for this would be a creation close to his heart, an intimate relation.

After he finished with them he went to his freezer for more parts. His mind danced with imaginative multiple-headed creatures, three legs and no eyes, muscle and bone outside of skin. But these were only previews of the climax of his talent. A kind of frenzy overtook him. He had the answer floating about in his head, not to hide the manipulations of the flesh, but to show-case them, emphasize every unnatural joint and union.

For this he took a coroner's needle and thick, black thread, working with slippery skin and mating it to bone. A woman's breast became a truncated child's limb, a fingerless hand punching its way through exposed ribs. Eyes without lids glared upward through a membrane of stomach lining. A layer of teeth planted themselves amid a pucker of flesh. Ian sliced and hammered holes, brought flesh together and ripped it apart with a violence he had previously held in check. Layer built upon layer, both intricate and roughly sculpted visions of death.

He worked through the dawn and into the afternoon. The candles burned down to nubs. The only sign of time passing was a slight glow around his heavy blinds. He lost himself in a feverish, glittery delirium.

Finally, as night fell once again across the city beyond, he stood in aching silence and observed what had grown up out of his studio floor. Candlelight flickered upon the backs of the dead. Black thread like veins lay everywhere, up one seam and down another. Toothless mouths turned to wombs, gave birth to things unmentionable. Limbs reached up and clawed the sky in agony.

Ian retched into the drain as traces of old booze turned his insides out and left him shaking and sore. A hand wiped across his mouth left a foul-smelling, slippery trail. He stood and held the heaves in check. His camera was within easy reach. Ian fumbled for it, every pore tingling at the raw power of the thing, stomach lurching and rolling. He had never before had the feeling that he had captured what his mind had been striving to create; he always felt empty, unfulfilled, as if somewhere along the line he had stumbled off track.

But this, this was perfect.

~φ~

He took to the streets the following evening to work off the ache in his legs. He had slept like the dead for a full day and woke to a clear head. He had created something unimaginable. Pornography for the supernatural. Demons did not exactly orgasm, as he understood it. But the pictures set off an erotic reaction that was both frenzied and powerful. And the Taratcha always wanted more, however satiated they might seem at first. How he could create something that might satisfy them the next time around made his blood run cold.

Anna wouldn't understand any of it. He had kept her from his secret so far, but it was only a matter of time before she saw something.

Then there was the matter of his immortal soul. Ian had begun to sense the changes. Driving past the scene of a car accident, he would catch himself drooling a little, wanting to stop and run his fingers through pools of blood. The visits to the morgue were swiftly becoming less business-like and more pleasurable, the sight of those lifeless, cold-blue limbs making him hard in the trousers. Not such an unusual reaction, he reasoned, after so much effort and time spent in the company of such things, but nonetheless it was dangerous. He had never intended this to be his lifetime work.

By full dark he found himself in an area of nightclubs and movie houses, neon lights blinking in and out. Twenty-four hour peep shows beckoned from behind half-lidded windows. There were people of all sorts here, businessmen scurrying home in trench coats like roaches before the sun, hookers and transvestites, bikers, drug addicts with starved faces and bruises up their arms.

Sandwiched between a tattoo parlor and a sex toys shop was a tiny wooden door with a sign above it that read *Gatehouse*. Ian ducked through into a narrow stairwell that smelled of urine, and followed it down into dim silence. The stairs seemed to go down much further than they should. The last time he'd been here was almost five years ago, when he first grappled with the details of his craft. The Gatehouse had likely saved his life then, and now with a little luck it would give him the key to saving himself again.

The place was like an oasis between worlds. Occult objects, books and charms crammed the walls, alongside the latest scientific texts. Drugs of all kinds helped prepare the mind for new experiences. If you sat down at the table near the back and had your fortune read you might never get up again, for this fortune was real, and as so many customers had found, reality was often painfully blunt.

"So what is it this time?" The voice came seemingly out of nowhere. "Looking for demon repellent? A little soul patching? Or are you already too far gone for that?"

"Come out where I can see you, Frost."

"Nervous, eh? Ah, you're human yet." A shadow flickered and a small, lithe form materialized from the back. It was difficult to say whether the wrinkled, hairless creature that came forward was female or male, or whether it had been hiding or simply appeared out of thin air. Ian chose to believe the latter, in both cases.

"I thought you would have come earlier," Frost said. "I imagined you were dead. You've held up well, considering." He stepped closer and peered into Ian's face. One claw-like finger reached up and traced the line of his jaw. "Though they've taken their toll on you, haven't they?"

Ian nodded. "I want out."

Frost chuckled. "We all say that."

"I mean it. I've done it for the last time."

"But you like it, don't you? Or is that what you're afraid of, that you'll become like them?"

Frost had always had an unsettling ability to find the heart of the matter. He had his feet firmly placed in both worlds. Knowing someone had been there before was an odd comfort. "Fowler's lost already," Ian said, surprised to find his voice shaking. "He wants me to keep going as much as they do. He gets off on it now. I can't get rid of him."

"You're afraid he'll come after you? Why don't you just kill him?"

"I don't kill people. And I'm not sure he wouldn't just... come back."

"I see." Frost stood almost a head shorter than Ian, his skull moist and gleaming under the yellow light. There was no way of telling his age. His ears were curiously withered and his face looked like a half-eaten apple. "He might at that. Unless you catch him."

"What do you mean?"

"You've heard of the tribes in South America that are afraid of cameras? Do you know why? They believe the camera has the ability to trap the soul. Not entirely true. But they can trap other things."

"I don't get it."

"Taratcha are creatures of the night. They live off fear, the inability to see what might be coming. If you are able to photograph one it will remain caught on film."

"Forever?"

"Until such time as you choose to look at the prints." Frost smiled. "They can get very angry at a trick like that. I'll leave the details up to you. But it seems to me that it could be the answer you're looking for."

"Thank you, Frost."

"There's the matter of payment? Even otherworldly advice isn't free."

Ian handed over a wad of bills and turned to leave. Frost caught him at the door. "Ever wonder where things like that come from?"

"What do you mean?"

"Demons. Taratcha. The sort that you might call your customers."

"I assumed they were once like us. In Fowler's case, he's a greedy bastard. I always thought he would change completely, given the time."

"It's something to think about."

"Are there other things I should be thinking about?"

Frost shrugged. "I won't tell you everything, that wouldn't be fair. But I will tell you this: be true to yourself. And be careful, Ian Quinn. They're closer than you think."

~φ~

Closer than you think. Frost's words followed him home. Had he made an unforgivable error in judgment? Was getting rid of Fowler not the answer after all?

As he stepped around the corner near his building, a shape slipped from the shadows into the light of a streetlamp. "If I didn't know any better I'd think you were avoiding me," Anna said. She wore a white tank top and jeans that clung to her curves. She'd put her black hair up, loose strands curling down to kiss her neck. "I've been calling your cell and getting voice-mail."

"I turned it off," Ian said. "Needed some sleep. And the landlord's been looking for rent and I'd rather not talk to him."

"You want to know how I found you. I knew you lived in this neighborhood and drove around a couple of blocks until I saw your van. It needs a wash." She wrinkled her nose. "*You* need a wash."

"Water's off." He shrugged. "What can I say, I'm a little behind..."

"Why don't you come back to my place. I can cook you something nice, get you cleaned up."

"I really should get some work done."

"We need to talk, Ian." She crossed her arms over her breasts and did not step any closer. "Come with me right now, please. I need to know what's going on."

Back at her apartment Anna busied herself in the kitchen while Ian stood under white-hot needles of spray, washing what felt like months of grime from his skin. He hung his head under the water and breathed slowly through his mouth. Something floated and spun in the circling pattern of drain water. He waited until the water finally turned from light gray to clear, and then he stepped onto a fluffy, sage-green bathmat and toweled himself until his flesh stung.

He dressed in one of Anna's oversized t-shirts and sweat-pants and went into the living room while she worked in the kitchen. He took a photo album from the bookshelf, sat on the couch and flipped through its pages. Here stood Anna as a girl with a smiling man and woman, in front of a Tudor with well-trimmed shrubs; Anna in a softball uniform; vacations with white sand beaches and cruise ships the size of small continents; a series shot against a lush mountain backdrop with another woman with similar features. They wore backpacks with sleeping bags strapped to the sides. Each shot perfectly captured a smile or look, a gesture or a thought held in someone's expression.

The smell of food made his mouth water. In the kitchen, Anna had placed a full plate of chops, rice and beans on the wooden farmer's table. She watched him rip into the meal with a half-formed smile on her face. "It's almost morning, but I thought you needed something meaty. At least someone will eat my cooking."

"Right now, I'll eat anything."

She elbowed him in the ribs and tucked one foot under her in the chair. "So where were you coming from tonight?"

"I had to take some photos of the waterfront for a client. They're going to rebuild."

"You didn't have a camera."

"Yeah, well." He shrugged. "I was scouting the location."

"Are you seeing someone else, Ian?"

"Of course not."

"Then why won't you tell me the truth?"

"It's none of your business, Anna."

"When I've been sleeping with someone for a while I kind of expect things to move forward. I like you, Ian, you're funny, sweet, sensitive. But I don't like your secrets."

"I've got a dark side."

"I want to see that too."

"You've got to understand something about me. My work, it's like another woman I'm in love with. I can't just let her go, and I can't share her with you. The two of you wouldn't mix."

"How do you know? Maybe that could be fun. You should try me, you might be surprised." She took a deep breath as if gathering courage. "You know what I think? You're scared of a boring life. Wife, kids, house in the suburbs. You think it's death. You think you can't have that and still do what you do. Maybe you need the darkness, depression moves you, am I right? If you were happy, you'd lose your hold on that creative muse. But what good is it to shut yourself off from everyone who loves you, just because you're afraid of what might happen?"

"It isn't like that."

"No? You tell me then. I'm in love with you, Ian. I'm willing to take the next step. I'd like to meet that other woman. But I can't be in a relationship like this, not anymore. You let me know if you ever decide you'd like to let me in."

~φ~

He had left the blinds in his apartment closed. But when he opened the door they had been pulled back, bright early morning sunlight streaming down onto the stinking flesh on his sheet metal stage. A moment later, Fowler came strolling out from the little kitchen alcove, eyes hidden behind dark glasses. "Magnificent," he breathed. His jowls trembled with something like lust. "You've topped yourself yet again. I didn't think you had it in you."

"You son of a bitch," Ian said. "If any of them followed you here —"

"Get real." Fowler swept a hand towards the window. "It's light out, or haven't you noticed? Tends to hurt my eyes, and it makes them scream. If they want to know where you live, they'll find you without any help from me."

Ian grabbed his camera from the table. He fixed Fowler through the sticky lens, found the image of the man with his palms up, gesturing. "Hey —"

Click. The flash popped and whined; bright light painted the interior of the room. Fowler winced. "Jesus Christ, will you cut it out? Hurts my eyes..."

Click. Pop. Another wince and a muttered breath. Ian let the camera drop to his chest. Fowler was still there.

"What the hell did you do that for?"

"You looked good standing next to it."

"Yeah. Well, don't do it again." Fowler's eyes momentarily glowed red through the dark lenses and then faded. "You ain't so cute either, you know that? You ought to look in the mirror once in a while." He moved to the door. "Get me those prints." He stole one more glance back at the creation lying still upon the bloodied silver platform, the longing plain in his face. Ian imagined him caressing its gory flanks, leaning down to touch his lips to slippery flesh. And then he was gone.

Not yet. Ian pounded a fist into his palm. Fowler would not be so easy to trap. He would have to find another way.

~φ~

Late that night the solution came to him. Like most solutions born of desperation, this one came upon him by chance.

He had long since gone to bed, but sleep wouldn't come at first. He couldn't yet bring himself to disassemble his masterwork. And so it sat, alone on its altar like the remains of blood worship. Ian had begun to think of it as more than his Art, a testimony to all he had accomplished, a showcase of his talent. More than that, it was his child; and as frightened as he was with that thought, he no longer had the strength within himself to be disgusted by it.

He did not know when he slept or when exactly he awakened, but for a moment the flitting shadow shapes and crawling, tentacled dream creatures remained with him. The huge loft sat black and silent as a tomb. He lay there blinking up into the dark until his bladder forced him out of bed.

When he flicked on the bathroom light he almost screamed at the image glaring back at him through the mirror. Heavy brows overshadowed sunken, bruised eyes with a spark of red at their centers. He flicked the light off again and stood blinking in the dark. Fowler was right. He hadn't noticed how far it had progressed. But it was a reversible transformation. It had to be.

Something nagged at his mind. It was all too easy to think of the *Taratcha* as simply evil given form and substance, part of an ongoing underworld war, a system of checks and balances between lightness and dark. But that alone did not give them definition. It did not make them real. Now, with the image of his own face floating like a ghost in the blackness that surrounded him, he began to understand their true essence. Creatures born from a collective unconscious. Trace memory of a human race too savage to bear the light. The monster under the bed, the spark behind a pedophile's eyes. The stuffing of a madman's brain. They were *human* creations, weren't they? And what better place for the birth of a demon than within the dark heart of an artiste?

He was almost too late. When he heard movement behind him he whirled, aware of a dim, reddish glow that wholly human eyes would never have registered. The bathroom door hung open, and beyond it came the sound of something sliding across a slick surface.

Padding silently on bare feet he slipped around the door-frame, and kept to the wall as he felt his way around the circumference of the room. His camera hung with the rest of his tools. With one motion he turned, stepped forward and brought it to his eyes. Only then did he look at what it was he had created.

It dragged itself slowly along, tiny child arms waggling, grasping with bony fingers at the place he had been. Seams of black thread joined and divided an endless expanse of puckered flesh, opening and closing like a thousand tiny mouths. Ends of bone poked out like porcupine quills. Eyes like white-fisted tumors bulged and rolled under skin stretched tight as a bruise. A snail's trail of dark fluid marked its path from the metal stage to the floor.

A demon's first steps. Laughter was Ian's first thought; this thing, searching blindly out for *him*, its creator, whatever purpose that drove it held deep inside its bloated depths and hidden from view. What would it do if it found him? Was this patricide? Or would it welcome him with open arms?

His second thought was less defined. As the creature turned and sought him with some blind sense and a voice like a thousand shrieks filled his head, he centered the frame and pushed the trigger. White light painted the room like a flare. The shrieks reached a sudden raging crescendo. He had the fleeting sense of a forest of waving limbs, frozen in time. For a moment the doorway opened itself to him as through the camera's window he glimpsed an army of impossible creatures writhing like a mound of earthworms within a tightfisted cavern of dripping stone. Then he remembered nothing, aware only of a strange feeling of loss, his own voice repeating the same phrase over and over like the words to a forgotten ritual in the sudden silence of the loft.

I'm sorry. I didn't know.

~φ~

Fowler waited for him in their regular booth. He looked up as Ian approached, and this time he could not hide the hunger in his eyes.

"Jesus, you take your goddamned time," Fowler said. His voice buzzed like a radio losing its signal. Or was it something more? The sound of a man slipping between the cracks?

"Sorry. It won't happen again, believe me."

Fowler seemed appeased by Ian's attitude. But he paused when the leather portfolio slid across the moistened table, something in Ian's own eyes making him uncertain. He sensed a change here, a new confidence and strength that made him curious. Then the hunger seemed to overwhelm everything else. Fowler's fingers touched the fold, opened it. "Wait," Ian said. "I don't want you to look at them yet."

"Why the hell not?"

"Trust me on this. Take the portfolio and bring it back to me later. You'll want to be alone."

Fowler's chubby hand shot out and grabbed Ian's forearm. The grip held a little bit of desperation in it. Fowler's fingers tightened, digging. "Ever see what the *Taratcha* do to a man? They're not happy with killing you. They want you to live with the pain."

Ian resisted the overpowering urge to shrug off the touch the way you might shrug off a bug. "I get it."

"If you're planning to cut out on me, think again. One word from me and you're gone. Anybody you love, gone. Get that?"

"Whatever you say."

"You know, I didn't take to your new look at first. But I gotta tell you, it's an acquired taste. Keep your chin up, as they say."

Ian remained at the table for a long time after Fowler had gone. He did not touch the thick envelope that had been left for him. He ordered a drink, then another, gathering his courage.

The feeling of loss had remained with him for the rest of that night and into the morning. He had seen something in the thing, as gruesome as it was. Some spark of recognition, some kind of empathy.

The Art was the only thing he had ever truly been good at, and yet a part of him had always been ashamed. In his younger years he had frequently been asked where the darker sides of his talent came from, and when he tried in vain to answer he would often be faced with a look of pity or even guarded mistrust. What are you hiding, they seemed to be saying. His only reply was that he did not know.

The dim light in the bar hurt his eyes. Ian walked to the empty bathroom, hit the switch and stood in the dark, bent over the sink and holding the cool porcelain with both hands. Finally he looked up. The mirror over the sink revealed a face that burned with its own light. He looked inward through his mind's eye and saw a sea of writhing shapes, breeding and dividing.

He imagined Fowler's trembling fingers as they slipped open the leather flap, drew out the photographs, brought them close to his face. Imagined the explosion of flesh as his offspring, his spawn, did the work it had been born to do.

You let me know if you ever decide to let me in. He dug his cell phone out of his pocket and switched it on. He didn't know if he could survive when these two worlds collided, but he had to stop hiding. It was time to find out whether his two loves could co-exist.

It took only a moment for Anna to answer. ◣

Gravedigger

Bobby DeCourci slipped a middle finger inside the dead woman, probing upward until he reached resistance. In up to the third knuckle. The feeling was like the pocket of a windbreaker on a wet day, slick and cool and loose, nothing like a live one. Not that he'd felt that in some time. He wasn't one to get a lot of pussy, not since the accident. And Damon never let him forget it, the shithead.

He hooked his nail on the package and pulled gently. It slipped out of the vaginal opening with a slight sucking sound and fell into his waiting hand. A simple plastic baggie, filled with what looked like white flour and coated with fresh semen.

"Gotcha," he said aloud.

"Yeah?" Damon said from across the room. Bobby glanced over. He thought (not for the first time) that Damon was like a boil situated at that one place on your back; a boil you want desperately to pop, but can't quite reach. They had been working together in this goddamn basement for almost five years now, keeping time with the dead, and he found that on the whole he'd rather spend time with a corpse than the only other living thing in the room.

The man's hunched shoulders shook as he scrubbed himself at the sink. Bobby grinned. He'd been worried for a moment, but Damon was so fucking tiny he hadn't even felt the package in there, even as he went at the woman on the slab like a rabbit on speed.

It had ended in a minute, tops. The pervert couldn't even satisfy the dead.

"Nothing," he muttered. *Keep scrubbing, Casanova.* He slipped the baggie in his coat pocket and went back to work draining fluids from the woman's body. She was in her late thirties, judging by her face and the flesh on her hips. Her breasts were like deflated gray balloons lying on her chest, and the skin around her eyes was unnaturally taut. Had some work done already, Bobby thought. Probably came from money. His family, money was a four-letter word. His own mother had lived off welfare in the same trailer for damn near thirty years after his father had run out on them, and when she died she turned it over to him along with a credit card bill and a kitchen drawer full of expired coupons. He had tossed the coupons, dragged one bookcase full of glass gnomes and crystal snowflakes to the curb, turned the rug in the living room the other direction and called it his own.

Bobby looked down at the bags of flesh and sighed. Embalming someone was a bitch. Most people thought being an undertaker would be creepy, but the bulk of it was damn practical. It was all just dead meat that had to be cleaned up and prepared for viewing. But it wasn't pretty. There was all the sewing they needed to do, and the makeup to cover up the damage. In the end, Bobby always thought they looked like a wax doll. Yessir, cremation was the way to go. The alternative, slow rot in a wooden box buried six feet under with the worms, was plain fucking nuts.

As he slipped a second needle into the woman's right arm, her finger twitched.

"Jesus!" Bobby said, jumping back from the table. His feet slipped and he nearly went down.

"What's the problem?"

"She moved."

"Fuck *off*." Damon rubbed himself with a towel and hitched up his pants. "Where?"

"Her finger."

"Oh oh oh, do me baby!" Damon sang in a falsetto voice as he slid across the room on his socks. *"Do the humpty hump…"*

"Shut up," Bobby said.

"Tell me the truth. You on drugs again? You know what happened the last time. Man, I'll never forget the way you looked – cheek like raw hamburger. That was some fucked up shit."

Bobby touched a hand to the nasty purple scar that ran across his left cheekbone, over his lips and underneath his jaw, a self-conscious gesture that had long ago become a habit. The dog had chewed on him for a while before losing interest. He'd been so high he hadn't felt a thing, and when he woke up and tried to light a cigarette he was shocked to discover his mouth wouldn't hold onto it properly. He'd looked at himself in the mirror and found his lower lip hanging by a thread of skin.

It wasn't until almost ten minutes later that he'd noticed Stella lying dead on the kitchen tile.

"No, dickhead, I'm not using." He shivered. He'd been clean ever since, almost three years now. *Never again.* Not that he didn't want it; not that he didn't crave it, every single day. He just knew that to start up again would mean death, that he would not be able to stop, no matter what happened to him, and that sooner or later he would end up on one of these tables, with someone else sticking the line into his veins to drain him dry.

Like Stella...

"Just look at the finger, okay?"

"Which hand?"

Bobby pointed to the woman's offending digit and swallowed, feeling the click of his dry throat. Dry as a bone. Like her pussy. Damon had squirted on the lube before he entered her, or even that baby carrot dick wouldn't have had a chance of getting up in there.

Damon leaned in close. He sniffed the finger and licked it. "Mmmm, chicken."

"You are a major asshole, you know that?"

"Reflex, Bobby-G. She's dead as a doornail. Don't you want a piece? You gonna stay all high and mighty forever?"

Bobby shook his head. He didn't want to go anywhere near that thing. *Reflex, my ass.* She'd been dead at least twenty-four hours. He told Damon so.

"Okay, wait. You put that line in there. That's your answer. Must have missed the vein and pumped her muscle."

"I didn't miss shit."

"Sure you did." Damon was nodding. "See, right here –"

A noise from beyond the closed doors made them both turn. A man in a black leather jacket walked in. He was the size of a pro linebacker, and Bobby thought he'd probably played ball at one time, or maybe it was boxing, judging from his flattened, crooked nose. Hair shaved close to the scalp, ice-colored eyes. Looked sort of like Rutger Hauer on 'roids.

Had to be J.D.'s guy, but he was way too early and Bobby had never seen him before. He obviously didn't know the drill. Knock twice, come in like you're the janitor, clean out the trash basket by the door and leave the payment under the fresh bag at the bottom. Everything neat and simple. They'd been running this system for a long time, and Damon never caught on, which was good, because they all knew that first he would have demanded a piece of the action, and then he would have screwed things up somehow, most likely by opening his big fat mouth to the wrong person. J.D. knew Damon from way back (they'd grown up together, in fact), and he wouldn't trust him as far as he could spit. Bobby would trust him about two feet less than that.

"Who the fuck're you?" Damon said. Surprise made him look like a mental defective, and it took him a moment to recover. "You can't come in here."

"He's a friend of mine," Bobby said quickly. "Name's Sam."

"It's Rocko," the man said. "Fucking douchebag." He walked over to Damon's scraggly, chicken-winged form and put a hand the size of a dinner plate on his face, palming his skull. He gave a shove. Damon flew backward into a rack of surgical equipment, which clattered to the floor.

Damon sat up and skittered backward on his palms and feet until he reached the wall, little patch of hair on his chin quivering. A few strands of his dirty blond hair had come loose from the ponytail he kept tight against the back of his neck. "You – you can't do that shit!" he said. "What the fuck? I'm calling the cops! You hear me shithead? I'm calling —"

Rocko took a step in his direction and Damon put his hands up. "Hey, easy, listen, I'm kidding with you, man, understand? Just fucking around. No harm done, okay?" He swiped at a thin line of blood that trickled from the corner of his mouth. "Look, I'm fine, I'm cool."

Rocko nodded in the direction of Damon's groin. "Zip up your fuckin' pants," he said. Then he turned to Bobby. "Where is it?" he asked.

"Where's what?" Damon said from the corner. "We've got nothing of yours. I swear!"

Rocko stared at Bobby and sighed. His eyes were as lifeless as the corpse of the woman that lay next to him on the table. He hadn't looked once at her.

"Does he always run his mouth this fuckin' much?" Rocko said.

"Only after he's gotten laid," Bobby said. "Pillow talk, you know."

Rocko nodded, as if that was the most natural thing in the world to say at that moment. He slid a hand into his jacket pocket. "J.D.'s changing his approach. Seems to think you might be taking some off the top. I'm here to find out if that's true."

"You got it all wrong, man. Tell J.D. there's nothing like that going on."

"I wanna take a look myself. So. You gonna make me ask you for it again?"

Bobby shook his head. A bead of sweat slid from his temple and ran down his cheek. He didn't want to look rattled. "I'd prefer to talk outside," he said.

It was then that the woman on the table sat up.

~φ~

"*mmmmmmph,*" the dead woman said. "*plmmmmmnnnnahhhh-hhhlrrrrrm.*" Her neck cracked as she turned to stare at them. Her dead eyes rolled, purple skin across her cheeks shiny-tight with bloat. She lifted a hand, fingers plump and gray as uncooked sausages, and reached out, as if in pain.

Stella she looks like my Stella dead on the kitchen floor—

"Holy fucking shit!" Damon jumped up, stumbled against the equipment scattered at his feet and pressed his back against the wall. "Sit the fuck down, you crazy bitch!" He picked up a stainless steel bowl and threw it at her. The bowl struck the woman in the shoulder and clattered to the floor.

Slowly, very slowly, she turned her head and looked at him.

"Bobby, what the fuck is this! Huh? What the fuck?"

"Shut up, Damon," Bobby said slowly. Something was very wrong here, but his brain just couldn't seem to process things properly. Somehow he and Rocko had ended up against the other wall near the refrigerator unit door, although for the life of him he could not remember moving away from the thing on the table.

His voice hadn't seemed to work at first either; now his eyes were on Rocko, who had pulled a very large gun from his jacket. The gun barrel went from the woman, to Damon, to Bobby and back again.

I must be losing my fucking mind.

Bobby tried to make his brain start moving again, but everything seemed to be coated in a thick fog. This could not be happening, of course. Somehow he had fallen asleep, or Damon had slipped him something in that Pepsi they'd shared earlier. Damon was having a good laugh on him.

Bobby could see Rocko's finger tightening on the trigger. The room seemed to sharpen at once and snap back into place. He showed Rocko both palms. "Take it easy," he said. He looked at Damon. "Go check on her," he said.

"Are you fucking *crazy?* I'm not going anywhere near that nightmare." Damon shook his head and blood from his split lip spattered on the wall. The woman moaned, as if in answer.

"Look," Bobby said. "Obviously she's not dead. We gotta help her."

"You *drained* her, man." Damon pointed to the needle and line that still ran from the woman to a half-full bag of dark fluid. Purple rigor mortis marks leered like old tattoos sketched across her right side. "You gotta be high if you think she's anything but worm food. She's been dead since yesterday, you said it yourself."

"I don't know what's going on, okay?" Bobby said. "Maybe some kind of coma? Just get over there and check her pulse. Just do it."

"Oh, man." Damon shook his head again, took a step and then skittered backward again, took another couple of steps, reaching out tentatively, licking his lips. "I gotta be nuts. They don't pay me anywhere near enough for this shit. Okay. Okay." He took another step, only a couple of feet away from the table now. "You okay lady? You hear me?"

The woman just stared at him.

A high keening noise escaped his mouth, sounding like air leaking from a balloon. He glanced back. *"Bobby?"*

"Her name is Denise. Just check her. Then we'll call 911."

"Hold on," Rocko said. "Nobody's calling no cops." He leveled the gun at Bobby's face. "Where's my stuff?"

Bobby moved his hand slowly, very slowly to his coat pocket. "Right here. No problem. Just take it easy, okay?" He reached in and pulled out the baggie, but something was wrong. It shifted in his hands and he felt the contents draining away, and when he looked down he saw the zipper lock had come open and white powder was falling in a soft, slow drift to the tile floor. In spite of himself, even as his gut dropped to his shoes, he licked his ruined lips, thinking of the feeling that powder would give him, if only he were able to use it. Such a terrible waste.

Oh, shit.

The package had drawn their attention away from the table, but two things happened at once to change things in a right goddamned hurry: Rocko cocked the gun, which sounded very loud in the sudden quiet of the room; and the naked woman on the table lunged forward with astonishing speed, grabbing Damon's head with both hands and burying her teeth in his right cheek.

Jesus, she...she bit him...like...just like a dog.

Damon screamed and threw himself backward, pulling the woman off the table and into his arms. They tottered across the floor like two awkward dancers in a lover's embrace, and the woman grunted and tore at his face with her mouth, then went lower, at his neck.

Something popped in there, and Damon screamed again, beating at her back with both fists. Bright red blood spurted across the woman's face and hair. She dropped to her knees and pulled Damon's pants down with one savage yank, exposing his tiny, shriveled penis in its thatch of gray-blond hair. The dead woman grimaced, showing bloody teeth, or perhaps it was a smile.

Then she leaned in and bit down hard.

Damon let out a gurgling scream. The sound of gristle tearing and ripping could be heard clearly across the room as she jerked her head and came away with a morsel of flesh.

A moment later her head came up and she turned on her knees, sniffing the air. She let go of Damon, who fell to the floor, legs kicking, blood still pumping from the gaping wound in his neck, flap of skin dangling from his cheek. His heels drummed on the tile.

The woman sniffed again like a blind dog on a scent. She cocked her head at where Rocko and Bobby stood near the refrigerator door.

Rocko's gun barked and the woman's head snapped back. A small, round hole appeared neatly between her eyes. She didn't seem to care much, just stood up and began to shuffle forward, gaining speed quickly.

If Rocko was surprised by this latest development, he didn't show it. "Get the fuck in there, now," he said quietly, motioning at the stainless steel door with the gun. Bobby nodded and swung it open, and the two of them ducked in, slamming the door shut and putting their backs against it a second before the woman hit it with a shuddering thump.

"Did you see that? Did you see it?" Bobby shook with adrenaline, his stomach churning. "Bit him. Jesus Christ." He still held the now half-empty baggie, and he stuck it back in his pocket, wiping his hand on his jeans. He shuddered.

Then he threw up.

Dear Lord, Bobby thought, retching again, the smell and taste of vomit thick in his throat, *I know I've been a useless mess most of my life. I know I don't deserve it. But if you get me out of here I swear I'll turn it around. I'll—*

"The fuck happened to your face, anyway?" Rocko said. The woman was still throwing herself at the door, thumps and bangs rattling their teeth.

"My…" Bobby wiped puke from his mouth with the back of his hand, and touched his cheek again. "Who cares about my goddamned face? There's a goddamn *zombie* in the other room. How about that, huh? How about we hash *that* one out before I tell you my life story?"

"Just making conversation," Rocko said. He checked the

gun and snapped the clip back into the handle. "Thought it might be relevant, you know, to the situation. Give me an idea on whether you're going to flip out on me. That bitch may be stupid, but she's still dangerous. I gotta know who I'm dealing with in here."

"How do you know she's stupid? What happens if she figures out how to open this door?"

"She won't."

"Says you. Who the fuck are you, anyway? Where's J.D.'s regular guy?"

"He's dead," Rocko said. "I killed him."

"You *killed* him? Why?"

"It's a long story." Rocko seemed to look around the room for the first time. "Goddamn meat locker in here. What is this place?"

Bobby looked up then, finally focusing on where they were, and what he saw chilled his blood more than the refrigerated air ever could. Three dead bodies lay under white sheets on rolling steel gurneys, and he knew that several more lurked behind the closed doors of the storage units. *Latched, thank God for small favors.*

The Augusta morgue pulled bodies from no less than eight different small towns in the immediate area. There had been seven deaths during the past two days. An Edward Needleman from White Falls, Marlene Marcus and a John Doe from Augusta, a Jen Seigel from Wiscasset, and the lovely and talented Denise James *(currently starring in Lifestyles of the Rich and Dead, right outside your door)* – those were the names he remembered. There were others. Maybe more than seven in here, behind those locker doors, waiting patiently for their time on the slab.

Or waiting for something else. For some reason his mind flashed to a scene he'd imagined many times over the past three years, his Stella, the love of his life, dead of an overdose that should have been his, lying silent and still inside a coffin buried six feet underground, her arms crossed on her chest, her body collapsing into itself, lips and eyes slowly melting away to nothing. Waiting.

"It's...where we store all the corpses," Bobby said. He hesitated, staring at the nearest bare toes peeking out from under the sheets. Feminine toes, still painted pink. "You don't think…"

"Let me see your hands," Rocko said. He stuck the gun in his pocket and pulled out a metal flask.

"Why —"

"Just do it."

Bobby stuck out his hands, palms up. Rocko unscrewed the flask and poured liquid over them. The smell of high-proof alcohol burned Bobby's nostrils. Rocko rubbed it into his skin. "Everclear," he said. "Gets rid of the residue. Where's the baggie?"

"In my pocket." Bobby started to reach for it, and Rocko slapped his hand away.

"Don't touch it," he said. "Did you reseal the bag?"

"I think so. Why? What the hell's going on?"

Rocko didn't look at Bobby, and at first it seemed it might be out of embarrassment, but then Bobby realized he was watching the corpses. "I'm not exactly J.D.'s best friend, you catch my drift. I knew what you guys were doing here. Smuggling blow inside of dead bodies? Fucking genius, I said. But J.D. didn't like me cutting in. I had to get creative."

"You killed him," Bobby said.

"No, I killed his partner, like I told you. That part was true. They were faggots, you know. J.D. drew down on me. I needed leverage."

"What kind of leverage did that get you? Why wouldn't J.D. just kill you?"

"Because he was in love with the guy, and I was the only one who could get the stuff that would bring him back."

Bring him…? Bobby shook his head. "You're crazy," he said. "Plain as vanilla, shit-house nuts."

"Oh yeah? What about Denise out there," Rocko said. "She a figment of my crazy imagination?"

"I…" and then he understood. "It's the powder," Bobby said. "That's right, isn't it? Some of it got into her, down there."

"Regular Shiloh Holmes," Rocko said, and Bobby didn't bother to correct him. It didn't matter.

What mattered was that the flask was back in the man's pocket, and the gun was out again.

And what was worse (much, much worse, in fact), was that said gun was pointing directly at Bobby's face.

A bullet between the eyes might not slow down Denise James, Bobby thought, but he was pretty damn sure it would put a real damper on *his* future plans.

"Here's the deal," Rocko said in a low voice. "That woman's been dead too long for her to do more than stumble through the dark. Her bulb's burned out, you catch my drift? And they need a little more of that Gravedigger powder every few minutes to keep walking around. I haven't heard a noise from the other room in a while now, which makes me wonder if maybe she just fell back down dead again."

He was right, Bobby realized; the thumpings at the door had stopped.

"What do you want from me?" he said.

"I want you to open up that door, real slow, and stick your head out to see what's going on. You do that, and if it's cool, I'll let you leave. You don't, and I'll shoot you in the leg first, before I throw you out there. They love the smell of blood. You can play spin the bottle with Denise. Or something else. Maybe she'll give you one of those special blowjobs, on the house."

Bobby looked at him. Rocko smiled, but his eyes were still dead. He motioned with the gun. "Get out there, hotshot, before I change my mind."

~φ~

By the time he'd gathered up his courage enough to crack open the door, Bobby had it all pretty much figured out; Rocko was smuggling something way beyond regular old blow, something that might just be goddamned near the holy grail. *Live forever, even if you're dead.* Where it came from, who the hell knew, but J.D. must have had a pretty good idea of how the stuff worked for him to believe his partner could be resurrected. Whether he was in on all this from the beginning or not didn't really matter.

The simple fact was, this stuff was worth a lot more than any other shipment that had ever come through here. And that meant it was way too valuable to let little old Bobby live to tell the tale.

So you're a dead man if you stay in here, and you're very likely a dead man if you go out there. Pick your poison.

Bobby ached for a little bit of something to calm his nerves. Just a little pinch would make all this go away for the wet parts, or at least not matter as much. But that wouldn't really help him, now would it? No. So what if it dulled the pain when Denise started ripping out his throat. The end was the same.

Rocko tapped the gun barrel against the back of his head. Bobby took a deep breath and cracked the door.

The room outside appeared empty. He could just see Damon's shoes, speckled with blood. No movement.

He pushed the door open a little bit wider, heart hammering in his throat, and got a full view of Damon's bloody corpse lying on the floor. No sign of Denise.

As he peered into the other room, Bobby was aware of a familiar sense of loss. He wasn't quite sure what the feeling meant, only that it was about himself and who he was and why he'd ended up here, of all places. *Always wondered if I had a death wish. Way I grew up, always into trouble, like I was looking for it every place I went. Drugs, using and dealing, sort of like dying and coming back to life and then dying again. Little deaths. Waiting for the wrong guy to come along and put a bullet in me. Or maybe just waiting for the wrong pills to fry my brain into oblivion, a dog to tear off my face.*

Stella had been his lifeline, or so he thought. They would get married, move out of his shitty trailer, he'd take a steady job and they have some kids. She was supposed to make it all better. But somehow they'd never gotten there, and now she was dead, just like he would be if he didn't think of something pretty damn fast.

He swallowed and pushed the door all the way open. He could see the dusting of powder that had spilled from the bag when he took it from his pocket. He could not tell whether it had been disturbed. Had there been an entire pile of it before, or just...

"What'd you call that stuff?" he said. "Gravedigger powder?"

"Keep moving," Rocko said at his back. Bobby inched out into the room and scanned right and left. The woman was not there. Equipment was scattered across the floor; bone saws and shears, dissection knives, lab pans and trays, exam gloves spilling from an open packet, Mayo stands tipped like drunken soldiers. Blood from Damon's carotid artery had sprayed like a whipping fire hose across the wall and high window and speckled the storage closet doors, deep sink and centrifuges, making the entire scene look like some kind of surreal modern art exposition in gore.

The door to the hallway was standing wide open. Bobby could just make out what looked like a single faint footprint in blood near the threshold.

"I don't think she's here," he said, legs shaking with relief as he turned back to Rocko. "I think maybe she —"

He heard a sudden scraping noise, and turned to find the naked dead woman exploding out of the storage closet,

(not so stupid after all, now is she)

gray mottled breasts flapping, hitting him low around the waist, like a free safety coming up to stuff the run, and he was flying backward and into Rocko as the gun went off and stitched the ceiling, scattering plaster chips and dust. The impact took him off his feet and drove them both through the door and back into the refrigerator unit, the woman already scrabbling at him as they hit the floor hard and came to rest below the nearest gurney.

Bobby rolled over, then felt his bladder let go with a warm rush as the dead woman's cool, dry fingers ran over his face and neck. He kicked at her and tried to scramble away. He could smell the chemicals on her, the dead flesh already beginning to rot. She bared her teeth, but her hands kept moving lower, and at the same time he became aware of a strange film in the room, coating his face and softening the light until he could see nothing but haloed shapes.

He blinked to clear his sight, and looked down to see Denise James licking white dust from his jacket with a long, gray tongue, her eyes rolled back to whites as her body shuddered as if in release.

Oh, God. God, no. She'd hit him full speed right at the jacket pocket level, and what remained of the bag of gravedigger powder had burst all over him and into the air.

Rocko had smacked his head against the tile floor and was lying motionless, the gun somewhere out of sight. A trickle of blood ran from his mouth. Bobby shoved the woman away from him and tried to get to his feet, but she grabbed him by his legs and began to pull herself up his body with claws as strong as iron. Her wrinkled buttocks clenched, bare feet scrambling against the tile, and he thought of a possum he'd seen as a kid that had been run over in the road, its hind legs crushed, dragging itself across the asphalt.

The powder was everywhere.

He managed to get a hand on the edge of the gurney table, and he was almost upright when something brushed against his fingers. He looked down at his hand to see naked toes wiggling against him from under the gurney's white sheet.

Near hysterics and summoning more strength than he knew he had left, he drove his knee upward and caught Denise James smartly under the chin. Her head snapped back and her grip loosened, and he lashed out at her again in a roundhouse kick, catching her flush on the temple with the top of his shoe. She went down hard, her head hitting the floor with a sickening crack.

Her tongue, her tongue is severed, bitten right through—

The tongue lay on the tile like a fat, purple worm, wriggling of its own accord as if trying desperately to reach him. At that point Bobby very clearly felt one corner of his mind unhinge, and he grinned through what appeared to be a reddish mist that had begun to descend over his eyes. He realized that he'd been wrong before; it wasn't a possum she reminded him of, but a dog. A big, mean bastard that liked to rip into flesh. One with a taste for human blood. He'd seen that dog before, in fact it had haunted his dreams for years; that dog had had a taste of him and found it good, and now it was back for more.

"Gimme back my face!" he screamed, and as she tried to rise he stomped down on her head with everything he had, feeling something crack and give, and then he stomped down again, and this time the feeling was like stepping on a rotten pumpkin out in the field, a bit of resistance and then soft, gooey sickness. He raised a red, dripping sneaker and brought it down one more time, until Denise James's skull was nothing but a shuddering, oozing pulp of cartilage, teeth and muscle. Dimly he heard himself shouting, the sound of a damned man, and through that sound a single clear thought cut its way to the surface: maybe his was not a death wish at all, maybe he was the dead one, maybe death was your mother's trailer in Indian Road park with cinderblock front steps and a clothesline in the back, and a job cutting up corpses with a sociopath for a partner, a fiancé lying cold in the ground from your own bad stash and $75 in the bank with no real way to pay the bills other than smuggling the very thing that had nearly suffocated him before the dog's jaws finally brought him to his knees.

Maybe death was having nothing ahead of you, and nothing behind.

Or maybe it was the face of the stranger that stared back at you from the mirror every morning.

"Gimme back my face," he muttered again, and stumbled backward, away from the ruin that had been Ms. Denise James. Her foot twitched on the tile. He tried not to look at it. His pact with God earlier was no good, he realized now. Because God was dead too. He had to be, if this was how the world ended up.

The wetness of his urine had grown cold and his pants stuck uncomfortably to his skin. He became aware of other sounds in the room. Wet, ripping sounds, and other draggings and hollow thumps. He looked up to see the young, naked woman from the gurney (Jen Siegel from Wiscasset?), her of the pink, wriggling toes, her back to him as she sat astride the jittering body of Rocko. She lowered her face to tear at his neck, and if Bobby hadn't known better, he might have thought it was a lover's embrace and tender kiss.

Gravedigger…

He glanced around the room to see the two other corpses (Edward? Marlene?) rising up off their gurneys like puppets pulled by invisible strings, and he could now clearly make out the sounds of other things thumping against the closed and latched doors of their lockers, the sound like someone beating the hull of a wounded submarine.

Bobby DeCourci screamed.

Jen Seigel's head whipped around at the sound, and she

hissed back at him like a cat before leaping to her feet. Edward and Marlene were up and moving now too (Edward had a bum leg, which made him limp in death as surely as it must have in life), and Bobby stumbled backward, sobbing helplessly now, until he was up against the wall.

It's funny now that I'm facing my own end for real, I find out I wanna live.

Jesus, yes, he did.

I want to live.

He looked around desperately for an opening. There, under the third gurney, was Rocko's gun. As Jen Seigel leaped at him he went low in a baserunner's headfirst dive, sliding across the bloody tile on his stomach and then pulling himself the rest of the way with his arms until the gun was in his hand. Then he rolled out from under the gurney, scrambled to his feet, turned to Edward Needleman and pulled the trigger.

Nothing happened.

Check the safety, you idiot…

He pressed the orange button on the side and then pulled the trigger again.

The gun bucked in his hand and Edward stumbled. He turned to fire twice at Jen Seigel, who had almost reached him now, and she fell sideways. Marlene hung back, watching him warily, a glint of intelligence in her eyes. Was she the freshest corpse? Bobby wondered. He tried to recall what Rocko had said. Something about Denise James being dead too long to remember…

Edward and Jen were back on their feet and coming at him again. He didn't know how many more bullets were left in the gun, and there were too many of them between him and the door. There was no way out.

Something nagged at him as he waved the gun from one to the next, trying to figure out which one to shoot, something about how these people were acting, not quite like animals, but as if they had some semblance of intelligence; Denise James biting off Damon's cock as if in retaliation for his earlier violation, her hiding in the closet and waiting for just the right moment to jump him, and now Marlene looking almost as if she were trying to plan a path of attack.

But it wasn't until Rocko stood up that his way out clicked into place.

And even then, the sheer magnitude of what he was about to do nearly overwhelmed him. He had lived the past few years swearing on his mother's grave he would never touch the stuff again, and yet his body always ached for it. Even now, he felt that ache deep in his belly. Once he stepped back on that path, there was no turning away again...

(...*that to start up again would mean death, that he would not be able to stop, no matter what happened to him, and that sooner or later he would end up on one of these tables, with someone else sticking the line into his veins to drain him dry.*)

But what choice did he have? If he tried to make it to the door, they would rip him apart. None of the corpses seemed to have any interest in each other; for whatever reason (and did the why really matter?), they were interested only in the living. That and the powder that kept them animated.

"Gimme," Rocko said. His voice sounded like he'd swallowed an aquarium full of gravel. His throat was half torn out. One eye was gone, in its place a bloody socket touched with the white gleam of fresh bone. He stumbled forward, silver buckles on his biker jacket tinkling. "I can smell it. Gimmmmeeee..."

Bobby stared at Rocko's ruined face and wondered if he had perhaps lost his own mind. Yes, in fact, that seemed to be a distinct possibility. He put the gun on the gurney, then dug into his jacket pocket and withdrew the popped baggie. A bit left in one of the corners. Then he dumped a small amount of the powder into his other palm and took a deep breath.

Well ain't this ironic, Bobby my man? You spent every waking hour the past three years trying to keep from stuffing blow up your nose and ending up feet first to the furnace, and now it's the only way for you to stay alive. After a fashion, anyway.

He chuckled. Ironic, all right. And as he lifted his palm to his nose, he found himself wondering what Stella might look like after three years in the ground.

The rush hit him almost immediately, that great, sweeping rush, prickles running up and down his limbs and turning his blood to glass. The red haze that had obscured his sight returned, and with it came an almost unbearable itch.

When he opened his eyes again they were almost upon him.

Bobby DeCourci didn't hesitate. He swept the gun up and pressed the barrel to his own chest directly over his heart.

He figured he had just enough powder in him to find J.D. and the source. After that, maybe he'd pay Stella a visit. He wondered again how bad she might look after three years. And after that long, was there enough left of her brain to make her function again after some of this gravedigger powder?

Gravedigger. Keep me sane. Bury me deep, so that I can't rise again…

DeCourci pulled the trigger. ⋈

One With The Music

*A*s soon as she glimpsed it, sitting back there among the dust and clutter, she knew she had found something special. Though if it was the one, if it was the very one she had been searching for, she heard no sudden voice from the heavens, felt no chill, no spark of recognition. Of course I wouldn't, she thought, how could I? I've never seen it before in my life...

Though she had seen it, in a way. She had seen it in her dreams.

"Ah," the old man said, coming toward her through the darkness of the little shop. "You've found it, then. Wasn't sure it was still around." He hobbled by her, past an ancient oak bed and headboard carved with tiny figures and designs and standing on its side like a gnarled old tree growing up out of the floor. Next to that was a lamp with a yellow paper shade, a rolled up rug that smelled of dust and mold, and a bird's nest of kitchen chairs stacked on and in and around each other. The old man reached up, leaning over a bunch of rotting cardboard boxes, leftovers of someone else's life, the dust swirling around his legs like a tiny, yapping dog at his master's feet.

"No," Laura said. The sight of him there, his withered fingers about to touch the precious wood, brought bile to her throat. "Please. I'll get it." He stepped back obediently, hawk nose dripping clear fluid, thin gray lips rimmed with white crust.

The violin sat on the second shelf from the top and she had to get up on tiptoes to reach it. When she brought it down the dust flew into her face and down her nose and throat. "Yep, that's the one," the old man said as she dissolved into a fit of coughing. His voice was rough and high-pitched, as old and unused as the clutter that surrounded him. "Been here for two years at least. Young fella brought it in, as I remember. Was his grandfather's, he said."

"Giovannetti."

The old man looked at her in surprise. "That's right. A famous musician in his time, I guess he was."

A famous musician indeed. Laura held the violin gently in her hands, rocking it like a baby. It seemed she felt a tremor run through the wood, like a distant memory of forgotten music.

She had found it. She had found it at last.

~φ~

After making the purchase she left the tiny second-hand shop and walked through the streets of Soho, ignoring the crowds as best she could. The gunmetal sky hovered just above the rooftops. It would rain soon, and with the rain would come the steam and the rush of dirty water through the gutters, fractured reflections off car windows and wet pavement, the sound of umbrellas flapping in the wind. How she had grown to hate this city, the noise and people rushing everywhere at all hours of the day and night. But here, she thought, only here could she pursue her dreams of becoming a star. Only here had she found the resources to finish the search that had come to consume her every waking moment. She clutched the paper bag closer to her chest and thought of all the hours that had led to this day, hours crouched over history books in silent library rooms, smelling the dusty pages, the phone calls overseas to more old men who sometimes spoke broken English, and sometimes spoke none at all. After all this time, and all this work, who could have known that she would find it here, in New York, not ten blocks from her apartment! Almost as if it had been waiting for her. She shivered and felt the tingle go all the way to her toes.

In her studio she closed the door and locked it, throwing the three bolts and slipping on the chain. Before she had thought the locks to be a bit of overkill, even in a city like this, but now they were a godsend. If anyone knew what she had...

She unwrapped the violin by the big bay windows and sat on the couch to examine it more closely. The wood had been dulled by time and neglect, but the grain was still visible, the quality of craftsmanship undeniable to anyone even vaguely familiar with the subject. And she, of course, was an expert. She wiped her palm gently over its surface and it was like wiping a clean spot on a foggy window, the smooth wood seeming to breathe under her skin, the beat of life there, faint but audible. She picked up the bow and felt along its length; the horsehair was in decent shape. It would be possible to play.

Faced with the reality of it at last, she almost lost her nerve. Who was she to think that she could walk in the footsteps of genius? Just an ordinary, average music student of mediocre talent, who worked hard but would never be a great musician, a girl who hadn't played in front of a crowd of over twenty in her life (and that at her seventh grade recital back home in White Falls). A girl with a dream, sure, but why should that make any difference? Everyone had dreams. Those who were truly great had something more, something she had always searched for but could never find. She couldn't remember when she had first realized it would remain forever out of her reach, but she remembered the terrible depression that descended like a black cloud over her life. Until now.

Laura Barnes, she thought. An average, ordinary name. She thought of her face, plain and broad, dark hair more like oil than the kind of coal-black she had always admired. She imagined the name up in lights in front of Lincoln Center and on posters plastered across the city, and almost laughed aloud. Did she really believe that a simple wooden instrument could bring her all this?

Still…

She lifted the violin to her throat and settled her chin against the soft leather rest. Raised the bow and placed it gently against the strings. Tuned each one as best she could.

And then, closing her eyes, drew the bow as her fingers found their places almost by their own accord.

A single deep, thrumming note leaped from the belly of the violin, and her heart jumped in her chest before a string let go with a loud *ping!* and the music stopped abruptly. Disappointed, she lay the instrument down on the couch next to her and sighed. What did she expect, anyway? After all, it had remained on a shelf in that crummy little shop for over two years, and if the old man had so much as dusted in its general vicinity she would be very surprised.

But that one note she had heard before the string let go had sent chills racing down her spine, her fingers tingling from their contact with the wood. She would replace the string, replace all of them. She would polish the wood until it shined, every last speck of dust and grime lifted from its precious surface.

And then we will see.

~φ~

"But Paganini played a Guarnerius. Everyone knows that. It's still in Genoa, on display."

"That's what everyone thinks. And they're right, of course."

"So what are you saying?"

"That's only part of the story."

They sat hunched over a small table in the rear of a crowded Soho bar. Danielle Aniston's face reflected the pulsing red, green and blue lights from the dance floor. Normally she was beautiful, with the sort of delicate china-doll features Laura had often wished she possessed. But now the lights and the noise and the skeptical expression on Danielle's face hardened her looks, making her appear as if she were carved from wood.

"I don't understand," she said. "You mean the one in Genoa is some sort of fake?"

"Of course not." Laura curled her fingers around the cool bottle of beer and found the smooth, slick glass repulsed her. Had she done the right thing, meeting her friend here? But she had to tell someone.

She wiped her hand on a napkin. "How much do you know about him?"

"Nicoli Paganini? Born in 1780-something, wasn't he? Italian virtuoso on the violin. Brilliant composer and musician. Traveled all over the world and died a very rich man."

"But what do you know about *him*? The person?"

"Oh," Danielle said, waving a hand. "I never pay too much attention in class. You know that."

"Maybe you should start."

"Spare me the lecture."

A young couple passed by on their way to the dance floor, two men holding hands. One of them bumped the table with his hip and sent the beer bottle into a drunken wobble. Laura steadied it with her hand (that slick feeling making her stomach lurch) and then continued, her voice softer now, so that her friend had to lean closer to hear her. "He was a gambler," she said. "Early in his career, he lost everything. They were coming after him to collect and he didn't have a penny to his name. How would it look if such a young, rising star was found with a couple of broken legs? Or worse, broken fingers? His career would be over. So he did the only thing he could do. He pawned his violin."

So then he bought it back when he had earned some money?"

Laura shook her head. "Soon after that a rich French merchant named Livron took him in. Livron bought him a new violin. The Guarnerius you see on display in Genoa today."

"Wait a minute." Danielle sat back in her chair. "You mean there was another one?"

"That's right. The real Paganini violin. The one that taught him how to play."

Danielle smiled. The lights pulsed and played about her features like a living bruise. "You've been working too hard, babe. Violins don't teach people."

"That's not the end of the story. The violin was bought from the pawnshop by a man named Hines. Hines unfortunately died young. Still, he made a name for himself before his death, in local circles. A brilliant musician, apparently. From there it was passed along to his daughter, who married a man named Giovannetti —"

"*The* Giovannetti?" Danielle's eyes had gone wide.

"Not the one you're thinking of, though it's the same family. The famous one, Roberto Giovannetti, was the great grandson of the woman who inherited that violin from Himes. She herself was a talented violinist, and she taught her own son, who passed it down, and so on —"

"So Roberto Giovannetti played on the same instrument as Paganini?"

"Before he disappeared three years ago, yes. A while after that his own grandson went through his things, and, not knowing what he'd found, pawned the violin to a shop in New York City for a few measly bucks." Laura leaned back and smiled. "And now I have it."

"You can't be serious." The look on Danielle's face had progressed from skeptical to incredulous. "First of all that's crazy. Too much of a coincidence, two brilliant musicians separated by centuries using the same instrument without even knowing it. And anyway, there's never been anything but junk in those second-hand shops in Soho. You expect me to believe a violin worth hundreds of thousands of dollars —"

"But don't you see?" Laura asked, he voice rising a bit in spite of her struggle to remain calm. "It wasn't just two brilliant musicians. Every single one of them who ever touched that violin, man, woman or child, had the gift. Or had it handed to them."

The music suddenly stopped and all activity around them paused while the DJ spun another album. The waiter hustled up to their table, balancing a tray on his palm, picked up their drinks (Laura's beer still almost half full and warm as tap water) and slipped away again into the crowd spilling off the dance floor. Through all this Danielle stared at her friend across the table. "You actually expect me to believe," she said finally, and this time the smile was gone completely, this time she actually looked a little pissed, "that this piece of wood has... magical powers? A way of creating genius?"

"I don't know," Laura said, unsure again after hearing it put that way. Out in the open for the first time. She remembered all her thoughts during the past few months, curiosity in the beginning, growing into amazement as her research progressed, her own disbelief and then wonder and finally utter conviction. The violin was real, it was out there and she would find it. And she had. Was she crazy, after all?

"I want to see it," Danielle said.

"No." The word came immediately to her lips before she had a chance to think about it. "That's not possible."

"Then I don't believe you. You're bullshitting me."

"I am *not*." But Laura wondered what had made her tell

in the first place. If she wouldn't show anyone, even Danielle, who she considered her only real friend in the whole city, what was the point? Through all this she had been alone, unable to share each moment of frustration and triumph as they occurred, afraid her discovery would be stolen from her before she even had a chance to see it. Now that she owned the violin, with a receipt to prove it, what was she waiting for?

"Come on. If you really have it then let's see. Put up or shut up, girl." Danielle grinned again, and this time Laura could see that there would be no backing down. Things had progressed too far.

"Okay," she said. "But you have to promise not to tell anyone about this. *Promise*."

"Tell anyone about what?" Still grinning.

"Just wait," Laura said. "You'll see."

It was raining as they left the bar. Neither of them had brought umbrellas, and it wouldn't have helped them much if they had; great gusts of humid wind blew spray in their faces, flipping wet papers across the shiny black pavement. The streets were jammed with slow-moving cars, their headlights stabbing through the rain, honking and swearing drivers hunched behind steering wheels. The whole city smelled like wet dog.

Laura's apartment was only two blocks away, but by the time they reached it both girls were thoroughly soaked. Neither spoke on the way up in the elevator, the only sound the drip, drip of water from their clothes and hair hitting the floor. Laura had become increasingly nervous since they had left the bar, and now wished desperately that she had never called Danielle in the first place. The story was crazy enough; and what would she think of the rest of it, the stranger things she had come to believe in the course of her research?

Then a worse thought sprang into her head. Suddenly she knew that when she opened the door to her apartment the violin would be gone. The couch would be empty, nothing but lint balls and dust gracing the red-wine cushions, and she would have to face the fact that she *was* crazy, after all.

But when she opened the door and switched on the lights the violin was there. She could see its reflection in the big windows, streaked by rain, its shape seeming to ripple and bulge as the wind rattled the glass. She breathed a sigh of relief.

"Well," Danielle said, slicking her wet hair back into a ponytail and securing it with a rubber band. "Let me see this miracle, will you? It's getting late and I shouldn't stay long. Billy will worry."

Billy, Laura thought as she closed the door and locked it. She pictured a young, bronzed creature with sculpted pecks and washboard stomach, and jealousy washed through her like a bitter wave. She had never had the chance at a man like that, while Danielle seemed to attract them at will. She crossed the room to the couch, wishing again that she had never brought her friend here. But when she picked up the violin all those ugly thoughts disappeared. Under her flesh the soft wood seemed to hum at a pitch too high for human ears. She felt a gentle tug begin somewhere below her breasts, an urge to cradle it in her arms like a baby. Who had crafted these strange curves? *Does it matter?*

"Ugh," Danielle said, coming forward with her nose wrinkled as if she had just smelled something rotten. "It's dirty."

"Nothing a little lemon oil won't fix."

"Strange shape, isn't it? Something about the neck. And what kind of wood is that?" She reached out a hand and Laura jerked the violin out of reach.

"Don't."

"Hey, relax. I won't touch your precious instrument. Though I have to say I don't see it, I really don't. It doesn't look anything like a Guarnerius —"

"It's *not* a Guarnerius! Haven't you listened to anything I've told you?"

"It's just a crazy story. Come on, seriously."

"I wouldn't expect someone like you to get it," Laura said. The blood had risen to her cheeks. Her heart was pounding and she gripped the violin tightly against her chest. Rainwater trickled from her hair down her face. "You don't even care about music. You're just happy lying around all day letting Billy screw you."

Danielle turned back to her and her eyes glittered like cut stones. "I think I'd better leave."

"Go ahead then. There's the door."

"You're nuts, you know that?" Danielle said. "Honestly." When Laura did not respond she spun on her heel and left, slamming the door behind her.

Laura collapsed on the couch, struggling with tears. Why she had gotten so angry was a mystery; after all, she was the one who had called Danielle in the first place. It was a stupid idea anyway, telling someone that story and expecting her to understand. *It does sound crazy.*

Except it was true. All of it.

She touched the violin and brought it to her cheek. The wood was warm as flesh. Outside the big bay windows lightning flashed, and a crash of thunder rolled past the building like the distant sound of drums. She had hidden from those storms as a child, cowering under the covers of her bed. How silly it seemed now to be frightened of a storm.

Go ahead. Play it.

She got up and went to find her spare string and lemon oil, and when she returned she began to polish the wood slowly, gently, washing away the dust and the old caked resin and human fingerprints, watching as the varnish began to shine under the lights. It was a strange wood. Danielle had been right about that, anyway. Soft in appearance like pine but a different color and pattern. And a strange shape, not like the old Italian designs at all, too long and thick in the neck and bulky around the base, belly rounded as if each rib and panel hadn't been glued together but rather had grown up out of each other like some sort of polished, sculpted tree. She wondered again where it had come from, what kind of man had built a thing like this.

So beautiful, she thought, no matter if it *is* different. Or, rather, *because* it is.

She wound the new string into place, tightened it and then admired her work. Danielle would hardly recognize it now. The violin sparkled. No, blazed was a better word, its varnish perfectly intact after all these years, not a crack or dull spot. A yellow-orange tint to it, like hundreds of tiny flames licking over its surface.

A little voice spoke up from the depths of her brain. *What about the other things? What about all the tragedies, the disappearances...*

And the way she had begun to suspect lately that Giovanetti's grandson had known exactly what he was doing when he pawned the violin to that store in Soho. That he had *wanted* to get rid of it.

Ridiculous. But how else to explain such a valuable instrument sitting untouched on a dusty shelf for two years?

Talent, it seemed to whisper. *What you've always wanted. Right here.* She let her finger run across the wooden surface. Traced the path of the grain, down across the belly and over the base, searching for the empty space within. Violins are like people, she thought, like women with their empty wombs, waiting for something to fill them up.

She began with a simple piece, a Haydn sonata, letting herself become familiar with the finger board and the way the instrument melded to her body. The sound that came from within the violin was like nothing she had ever heard in her life, at once full and strong, and yet blessed with the most delicate pitch. The strings responded to her rosined bow with a firmness that at first surprised and then delighted her; never in her life had she played such an instrument! It was as if the violin could anticipate her every move. Nothing she had ever owned – none of the practice instruments at the school – had ever felt like this. She always knew, even after hours of playing when the blisters came and her neck began to ache, that she was holding a piece of dead wood in her hands and not an extension of herself.

She tried a more difficult piece, a Mendelsson concerto that until now had eluded her. The opening faltered for a moment before she began to find the rhythm again and the violin responded, the music like a swelling wave. Give and take, an exchange as intimate as any other. The leather rest felt like soft lips against her throat, nuzzling her skin. She watched her reflection in the windows as if she were a spectator at a concert, her fingers growing a mind of their own, flying over the board at an ever-increasing pace as the concerto took flight and soared about the room, filling the high spaces and echoing back to her ears. Laughter welled up and spilled from her throat; this music, this beautiful music was coming from her, Laura Barnes! She closed her eyes against tears and felt her wet hair swinging in her face and the sweat trickling down between her shoulder blades, imagining herself on the stage of a gigantic hall filled with silent faces, spotlight hot on the back of her neck, the air alive around her as the violin melted into her flesh, obeying her every command, becoming one, beating with her blood. She sobbed with happiness as her mind lost itself among the lilting notes, and suddenly she *was* on stage, the packed house hanging on her every move, the air vibrating with the beauty of her music.

She played on, losing herself as the violin worked its magic. Time passed, how long she didn't know. Gradually she began to realize that something had changed. The music was no longer familiar to her; it was a moment before she recognized it. She was playing a Paganini concerto.

Or rather, it was playing her.

The music had grown louder, fuller, as if an orchestra were accompanying her somewhere out of sight. Her hand had begun to ache. She felt as if something were being drawn from her, like the feeling of giving blood. Alarmed now, she opened her eyes.

The impossible sight that greeted her in the window as she raised her gaze to her reflection made her cry out. Impossible, and yet there it was; and this was not what she'd expected, though she had expected *something*, hadn't she?

The violin had swelled like a tick against her throat, its round belly becoming ever rounder, hard edges beginning to soften. She could no longer tell where the wood ended and her flesh began. And her hand, her hand was melting into the bow, the tips of her fingers running like taffy in the sun, white bone showing through strings of reddish, liquid skin. The wood was absorbing her, the two forms meeting and swirling and blending together.

Who had made this thing?

Terror overwhelmed her as the temperature rose in the studio apartment. Flames of a distant fire licked about her feet. Still she kept playing, helpless to stop now, muscles moving of their own accord. She tried to scream and found that something had happened to her vocal cords. *Wait*, she thought, *you were supposed to teach me, you were supposed to make me a star.*

And yet she knew. A talent like this was only on loan, and she had known all along what the price would be, hadn't she? She was no equal for such a thing as this. How could she expect to match its strength when even the great Paganini had only played it to a draw?

Her fingers had disappeared up to the third knuckle. The pain was sharper now, like a series of needles digging under her nails, except her nails were *gone*, they were…

Laura tried to scream again and managed only a weak bubbling noise. Her hand had completely melted, the flesh of her forearm becoming part of the bow, still running over the strings as the cords were pulled from her neck. She strained and tried to tear herself away, muscles standing out in her shoulders, oh God the pain, it was too much and still it kept eating at her.

Her vision filled with red. She felt something snap in her neck as her head bent back and touched her shoulder blades. She realized too late that there was something else she hadn't counted on.

The violin was hungry.

~φ~

Danielle Aniston let herself into the dim apartment with Laura's spare key. The rain was coming harder now, wind rocking the old brick building, moaning around the windows like something big and mean trying to get in. Water dripped from a dark spot near the ceiling and pattered softly against the worn wooden floor.

She didn't know quite why she had come back. She was angry at Laura, true, and wanted to get back at her for that crack about only caring about getting laid all the time. That wasn't the case at all. Danielle worked as hard as anybody and wanted to be the best, it was just that she was more of a realist. The number of people who actually made it big playing the violin… well, it was like winning the lottery. And of course you had to have the talent. You had to have the *gift*.

But that violin had disturbed her tonight more than she had let on. She hadn't wanted Laura to see the way she felt, the way she wanted to touch it so badly her hands shook. So beautiful, but so strange. Even covered with dust, she could see it was something special. Those stories Laura had told, they were silly of course, but what if...

It was warm in here. Laura must have turned the heat all the way up. She tiptoed into the living room, but when she saw that the bed against the wall was empty, she relaxed. Laura wasn't home.

The violin was still sitting on the sofa facing the windows. It looked different somehow, full. Laura had given it a thorough cleaning, that much was obvious. The pattern of rain-streaked glass played about its rounded surface, making it appear almost like it was breathing.

She stepped closer, fascinated. Lifted the instrument to her throat and settled her chin on the soft leather rest. It seemed to hum against her flesh, nuzzling her like a child at his mother's breast. She raised the bow, placed it gently against the strings, and closed her eyes.

A single deep, thrumming note leaped from the belly of the violin before a string let go with a loud *ping!* that startled her.

Disappointed, she put it back on the couch and stood looking at it. Of course it was nothing but a fake, a cheap imitation that had fooled Laura.

And yet. That one note had sent a chill along her spine.

She picked it up again and traced a finger along its warm, smooth surface. She would replace the strings, replace all of them. She would clean every inch of its flesh once again and make it shine. *And then we will see.*

For a moment, somewhere deep within, she thought she felt a heartbeat. ⟍

The Buzz of a Thousand Wings

The open apartment door stood at the end of a furry tongue of mustard-colored shag carpet. Owen caught the flash from a camera and the sound of voices drifting toward him from inside. The building bred things that shunned the air and scuttled away from him, and he kept to the center of the hall, aware of the floor's flesh-like give under his feet and the smell of rot that clung to his clothes.

Inside the stink changed to something vaguely human. He allowed himself a moment to capture the scene – rat droppings near his feet, wallpaper bubbled and torn like the flesh of a burn victim – before he focused upon the bodies laid out in supplication beneath the single high window.

"Never seen anything like this," the photographer said. "I swear to God, thirteen years, gunshots, hangings, car accidents. This is the worst."

If the victims had been wealthy the story might have hit the national news. But in the slums death was a daily event. A little wetness and discomfort, quickly forgotten.

A gust of wind sent a splatter of raindrops against the window, and a puff of air caressed Owen's sweaty face. His pulse quickened as he snapped on gloves, kneeled and forced himself to look into the corpses' eyes.

It was like staring into a pool of murky water. The man and woman were stretched out side by side, their torsos split from neck to groin so that whatever had been chewing at them could get its fill. What was left of their skin slid from their bones like a peel of rotten fruit.

A pair of scissors lay next to the bodies. He turned them over gently, saw clotted blood, and caught a psychic whiff of what death must have been like for these people. It was as if he were there, in the room with the killer. Scissors slashing, ripping, giving birth to blood. He swallowed until the feeling passed.

"Just moved in a month ago," someone near the door was saying. "Damn shame, you ask me."

Owen stood up and brushed wetness from his knees. A man with a starved face was talking to the beat cop. The man was in his sixties and about Owen's height, a little under six feet.

The man pointed a thumb in his direction. "Who's the raincoat?"

"Homicide," Owen said, walking over and shaking his hand. "And you?"

"Julio Guerrero. Down the hall, B17. I called it in, on account of the smell. The hallway stank to high heaven."

"How could you tell the difference?"

"Whattaya want for six hundred a month? The landlord jacks up the rent it'll put us all out on the street."

"Did you know these people, Mr. Guerrero?"

"Guy was running from a gang that thought he'd snitched on certain illegal activities. Said he was trying to get his family out."

"His wife?"

"Kids too. A little boy, four, maybe five years old."

The cop had been watching them with his arms crossed over his meaty chest. He shrugged. "No sign of a kid."

"Call it in to social services and make sure we put out an APB on a possible kidnapping," Owen said. "And could someone find this guy some coffee?"

"Sure, no problem," the uniform said. He reached out to touch Guerrero's arm, then evidently thought better of it. "Let's go, Pop. We'll take a formal statement outside."

Owen watched the old man shuffle away. Blood and scissors flashed once again before his eyes, and he hunched his shoulders against the images trying to burrow deeper inside.

The photographer's camera popped. Owen stepped carefully around an ancient kitchen table, past the stains of something unrecognizable and into a little alcove with the sink and faucet that dripped blood-colored water. Some canned food and a box of opened cereal still sat on a shelf. This place used to be a storage room back when the neighborhood was still middle class. Right here would be the stacks of boxes, books and broken toys.

He stepped past the bodies to the only other room in the apartment and flashed his light around a tiny bedroom, illuminating the blunt ends of pipes protruding from the wall. It was empty except for twin mattresses on the floor and clothes piled in the corner.

He played the light around the ceiling. Strips of floating white ghosts hung from the corners, drifting in unseen drafts.

Webs.

~φ~

Owen crossed the street with his jacket up over his head. Rain dripped into his collar. Graffiti scarred the walls and hookers languished on street corners or huddled in doorways. A horn blared and someone shouted out a rolled-down window as the car splashed dirty rivulets of gutter water.

He trudged through massive wooden doors and into sudden, heavy silence. Chipped mahogany pews marched away on both sides as the ceiling arched far above his head.

Someone coughed, the sound echoing through stone and hollow as Owen slipped up the aisle and into an empty booth.

"Forgive me Father for I have sinned."

He thought he glimpsed movement behind the dark screen.

"What are your sins, my son?"

"I have had bad thoughts, dreams I can't describe."

"Dreams are God's work."

"Not these. Terrible things, Father. Death and blood. Children screaming. Maybe it's penance. I have failed to catch a murderer when it is my job and my duty to do so."

"Sometimes it is not humanly possible to do what has been asked. Such sacrifice is too large a burden for one man to bear."

"Palowski's written it off as a gang hit. Me, I'm not sure. My partner is too eager to see everything in black and white."

"You see shades of gray."

"I see too much. Sometimes I wonder about this world.

Maybe I'm wrong, maybe it's always been this way underneath.
The people living in filth. What they do to each other. I've
been disgusted by them and I'm ashamed."

"As they are disgusted by you."

The priest's words took him by surprise. Owen pressed his
forehead against slippery wood and closed his eyes. "Do you
know how hard it is to investigate a crime in this city? The
dealers and whores scatter when you arrive and hide in the corners like cockroaches. You go walking around out there and
you know they're watching, you can feel them."

"They don't trust you."

"Likewise. You know what was strange about these murders? The bedroom was full of cobwebs. What do you make
of that?"

There was no answer this time. Owen sat forward, hair
standing up on his forearms. He waited, strained to see through
the darkness.

"Father? Are you all right?"

The confessional was quiet for a moment. The hiss, when
it came, was sudden and close. *"And in those days men will seek
death and will not find it; they will long to die, and death flies from
them."*

Owen recoiled backward so quickly his head cracked against
the wall. "Father?"

The confessional door banged open as something slipped
out and away.

He got to his feet and flung his door open, looking to the
right and left. Nothing but an old lady with her head down in
the third row. "Did you see anyone come through here?" he
shouted at her, pulling out his badge.

Startled, she looked up and shook her head no. "Only you,"
she said.

He ducked inside the priest's booth and found it empty and
smelling faintly of mold. A trail of wetness dripped from the
screen to the floor.

He followed the trail down the empty aisle, through a stone
archway scrawled with black spray paint, to stone steps that
led into a dark pit below the church. He held his gun clutched
in one hand as he went down, trailing the other hand against

the slippery wall, and emerged into a basement chamber with a single bulb flickering weakly from a high socket. Huge blocks of granite made up the walls, and bits and pieces of broken furniture had been thrown into corners.

Owen swept the gun from side to side and saw nothing.

The rattle of metal led him to a far corner. Set into the floor was a circular grate covered in rust.

A soft, distant moan drifted up from the depths, then faded away into nothingness.

~φ~

The bodies were identified and a search began for the missing child. Then another name was added to the list. Mr. and Mrs. Arachi had a teenage daughter who was last seen at a nightclub about three blocks away. They had found a faded photograph in the bedroom closet; a picture of a boy of about four with greasy hair and black eyes. A girl stood next to him, her face cut off at the nose by the top of the photo.

Owen turned the photo over in his hands for a long time. Something was wrong with their faces, but he couldn't put his finger on exactly what.

"The girl's a whore," Palowski said later, as they drove slowly down a slick city street. "Put your money on that. If she's still alive, she's gone into hiding. But they probably raped and killed her and dumped her in the river."

"And the boy?"

"He's young enough, they might use him." Palowski spat into the wind through his open window. "Let 'em all kill each other, I say. What good are they? You see 'em shooting up the streets every night. It's like a law of nature, like one of those bugs that bites the head off of its mate. What do you call 'em?"

"Praying mantis."

"That's the ticket."

Owen stared at the dashboard as hot, ripe air from the open window swirled around him. He thought of all the microscopic creatures swimming in grease, bits of doughnut and dead skin.

He wanted to scrub the world until it bled.

"You gotta love 'em, the whores," Palowski said. "They

keep us in business." He pulled the car over to the curb and paced a young girl in hot-pink spandex pants.

"Say, honey! You got a minute?"

The girl walked with arms crossed over her chest.

"We're searching for a young girl your age, fifteen or sixteen, works the streets. Used to hang out at the Hideaway." The girl kept walking. "Listen, you wanna talk here or should we take you downtown?"

"Go fuck yourself."

Palowski stopped the cruiser with a lurch. He ran around the front end and took the girl roughly by the elbow. "You don't want to talk to an officer of the law that way, you fuckin' tramp."

The girl muttered and twisted in his grip. She kept her head down the way dogs did when you tried to get them to stare at you.

"You know about a hit on a family from Queens?" Palowski asked her. "Gang action, Bloods, maybe someone else?"

"She doesn't know anything," Owen said. "We're wasting time here."

Palowski let go of the girl's arm. Terrified, she flashed Owen a look. Something in her eyes made him pause. A glint of metallic green-black.

"Hey," Palowski said. "What the hell —"

The girl bolted past them both and darted down a narrow alley. They gave chase, tripping over garbage cans, Palowski going to his knees in slippery trash as Owen ran ahead.

The girl slipped through the shadows, a lighter spot within the dark, and then she twisted and leaped at a chain-link fence, pushing off the wall with impossibly strong legs. She touched down lightly on the other side and was gone, the sound of her footsteps echoing into silence.

A chill wind swept down the alley, raising gooseflesh. Owen shivered.

"What happened?" Palowski shouted as he ran past and stopped near the fence. "Where the fuck did she go?" He turned back with an expression of confusion across his broad, brutal face. Everything about Palowski was logical. It was how he was wired. He could no more accept what they had just seen than he could accept that the girl was the Virgin Mary.

"Gymnast," Owen said. "I've seen that move before, like when guys run right up a wall and flip over backward. It's simple physics."

He didn't believe it himself. But Palowski just shrugged. "Freaky little bitch. I didn't see that coming."

A siren sounded in the distance. Somewhere beyond the fence a dog barked, and another howled in return. Owen wondered what else was out there, watching them. He could not see them, but he could feel their eyes.

~φ~

Soon there were more. In abandoned buildings, the waterfront. All of them eviscerated, all of them rotting away to nothing. Owen saw the corpses when he slept, their eyes like the whites of eggs, meat slipping away from bone as they reached out and caressed dark confessional walls.

He lost weight, drank too much coffee and watched black and white movies with all the lights on. He caught a news report where chicken breasts were painted with phosphorescent dust, then carefully prepared, the utensils washed, counter scrubbed with soap. The reporters turned out the lights to show phosphorescent fingerprints all over the kitchen. Imagine that dust is salmonella bacteria, the announcer said. *Imagine that this is your home.*

Owen began scrubbing the kitchen sink and walls with bleach, rubbing at black spots on the linoleum until his fingers were raw. He thought about the warm, dry breezes of summer and clothes hanging on the line, the smell of hay in the barn and the sounds of horses snorting in their stalls. Walking down to the brook, rolling up his pant legs and chasing crayfish through the cold, clear water.

He called Emma. "Come home," she said, and her voice echoed and buzzed as if entire worlds separated them rather than mere miles. "What's there for you? You always want to help everyone, clean up other people's messes. But you have to let go. You have no one to love."

Owen closed his eyes against the sudden slice of pain. He

imagined their little boy laughing and playing around her legs as dusk settled across fields of baled hay and the air turned crisp and clean with the dark.

"It wasn't your fault," Emma said. "You know that, don't you?"

"Charlie," he said. His voice broke and he hated himself for it. "My Charlie."

"I know," she said. "You loved him. It doesn't mean you had to leave everything else behind. If you have to blame someone, blame me."

I've blamed you for too much.

"I love you too, Emma," Owen said. "I always will."

Something was wrong. He paused in confusion and looked down at the receiver in his hand, listening to the steady hum of the dial tone. He placed it gently on its cradle.

~φ~

Much later, the sounds of the couple next door began, muffled voices sighing and mingling in sensual embrace. Soon they grew louder and more violent; rhythmic thrusts pounded the walls as something shattered on the floor. A female voice cried out in passion or anger. Owen thought he heard a third voice along with them before rock music was turned up loud.

He drifted. Foul water dripped onto his upturned face from somewhere in the dark. Somewhere a child was crying. He lay spread-eagled as moisture seeped up through his shirt. His arms and legs were wrapped in something soft and very strong. He struggled desperately, hearing the child's cries grow more frantic, but he could not break free.

"Daadeeeee…"

Carved-stone walls rose up high on either side. Echoes of water dripping and gurgling came to him from some distant place, and with it the sound of a thousand legs scrabbling across concrete. Roaches flowed up over his chest, their little chittering faces grinning as they bent to do their work.

He woke to find the bed sheets twisted around his legs so tightly he could barely shake free.

~φ~

Days went by without any leads. The murder weapon had uncovered nothing but the victims' own prints. The killer knew what he was doing. The Sergeant wanted to look for someone who had close ties to the police department, but Owen didn't buy it.

What the priest had said in the confessional bothered him until he finally managed to place it. It was from the Book of Revelations. The locusts were the plague brought forth by the fifth angel of Heaven; they held mankind for five months and tortured them with scorpion stings as punishment for their sins. What it meant, he wasn't sure, but it seemed to fit somehow.

He did not know what started him thinking about Guerrero again. Just an old man eager to talk to anyone who would listen. But some of the things he had said, Owen remembered, didn't make sense. He recalled how Guerrero was the one who put them onto the idea of a gang hit in the first place. Now hundreds of police officers across the city were out looking for gang members to shake down.

There were other things that worried him, now that he thought more about it. How the man didn't seem bothered in the least by the two dead bodies lying at his feet. And Owen was sure that Guerrero had said *kids*, when they were talking, but then he had gone on to mention only the boy who was missing.

He needed to pay the old man another visit.

~φ~

The neighborhood was worse than he remembered. The building stood on trembling legs, surrounded by overflowing dumpsters and patches of weeds. Burned cars on rusted rims lay slumped at its feet.

Owen stepped from his department car and paused on the sidewalk while Palowski stayed in his seat.

Palowski usually led the way in this sort of situation. It would be stupid to go in there alone. But Owen knew Guerrero would never talk with Palowski around. Besides, Owen had started wondering about Palowski lately. He seemed even more wound up than usual. His temper was growing worse. Who knew when he might suddenly explode, and do something stupid? Something truly dangerous?

Owen took his flashlight out and descended into the gloom. Nothing moved in the ancient stairwell, or in the basement hallway below; there was nothing to suggest that people lived here.

He located B17 and knocked on the door, and it swung open at his touch. He pushed through into a place that had obviously been abandoned long ago. The flashlight beam picked out plastic bags and rusted cans floating on a murky skin of water. A broken chair squatted beneath the single window. Guerrero was gone, if he had ever lived here at all.

Perhaps he had been wrong to come, Owen thought. Who was he to think they would welcome him to this place any more than they would have welcomed a brute like Palowski? What he remembered of his conversation with Guerrero might well have been all in his head.

Emma was right. You don't have to leave everything behind. You can remember what hurts you the most, and survive.

He waited for the words to mean something. But it was too late. He could not live his life any other way.

Owen stepped out of B17. The door at the end of the hall was closed, but he pushed it open and walked inside. With the beam from the flashlight he could clearly see the empty floor, the bloodstains where the two bodies had slept. Ants swarmed in a seething carpet.

Fear prickled his skin as a draft washed through the open door. He looked up, playing the light along the walls. Webs hung silently from the ceiling like drifting strands of white-blond hair. They draped across the kitchen alcove, caressed the floor and framed the door to the bedroom. They hung blanketing sound, a mute witness, turning the room into a tomb of black and white.

He looked towards the bedroom and caught a glimpse of something dark moving inside.

"Who's there?"

Something giggled in the shadows beyond the door.

Owen stepped quickly into the little room, holding the light out. Webs had transformed the walls into an alien landscape of drifting white contours and soft sticky mounds.

He flashed his light into the corner. There he found Guerrero, only his face visible above a cocoon of white sticky strands. A pair of surgical scissors lay at his feet.

Guerrero's eyes were open. When he saw Owen he began to struggle.

"The bodies we found," Owen said. "They did it to themselves, didn't they? Cut out their own bellies."

Guerrero coughed wetly, and something like a moan forced itself out his throat. "Why?"

Owen heard a scratching sound like claws against concrete. He spun and flashed the light across the white-draped room. The web funneled down to a place where the mattress had been slid aside, and beneath it gaped a round sewer hole.

More giggling. Wings buzzed and wafted damp sewer air. Metallic eyes flashed at him from the dark.

Something climbed up out of the hole. In the sudden trembling of the flashlight Owen could not see clearly. The boy's body looked distorted, as if pieces of him had exploded and then healed in sheets of reflective armor. His abdomen was round and tight and glossy black, his arms long and multijointed, ending in three prongs like black daggers. His face was a shining plate of eyes and a toothless maw.

"You see it?" Owen shouted at Guerrero. He drew his service piece and pointed it at the old man. "What is that? Tell me, Goddamnit!"

Guerrero screamed, heaving, twisting against the strands. Flecks of spittle wet his sunken cheeks. "Nothing there!" he shrieked. "Nothing!"

Something snapped inside Owen's head. He shot Guerrero between the eyes.

The thing at the sewer grate chittered. The sound was answered by several more, and as Owen swung the light quickly back again, the beam caught the Arachi boy hovering several feet above the floor, the buzzing of his wings fanning the webs into flapping white ghosts.

Owen kept the gun up where it could be seen, and backed

into the hallway. Then he turned and stumbled back through the choking debris, his back itching in its nakedness as the buzzing of wings and the sounds of feeding grew fainter.

Outside the light had changed. Owen climbed into his department car and rolled up the windows, turned the air conditioning up high. He did not look at Palowski at all. Owen filled his mind instead with thoughts of huge fields and orange sunsets, cold water coursing from a hand pump, the smell of fresh sheets and wood smoke. His wife waved at him from far away, long dress flapping around her legs, dark soil from the garden caking her hands and the bottom of her bare feet.

The buzzing filled his head. He struggled but the image would not hold. It dissolved into Emma lying naked across the bed, head thrown back and her mouth open. Her long white-blond hair scraped the floor like a gossamer web in the dusky light as she held her legs apart for some stranger who rutted at her with clenching buttocks.

He saw a roach skittering across the bedroom floor and a pair of scissors on the nightstand. He watched them cutting and slashing and laying waste to filth. He saw a little boy's face in the doorway, wide and white and screaming.

He saw two skeletal faces in the crawlspace under the floorboards of his farmhouse, their mouths filled with cobwebs.

Owen stared down at his hands, his fingers, blistered and raw. He glanced to his right, and the passenger seat was empty. He was alone.

Charlie, he thought. *My Charlie. I'm coming.*

Owen Palowski put his gun on his lap and he waited there until night fell, and the buzzing of a thousand wings filled the air, before he went to join them. ⩘